I0573972

ALL THINGS COME TO AN END

A THROUGH THE JOURNEY NOVEL

JENNIFER L. JOHNSON

ALL THINGS COME TO AN END

Copyright © 2020 by Jennifer L. Johnson

For information contact:
Jennifer L. Johnson
P.O. Box 5594
Suffolk, VA 23435
contact@iamjenniferjohnson.com
http://www.iamjenniferjohnson.com

ISBN: 978-1-7351740-0-6

CHAPTER ONE

Washington, D.C.

"This thing we got is forever," replays in my head. Alan has taken things to a new level. Last night was some bullshit, and I don't want to deal with him anymore.

The sun shines through the curtains onto my face, and I slowly peel my eyelids open. I don't want to remove the blanket from over my head because then I'll have to face the fact that it's time to get up and get ready for work.

The house is quiet. I can't tell if Alan is still here. Ever since I gave him a key, he acts like he lives here. He doesn't pay bills, but he wants to claim this as his home. Knowing my luck, he's waiting to finish arguing about whatever insecurities he was dealing with last night. I don't have the patience to deal with his fickle ass this morning.

I'm beginning to feel like there is something wrong with me. Why do I keep attracting these insecure, broken men? Everything seems good in the beginning, then they get hella jealous and act like I can't be out of their sight. They always want to be up under me and get upset when I don't want to do the same. Don't get me wrong—I want to spend time with my man, but I need time to myself, too. Shit, so does he.

I've heard people say, "Opposites attract." I thought that was a good thing, but not anymore. I'm a confident woman who has a lot going for herself. Alan, on the other hand, can't seem to keep a job or figure out what he's doing with his life. He's almost thirty years old. He lives with his sister and always wastes money on get-rich-quick schemes. Ugh, I'm getting too old to be dealing with the same relationship nonsense. The longer I stay with Alan, the more I realize we need to go our separate ways.

Between work and law school, I'm drained and don't have the energy to argue, especially about dumb shit. I made it clear when we first met that school and my career are important to me. I am focused on graduating, passing the bar exam, and starting my career as a lawyer. He knew what the deal was when he first met me, but he was so insistent on making a relationship work.

I'm starting to notice one constant thing in my life: failed relationships. Here I am at twenty-seven years old, and I've never been in a relationship that lasted over a year. Damn, maybe there is something wrong with me. All my friends question why I can't keep a man long enough for him to propose. It's because all these random men talk a good game but lack the desire to work hard for anything.

Everyone has the potential to achieve their goals. You might need a little encouragement, but you also need ambition and determination. I need my man to believe in himself and be willing to work for what he desires in life. I am a firm believer that if you want something bad enough, you should be fearless enough to go after it. There's a reason you believed in it to begin with. Don't give me bullshit excuses about how you're trying but never produce any results. I think I fell in love with Alan's potential, only to be disappointed and frustrated.

Kim called it when I first introduced her to Alan. She warned me that he was moving too fast and was controlling. "There's a reason they call it a one-night stand," she told me. I went way beyond my two-drink limit that night. What was supposed to be a one-night stand turned into a relationship. If I'm being honest, I got what I needed that night and was okay if we never saw each other again.

The next day, the phone calls started. How did he get my phone number? Was I *that* out of it? Everyone who knows me knows I don't answer calls from phone numbers I don't recognize, but he just kept calling. He was so persistent. I thought he wanted round two. Not to toot my own horn, but *toot, toot!* I am the shit. After the third time, he started talking about us being more than just a random hookup. He didn't match everything on my what-I-want-in-a-man checklist, but he had potential ... or so I thought.

I feel like I can't do anything right, and Alan might snap at me if I say the wrong thing. I promised myself I would never stay in another unhealthy relationship, but here I am.

The arguments have been senseless and consuming. Like last night. I was later than usual getting home from class, and he wanted to argue about it. "I was here waiting for you. Who you been with, and what y'all been doing?"

Don't be questioning me like you my daddy; he lives in Virginia. You know I have class on Tuesdays and Thursdays, and Wednesday nights are my study group nights. I never should have given him a key to my apartment.

After working all day and going to class at night, I don't have the energy for drama. I tried not to let his questions get the best of me because I didn't want to be up all night arguing. Plus, I knew it would still be an issue the next morning. So, I went straight to bed.

Morning always comes quicker when you're tired as hell. I close my eyes and say a prayer like I normally do before starting my day. Right after I say, "Amen," I know today is going to be the end of me and Alan. There's nothing like prayer and a talk with God to give you confirmation on something you've been holding off on doing.

With my eyes still closed, I reach out from under the blanket to grab my cell phone off the nightstand. I feel my books and laptop but not my phone. I open my eyes, pull the cover off my face, and sit up. I look on the nightstand, and my phone is not where I left it. When I turn my head to check the dresser, I see Alan standing in the doorway holding my phone.

"Looking for this?" He sneers, gripping my phone in one hand, leaning his shoulder on the wall like he's holding it up. It's too early in the morning for this shit. I let my body fall back on the bed.

"Alan, can I have my phone, please?"

"Yeah, as soon as you tell me why you were so late getting home last night."

"Come on, Alan, stop playing. It's too early for this."

I sit up, and Alan walks over and sits next to my feet. He tosses my phone onto my lap.

"Why were you so late getting home last night?"

"You know Wednesday night is my study group."

"I know, but you're usually home before eleven."

"I'm a grown-ass woman and don't need you to keep tabs on

me."

"Maybe I was worried."

"About what?"

"About you."

"Why didn't you call and check on me?"

He opens his mouth as if he's going to say something, but he doesn't. This back-and-forth arguing is draining.

"Alan, we need to talk."

"It's someone else, isn't it?"

"No, it's not. Time just got away from me last night."

"I don't believe you."

"Oh my gosh, Alan! I can't do this anymore with you. I think it's in our best interest if we go our separate ways."

A deafening silence fills the room. I don't remember ever seeing Alan at a loss for words. He's always got something to say and is quick with the comebacks. I look at his lap and see that his fist is clenched. I reach over to touch his hands, but before I can, he jumps up and punches the wall.

I leap to the other side of the bed, mouth wide open, eyebrows raised. "You put a hole in my wall. You gonna fix that?"

"You worried about a damn wall?" He turns and walks toward me.

He's staring at me with shrewd eyes. My heart is racing so fast, it feels like it's going to jump out of my chest. I pray that he unclenches his fist and doesn't release his anger on me. The wall was enough.

"Don't come any closer, Alan."

He raises his right hand, his finger inches from my face.

"You know what? You're absolutely right. We do need to go our separate ways. I'm too good for your bougie ass anyway."

"That's fine, Alan. I'll be that."

Before I can get another word out, he wraps his right hand around my neck. "Just remember, no one else will put up with your bullshit, and no one will ever love you the way I love you."

I force my left arm over his and manage to push off his hand. "Get out, Alan."

I take a couple of steps around him and reach for my cell phone on the bed. Before I can unlock it, Alan walks toward the front door.

"I'm leaving, but we ain't over."

My heart still races, trying to find its normal rhythm. I try to calm my breathing before I have a panic attack. There isn't that much love in the world. No man should ever put his hands on a woman like that, no matter how upset or frustrated he is.

I sit on the end of the bed and catch a glimpse of my reflection in the mirror on the wall in front of me. My eyes are puffy and red from crying, and I lift my shaking hands toward my face. I feel like I'm living a nightmare. *What are you doing, Destinee? Get yourself together. Don't let this man break you.*

Tears escape my eyes as I remember he still has a key to my apartment. I rush to get ready for work and pack an overnight bag just in case I need to stay somewhere else for the night. I'm not taking any chances.

If today was Friday, I would call out from work and drive home to Virginia for the weekend. In times like this, I wish I lived closer to family.

My mother calls me every morning when I'm on my way to work. She panics if she doesn't hear from me every day. It's been that way since I got my first apartment in D.C.

As I step out of the shower, I hear my phone ringing. I glance down and see "Mom" followed by heart emojis on my screen. I wipe my hands on my towel and swipe right to answer.

"Hey, Ma! I'm running late this morning. Can I call you later?"

"What's wrong? You're never late for anything."

If I tell her what happened, she'll worry, and tell my brother. He'll want to catch a flight from California to handle Alan. I don't need anyone getting into trouble or going to jail because of me and my bad relationship habits. I'll handle it on my own.

"Nothing, Ma. Just had a late night with my study group and overslept. I promise I'll call you later."

"Okay, Destinee. I love you!"

"I love you, too, Ma."

My mother gets on me about keeping everything to myself. If I tell her what's going on, everyone will hear about it and I will never hear the end of it. No one in my family cares for Alan. They keep telling me I deserve better. That is why I keep everything to myself. I don't have time for anyone's opinions.

When I go through shit, I go through it alone. I've learned that once family finds out what's going on in your life, your name comes up in every conversation. "Did you hear what happened to so-and-so?" Whether it's good or bad, best believe they're talking about it.

When I need to talk about what's going on with me, I'll call my therapist. She might tell her colleagues, but not my family.

CHAPTER TWO

I sit at my desk, staring into the corner office with the view of the D.C. skyline, watching the rain hit the window. I pray the rain will stop before it's time to get off work. I have class again tonight. No time for all the madness that comes with bad weather. Traffic is bad enough without the rain. Out the corner of my eye, I see someone walking toward my desk. *Please keep on walking.* Blaire, from accounting, stops at my desk and starts talking.

"You look deep in thought. Everything okay?"

I guess what I'm going through is written all over my face. Gotta fix that. I don't need anyone in this office knowing my business. I like to *hear* the gossip, not *be* the gossip.

"I'm okay, just praying the rain stops before it's time for me to leave."

"I know, me too. It's that good, sleepy weather."

"I know, right?"

As she walks away from my desk, I give myself a little pep talk.

Get it together, Destinee. Can't be at work thinking about the drama in your life. You need your job.

I feel and hear the vibration of my phone from my purse in my desk drawer. *Hmph.* It's Alan. Should've known. Seventh time today. With every call, he leaves a voice mail and sends a text message. I'm not responding.

It doesn't matter how many times he apologizes. What's done is done. It's over. My phone vibrates again, this time in my hand. Another voice mail. I tap the notification and listen.

"I know you see me calling and texting you. Answer your phone or call me back. Stop ignoring me. We need to talk. Don't make me come up to your job."

I have a feeling things are going to get worse before they get better. He's not going to stop calling, and he's the type to show up at my job and show out.

This is it for me. I tried the relationship thing, and it never seems to work out. It's time for me to focus on myself, finish school, and progress in my career, which is what I should've kept doing instead of getting involved with Alan.

Regardless of what happens in my life, I give it to God and move on. He can fix everything better than I can. Right now, I need the strength to make it through the rest of the day.

"Destinee, can I see you in my office?"

I look up and see Steven standing in the hallway by his office doorway.

Shit, what did I do wrong? The last thing I need is for my boss to get wind of the drama in my life right now. I've been busting my butt in this office day and night, all while being in school.

I walk into Steven's office. Todd, one of the firm's shareholders and the lead litigation attorney, sits in the chair across from Steven's desk. For the past couple of months, I've been assisting Todd and Steven with a federal case that is going to trial next month. I pray I didn't do anything wrong.

"Have a seat," Steven says.

Lord Jesus, they are about to fire my ass. Let me catch my breath before I have a panic attack. My mind is racing, trying to figure out what's going on. Steven closes the door, walks over to his desk, and sits down in his chair, leaving just enough space between him and his desk so his potbelly can breathe.

"How's your day going?"

What kind of question is that? I've been Steven's paralegal for five years now. He knows I don't beat around the bush, and I don't want anyone else to either, especially when it has something to do with me.

"My day is going well. What's going on?"

"I know you're wondering why we called you in here. Especially so late in the day."

Umm, yes. Please get to the point.

"Well, Todd and I were discussing the need to add another associate to help with our civil litigation case load. We thought you might be interested since you will be finished with school soon and taking the bar exam."

I want to jump out of my seat and do a praise dance. Slowly, I nod my head. *This is really happening.* I take a breath in and release it slowly, trying to contain myself.

"Yes. I am definitely interested. I have one more semester left, then the bar exam next summer. I would love to continue my career with this firm."

Todd nods and says, "Great, just what I wanted to hear."

"Thank you for thinking of me for this opportunity."

"No, thank *you*. Steven has said nothing but great things about you, and I've seen firsthand your work ethic and brilliance. Of course, we are relieved to hear you want to continue your career with us. We definitely don't want to lose you."

I glance over at Steven. He's staring at the ceiling, nose in the air and mouth tightly closed. I can tell he has something on his mind.

"Is everything okay, Steven?" I ask him.

"Well, yes and no. I will be losing the best paralegal I've ever had, but no one is more deserving of this opportunity than you. I know you will do well. Congratulations!" Steven scoots up closer to his desk like he's trying to shove his belly under the table, which looks uncomfortable. Like he's thinking about what to say next.

"Would you be okay with relocating to the Norfolk, Virginia office?"

I feel my forehead creasing. My eyes widen and my mouth drops open slightly. *What? Why would I want to do that?*

"Sir, in all honesty, I would rather stay in D.C. But if you need me in Virginia, I will go."

Todd gets up from the chair and walks toward the door. "Thank you for your honesty. We are still working out the logistics but wanted to run that by you. One more question."

I try not to roll my eyes, eager for the conversation to be over.

"Would you be able to travel to Norfolk next month to wrap up this trial you've been assisting with? I also want you to get the feel of the Norfolk office and the staff there."

"Sure, no problem."

"Perfect. We will talk details over the next couple of days."

As soon as Todd walks out of the office, I look at Steven and ask why the Norfolk office. Just because I have family in Virginia doesn't mean I want to live there. Turns out they only have one civil litigation attorney there who is not familiar with federal cases. They want to add another litigation associate—someone who is knowledgeable on the *Federal Rules of Civil Procedure* and the federal case process.

Maybe this is a sign from God that I need to be closer to my family. Being close to family is not always a good thing. They feel entitled to drop by unannounced and act surprised when I stare at them from the window. Call first so you don't get your feelings hurt. I do want that position, though, and getting out of D.C. might help me forget about everything with Alan and really focus on just me.

I know my family will be thrilled to hear about me moving back. Last time I was home to visit, I got fussed out because everyone thinks I don't come home enough or I don't tell anyone when I'm in town. If I can drive three hours, sometimes four depending on traffic, so can they. When I tell one family member I'm coming home and the whole family finds out, they get mad at me because I don't stop by their house to visit. How about you come visit me where I am? Plus, after being in town for two days, I'm ready to go back home.

The rain lets up right before it's time to get off work. I have just enough time to grab a snack and head to class. Alan is still blowing up my phone, expecting me to answer. Not gonna happen.

After being in class for a few minutes, I think maybe I should have skipped class. It feels like I'm listening to Charlie Brown's teacher lecturing, "wah wah wah wah." Nothing the professor says makes sense. There's too much on my mind. By the time class is over, I want to take a nice hot shower and go to sleep. I'm too afraid to go back to my apartment because I know Alan will be there waiting.

The Hilton is calling my name. I'll deal with Alan tomorrow.

On my way to the hotel, I glance at my phone to see if there are any more voice mails or text messages from Alan. No voice mails, but a long text message: "Your voice mail is full. Guess you haven't listened to my messages. I know you see me calling and texting you. Stop ignoring me and pick up your damn phone. Call me or text me back. At least let me know you are somewhere safe. I'm sorry about hurting you. It shouldn't have happened. I never should've put my hands on you. You didn't deserve that. I just want to talk to you. Destinee, please answer your phone. I'll do better."

Why do men want to do better after they did something wrong? How about don't do the wrong thing and you wouldn't have to be better?

Valet costs a grip, but I don't have the energy to find a parking spot and feed the meter. I arrive at the hotel and pull up to the valet. I grab my bag from the back seat, take my valet ticket, and walk into the hotel to check in.

My phone rings as I hand the front-desk clerk my ID and credit card. I silence my phone, toss it in my bag, grab my room key, and proceed to the elevator. As soon as I'm in the room, I plop down on the bed, my arms stretched out and legs dangling off the end of the bed.

Before I can gather my thoughts, there's a jarring knock at the door. I don't respond, hoping they have the wrong door. But the knocking continues.

"I know you're in there."

Shit! It's Alan. My soul sits up on the bed before my body has a chance to react. How did he know I was here? There's another knock on the door, this time harder than the one before. I tiptoe over to the door and look through the peephole.

"I'm calling hotel security," I say.

I look through the peephole again to see Alan staring at the door, simmering in anger. He has this stance like he's willing to knock down the door to get to me.

"So, call 'em. I just want to talk to you." His voice echoes through the hallway.

"I don't have anything to say."

"Open the damn door, Destinee."

The knock turns into kicking. *God, help me.* The tears begin to fall and I wipe them away as I pick up the room phone and call for security. I can still hear Alan yelling in the hallway about me not answering his calls. Telling me I should've went home instead of going to a hotel. He's stalking me now.

I hear security approach Alan and ask him to move away from the door.

"I'm not going nowhere. My lady is in there."

I look through the peephole to see what's going on and shake my head in disbelief at all the drama he's causing. I sure do know how to pick 'em.

One of the security guys knocks on my door.

"Ma'am, are you okay in there?"

I make sure the swing bar is latched before opening the door.

"Yes, I'm okay but would prefer that this gentleman leave the hotel."

Before the security guard can say another word, Alan turns and walks away.

"Looks like he's leaving now. If you have any more issues, just give us a call."

Unbelievable! I made the right decision not to go back to my apartment. Who knows what he would've done to me, especially with no security there to protect me.

A nice hot shower will do me some good. I can wash the day away and start anew tomorrow. While the shower runs, I wrap my hair up with my scarf, feeling like I'm moving in slow motion as I undress. The room fills up with steam, and I can no longer see my reflection in the mirror.

The hot water feels so good against my skin. If I wasn't so afraid of wetting my hair, I would stand under the water and let it douse me. But my hair appointment isn't for another week, so this hair has got to hold up. My mind races, replaying what happened this morning. I can take the yelling, fussing, and cussing, but when you put your hands on me, that's a problem.

I grab a washcloth from the shelf over the toilet, soak it with water, and lather it with soap. I hear a noise coming from the main door. I stop to listen. It sounds like something is scraping the door. I remember latching the door shut, so I continue washing up, rinsing all the soap from my body before turning off the water. As I reach for my towel, I feel a whiff of cool air enter the bathroom. Then I hear footsteps approaching. Quickly, I push the bathroom door closed and lock it.

"Didn't I tell you that this thing we got is forever?" Alan says.

How did he get into my room? He had time to figure out how to break into a hotel room, but he can't figure out how to get his life right. My clothes are still in my bag, so I wrap the towel around my body, back away from the door, put the toilet seat down, and sit on it. The door handle begins to rattle.

"Please, Alan, leave me alone."

"I'm not leaving here without you."

The lock clicks, and the door opens.

Alan walks into the bathroom, his face flushed and eyes squinted. He looks down at me and shrugs his shoulders. "See, I just want to talk. I'm not going to hurt you."

This is some shit you see on television, not something I thought would be happening to me. "Why are you doing this?"

He draws a deep breath and releases it before speaking. "Because I love you, and I know you love me too."

"Love is not enough. You put your hands on me. You hurt me." My heart is racing and my hands are shaking. I gotta try and get out of this bathroom and get some clothes on.

"I told you I was sorry."

"Sorry don't cut it."

I slowly ease up from the toilet and walk out of the bathroom. I put on my T-shirt and underwear. As I reach for my pants, Alan grabs me by the arm, making me lose my balance and fall to the floor.

"You pissing me off."

I have never seen this side of Alan before. Never did I think he would hurt me. I don't want to piss him off more, so I lie still on the floor.

"Get up so you can finish getting dressed, and we can go home."

Go home? We don't live together. Slowly, I rise up from the floor and reach across the bed for my pants. I put them on one leg at a time. Alan stands at the edge of the dresser, eyes lifeless and cold, watching my every move. Once I have my pants on, Alan's cell phone rings. When he reaches in his pocket and glances down at the phone, I make a run for the door.

I feel like my heart is in my throat and I'm moving in slow motion. I manage to get the door open, but before I can get out of the room he yanks my shirt and pulls me back. With his cold clammy hands, he pushes my head toward the door until my face collides with it. The force knocks me down to the floor in the doorway. It feels like he's got pure adrenaline pumping through him. As I try to get up, he kneels over me and wraps both hands around my neck. No matter how hard I try, I can't get him off of me.

"You so fucking hardheaded."

No words or scream can escape my mouth as his grip tightens, and it's becoming difficult to breathe. As I lie on the floor, I look up at Alan's scrunched face. His nostrils flare and his chin juts out. I've never seen him this angry before. Slowly, it feels like my body starts to drift. My arms fall to the floor and my eyelids flutter closed. He lets go. Before I can gather my thoughts and catch my breath, he gets up, steps over me, and leaves.

CHAPTER THREE

Being back in Virginia feels weird. Sometimes I feel like I'm being watched by my family, and it makes me uneasy. After everything I've been through with Alan, I believe this is where I need to be in this season of my life. Even though I'm only here for a few weeks, it feels good to be surrounded by friends and family who love and support me.

Every time I come home, I go to the beach. I love the warmth from the sun, the texture of the sand under my feet as I walk toward the water, and the smell of the ocean. There's something about the beach that calms my mind.

After getting settled at my sister's house and spending some time with my family, I decide to drive down to the oceanfront. "I'll go with you," Michelle says. After everything that went down with Alan, Michelle has been worried about me, a lot. I know she means well, but I just want to be alone. These last few weeks haven't been easy. I felt like I had to constantly pay attention to my surroundings, afraid that Alan would appear. I even stayed with Stephanie for a few nights because I was too afraid to go back to my apartment. I feel safer in Virginia.

When I say I'm going to the beach alone, she knows that means I'm going through something.

The weather is pleasant for a June night, and the sun is beginning to set. Perfect timing. I park in the parking garage and walk down to the boardwalk, removing my sandals before walking onto the sand. The sun setting on the water looks purple as the clouds close in, filling the sky with hues of red blended with a touch of orange. Such a beautiful sight. It's amazing how the sun is setting here, but on the other side of the world the sun is rising. Watching the sun set reminds me of how blessed I am—that even after the day has ended, tomorrow brings a new beginning.

My mother always tells my siblings and I that prayer is our lifeline to God. When I'm at the beach, I feel closer to that lifeline. Like God can hear me more clearly when I talk to him here. There's a sense of peace that comes over me, an extra reassurance that he's got my back.

I walk toward the water, my mind racing with everything that has happened over the past couple of weeks: the restraining order I got against Alan and the pure fear everywhere I went. Now it's time for healing and surrounding myself with people who love, care for, and support me. I'm excited for the new transition after I finish school in a couple of months.

Digging my toes into the sand, I wish I brought a chair or blanket so I could sit here for a while. I look around and see people packing up to leave the beach and couples walking along the seashore holding hands like they are madly in love. *God, I want that.*

Before making my way back up to the boardwalk, I put my feet in the water. I stand there, letting the water splash against my legs, holding my sundress up so it doesn't get wet. It's starting to get dark. I let out a big sigh and say a prayer.

"God, you know my every need and the desires of my heart. Help me find peace and have a forgiving heart for the pain I've endured. Today, I promise I'm going to wait on you to bless me with the man I am supposed to spend the rest of my life with. I will remain focused on you, myself, school, and my career. Amen!"

When I get back to Michelle's house, Jaiden is up waiting for me. He misses his auntie and I miss him. I feel bad that I haven't been home as much since I started law school. I plan on spending my free time with Jaiden, trying to make up for lost time. He's growing up so fast. I can't believe he starts kindergarten in September.

When I told Michelle I would be coming home for a few weeks, she asked if I was going to stay with Mom and Dad. My response was, "Hell, no." I love them both dearly, but I don't always get along with my dad. Seems like we always bump heads about something. My mom says it's because we are so much alike, but I beg to differ.

My dad has this way of talking to people like he's better than them. I can't stand it. Whenever I'm around him, I find myself defending someone from the foul things that come out of his mouth. I don't how my mother has dealt with him all these years.

When my dad found out what happened with Alan, he said, "You should've never dated him to begin with." Not the response I was expecting. I know I'm grown, but at least act like you have some concern for your daughter. Get mad, grab one of your guns, get in your car, and come check on me. Tell me you're gonna find

Alan and put a bullet in his ass. If my pop pop was here, he would have been in his car with the quickness driving down I-95 from Virginia to D.C. to find Alan.

I'm not thrilled about being back in the Hampton Roads area, but I'm going to try and make the best out of it. Trips to the beach, catching up with friends and family. Maybe Michelle and Kevin can have more date nights. They look like they need to release some tension. They are so busy with work and Jaiden that they never do anything or go anywhere. Maybe they can go to my place in D.C. for the weekend and get away from the everyday hustle and bustle of responsibilities.

It's Friday afternoon. Another hot, humid day in June. I want so badly to get back to my cozy little D.C. apartment and relax in my own space. I miss the narrow sidewalks and easy access to bars and restaurants. While I was in college, I would scope out different areas where I wanted to live. Everyone kept telling me D.C. was too expensive, but that was where I wanted to be. Especially the U Street Corridor section of the city. I think I was drawn to its history; it was known as the "Black Broadway" in the early 1900s.

I've been trying to fly under the radar at work today because I don't want to answer any more questions or do any more research. It's been a struggle to keep my eyes open since I got back from lunch, and I'm surprised no one has caught me nodding off at my desk. I normally eat a light, healthy lunch, but today I went all out. I met up with Kim, and we tried this new Peruvian restaurant that opened up around the corner from my office on Granby Street. Ever since college, Kim always finds new places to eat at. She'd rather support the small mom-and-pop restaurants than the big chain ones.

I keep checking the time at the bottom of my computer screen, but it doesn't seem to be moving as fast as I think it should. Feels like that's always the case when I want to be some place other than work.

Finally, at about 2:45, Todd walks out the conference room with his briefcase. He stops by my desk and places his briefcase on the floor. "I am leaving for the day and won't be back until Tuesday. You can take off early if you want to."

Don't have to tell me twice. I've been waiting to hear those words all day. It would've been better hearing them before lunch, but I'll take what I can get.

Without hesitation, I shut down my computer, lock my desk, grab my purse, and head straight for the elevator, trying my best to avoid anyone who would ask me questions. These low-ass cubicles make it difficult for anyone to be unnoticed.

As soon as I walk out the building, the humidity hits me like a ton of bricks. I have to stop for a minute to catch my breath before heading to the parking garage. I make it to my car, pop the trunk, toss my heels in, and slip on my flip flops. I collapse into the front seat and roll down the windows so I can breathe while the hot air flows out of the vents. Tipping my head back on the headrest, I wait for the cool air to circulate through the car.

The damn low-fuel light comes on as I exit the parking garage. Apparently, I forgot to get gas on my way to the office this morning. I tighten my hands on the wheel at the thought of running out of gas and being stranded on the side of the road.

I hate pumping gas. Especially in this heat or the freezing cold. I pull up to the gas pump with a sigh. As I stand there pumping gas, a black GMC truck pulls up to the pump across from me, music blaring. Usually loud music doesn't bother me, but I'm hot as hell and tired. It's been a long week.

I look over to see who's making all that noise and see a tall, thickly built, dark-skinned brotha get out of the truck. He looks pretty good in his military uniform. I try not to stare, but he catches me looking his way and nods as he walks inside the convenience store. On his way back to his truck, he looks my way, winks, and says, "Hello." He speaks in a calm, sensitive, yet deep tone of voice.

I'm surprised because he looks a little rough around the edges with his five o'clock shadow and overgrown fade.

I return the greeting and turn my head in the opposite direction, trying not to make eye contact with him. Back at his truck, he finally turns down his music.

"Oh my God, thank you," I say.

He peeks over at me. "Did you say something?"

I roll my eyes, smile at him, and shake my head.

As I twist the gas cap back on, I can feel his eyes on me. When I look at him again, he's watching me, smiling. I smile back as I walk to my car door. *Nope, I'm not falling for that. Now is not the time. Keep it moving, Destinee.*

As I open my car door, he yells, "Wait, wait, wait a minute. Let me give you my card."

Unwanted thoughts fill my mind as he gets closer to my car. Good lord, my hormones are raging. It's been a while since I've had some. I'm starting to feel like a born-again virgin. He's attractive, but I'm not falling for another man right now.

Clearly, he's in the military or he wouldn't be wearing a military uniform. What kind of business cards could he be handing out? I turn around and look at him.

"No, thank you. I'm good."

Now I got the stank face, the look of being pissed off and annoyed. He continues to walk closer to my car. "Here, you never know, it might come in handy one day."

Shit, you *might come in handy one day.* I'm glad I didn't say that out loud, but I think my eyes might have revealed my thoughts. He watches me as I stare him up and down then reaches over my car door to hand me his business card. It reads "Richardson Auto Repair Shop." Okay, a little confusing, but I don't have the time nor the patience to question him. I slide the card into my center console, tell him to have a nice day, and go about my business.

I'm staying true to the promise I made to myself and God: focusing on myself and waiting for God to send me my husband. Right now, it's all about school and my career. Plus, I need to get Alan out of my system.

I'm glad Kim isn't here. Every time we go out, she says, "There's nothing like a new man to help you get over an old one." No more one-night stands and one-year relationships. I want something real.

I call my mom to let her know I'm getting on the road, and I tell her what happened.

"Don't be out there chasing no man. Focus on Destinee. God will send you your husband one day."

"How will I know, Ma?"

"God will reveal it, and you will feel it. I promise."

She said the same thing to Michelle. Now Michelle's married with a little boy. Seems like all of my friends are getting married and having children, too. I swear, every couple of months I get a wedding invitation in the mail. As a matter of fact, Stephanie's wedding is in a few weeks. We ran track together at Howard and have remained close friends since. She wasn't too fond of Alan either. When she sent out the RSVPs, she asked if Alan was going to be my plus one. I told her I would come alone so I could enjoy myself.

As much as I miss D.C., I love the time I've been spending with my family and Kim. I remember when Kim and I got our acceptance letters to Howard University. Mine arrived first, but I wouldn't open it until she got hers. I knew no matter what that I was going away to college. I wanted that historically-black-college experience.

Plus, more than anything, I wanted to get away from the men in my life: my ex-boyfriend and Dad. The relationship with my ex was unhealthy, and my dad had a way of making me feel like I was the child he never wanted. I admired the relationship he had with Michelle and Landon. Whatever they had going on, he was always there to show his support. It wasn't like that with me.

That's why I always wanted to be with my grandparents. Plus, Kim lived down the street with her dad and stepmother. My grandfather always kept it real with me, and he felt more like a father than a grandfather. My grandmother was fun to be around too, and they both taught me so much.

Every time I went over to their house, I would watch how my grandparents cared for each other. They had a different kind of love that everyone could see and feel. The respect they had for each other is something you don't see these days. There were a couple of times I could tell my grandmother was upset with my grandfather about something, but she never let that get in the way of making sure her husband was taken care of. And my grandfather always made sure my grandmother didn't want for anything. They showed me that God, communication, respect, and love are key in a marriage. I want to experience that one day with my husband. Whenever he finds me.

CHAPTER FOUR

"Girl, you need to get out of the house," Kim yells through the phone. Whenever I leave the house, it's only to go to the office or the store, or out to eat. I've been content with staying in the house, watching movies with Jaiden and playing games.

"You've become such a homebody."

"And what's wrong with that?"

"You're never going to meet anyone if all you do is stay in the house."

"You're absolutely right. That's why I stay in the house." Mentally, I can't handle another relationship.

"Let's do brunch today."

If I say no, I'll never hear the end of it. "Give me a few to shower and find something to wear."

"Okay, pick me up when you're done. Text me when you're on the way." She hangs up before I can even respond. It's just like her to make a suggestion followed up with a demand.

Brunch with the bestie is always eventful. We catch up on each other's life and gossip about everything and everyone. Well, she does the gossiping. I just listen. I miss hanging out with Kim. We've been besties since the day we met in middle school. That didn't change when we went away to college together. I don't miss the clubbing, though. Before she got married, she would stay in the clubs. After undergrad, she moved back to Virginia Beach and married Troy, her HBCU beau.

Now she has baby fever and says she wants three little Troy's running around the house. I'm surprised Troy doesn't have any little Troy's running around somewhere else. He was always the player type in college. They say people change, but I don't think that's the case for Troy. He and all the other guys he hung out with on campus were always messing around. Troy would always try to hook me up with one of them, but I knew better. I tried to talk some sense into Kim but she was already too far gone, head over heels for Troy. Ain't no dick that good to want to share it with another woman.

I text Kim to let her know I'm on the way, and she responds back with the address of an auto repair shop to pick her up from. I knew when Kim snappishly asked me to pick her up that it was more than just brunch.

Turns out Troy is out of town this weekend, and she needs me to pick her up from the shop and drop her off after brunch to pick up her car. The nerve of her.

When I pull up to the location she texted me, I notice the name on the sign: "Richardson Auto Repair." I ask myself where I remember that name from, then it hits me. It was the name on the business card the guy at the gas station gave me a few days ago. If I tell Kim, she'll insist I call him. I pull up to the store next to the repair shop and text Kim to let her know I'm here. As soon as she gets in the car, I pull off.

"Someone's in a rush. Can I get my seat belt on before you get all reckless?"

"No rush, just hungry. Ready to eat."

Kim can't stand the fact that she's only five foot two. No matter what outfit she's sporting, it's a guarantee she will have heels on. I can't get away with the looks she pulls off. Like today, she's wearing some distressed jean shorts, a yellow-and-white blouse, and yellow high-heel sandals with the straps going up her legs. It's like a fashion show with her sometimes. I've always admired her long hair, though. She usually rocks a long bob haircut with a part down the middle, but today it's pulled up in a ponytail bun.

She always finds the best mom-and-pop restaurants to eat at, and the food be finger-licking good. This time, it's a new restaurant that only serves breakfast and lunch.

We sit down, glance over the menu, and order our food. Before I can take a sip of my mimosa, she asks me if I'm going to Stephanie's wedding. I already know where this conversation is headed, and I am not in the mood for it.

"Can we have a nice brunch without talking about men or marriage?" I place my drink on the table and lower my head.

"Destinee? When are you going to get back out there and start dating again?"

I cock my head back and let out a sigh. "Whenever God sends me my husband."

Kim tilts her head and asks, "And how will you know he's going to be your husband?"

I chuckle, shaking my head. "My mama said I will know and God will reveal."

"I love your mama, and I know she's ready for you to settle down just like I am."

The more she talks, the more my face scrunches up. I relax it, trying to regain my calm. Why is it so hard for her to understand that I can't handle a new relationship? I want to take time to focus on myself. Is that such a bad thing?

"I worry about you, Destinee."

"Why is that?"

"Ever since Troy and I got married, you've been a little distant. At first, I thought you were just giving me space since we were newlyweds. Now I wonder if it's something else."

"Something else like what?"

I need her to pump her breaks. I don't like where this conversation is headed, and I'm pretty sure she doesn't want to hear about how I'm worried about her too. I take another sip of my mimosa. I'm going to need another one if we keep having these types of discussions.

"I don't know. You've never been the jealous type, but maybe you're unhappy or lonely."

Before I can respond, our waitress brings out our food. Perfect timing. I order another mimosa and take a couple bites of my food before replying. I try to gather my thoughts—to think before I speak so I don't hurt Kim's feelings. Sometimes that works, and other times the thoughts come out before I can catch them.

"Listen, I'm not jealous. I'm happy for you and Troy. I just thought after graduating college you were going to stay in D.C. with me like we planned, but instead you married Troy and y'all moved back here. I still think you should've waited a couple more years before getting married, but I'm happy for y'all, and you shouldn't worry about me. I'm fine."

"Sounds a little like jealousy to me."

"I admit that when you guys got married, I was in yet another unhealthy relationship. But I wasn't jealous of you and Troy. I just thought you both needed time after college to figure some things out, especially Troy."

"Time to figure out what?"

Here we go. I can't hold it no more. "Life without Troy. Your career and other goals you had for yourself. Time to figure out who you really are outside of college and what you really want out of life. Same thing goes for Troy too. He wasn't ready for marriage, and you know that. He still has a lot of growing up to do."

Kim clicks her tongue, wraps her arms around herself, and slides back in her seat. "I knew what I wanted: to marry my college sweetheart and have his babies."

I always thought she wanted more in life than to be someone's wife and have babies. "That's all you wanted, and you were willing to settle?"

"Okay, where are you going with this?"

She won't let up. All I want is to eat my food and enjoy an afternoon out with my friend. Not argue about dumb stuff. "Nowhere, Kim. Just know that I am not jealous of you and Troy. If you are happy, I am happy for you. One day, I do want to get married and have children, but I am in no rush, especially with my track record of relationships. Right now, my focus is on me. I cannot handle another failed, abusive relationship."

"Troy and I are just fine. Yeah, we had our issues, but we're good now. I'm happy, Destinee, and I want you to be happy too."

"I am happy with my life right now. Taking care of me and working on my goals."

I look out the window of the restaurant and catch my reflection staring back at me. I see exactly who I am, imperfections and all. I see how far I've come in life. I'm much closer to the person I want to be. I lose track sometimes, get distracted, but I always return to the right path, walking toward my destiny. The waitress approaches with the check and breaks my concentration.

"What about your happiness?" Kim asks.

"Didn't I just say I am happy with the way my life is right now? It's busy with work and school and planning my move back to Virginia. I'm about to start a new chapter in my career, and I know Mr. Right will make his way into my life when the time is right."

She gets quiet for a few minutes and changes the subject, which is in her best interest because I am at my breaking point with this conversation.

After brunch, we get in a little shopping. There's nothing like treating yourself to a little retail therapy. As we're walking out of the mall, she gets a call that her car is ready. I will drop her off and go about my day. After the conversation we just had at brunch, I don't need her finding out about the other day at the gas station. Plus, I promised Jaiden we would watch a movie when I get back. I know he's there waiting for me to walk through the door.

As I turn into the parking lot, I see the same black truck from the gas station. I really thought he was handing me a bogus business card.

"Come inside with me so I can make sure everything is good to go," Kim says.

"I'll just sit here while you go check. I won't leave until you get your car."

"No, please come in with me. You know I'm not good with this kind of stuff."

That's what your husband is for. I catch that one before it escapes my lips. Kim grabs her bag and pulls the handle to open the car door.

"Come on, Destinee."

I am not a mechanic. What does she expect me to do in there? Plus, if the guy from the gas station is in there, I don't want to see him. Kim is still sitting in the car with the door open, letting out all the cool air. "Please, Destinee?"

I grab my phone and keys, turn the car off, and get out to follow her. As we walk up to the glass door, I see the guy from the gas station standing at the counter inside. Kim walks in and I walk in behind her.

"I knew my services would come in handy one day." The man leans on the counter, cheesing from ear to ear.

Kim looks at me and whispers, "Do you know him?"

I know he's talking to me, but I try to play it off. I look at Kim and then we both turn and look at the door to see if someone has walked in behind us. But no one is there.

"I'm talking to you, the beautiful lady from the gas station the other day on St. Paul Boulevard. You were wearing a tan blouse and a black skirt. I believe you were driving a black Infiniti Q50."

Kim scowls at me and asks why I didn't tell her about him.

There was nothing to tell. It's not like we exchanged numbers and went on a date.

Kim and I walk up to the counter. "She dropped her car off this morning. Kimberly Jones. Just here to pick it up."

I think about that day at the gas station. He was wearing a military uniform. Now, he stands behind the counter of an auto repair shop all greased up in some dirty, blue overalls. I can't help it. I have to ask.

"Are you in the military or a mechanic?"

"It's a long and interesting story. How about I tell you about it over dinner tonight?"

"No, thank you. We just want to pick up her car so we can go about the rest of our day."

Kim quickly interjects. She leans on the counter and lifts her head up to talk to the guy. "Yes, dinner does sound nice." She turns to whisper to me, "He seems like an alright guy. Dark chocolate with pearly white teeth. Just your type, Dee." Turning back to the guy, she asks, "And your name is?"

I look over at Kim as she continues to ignore me.

"My name is Christopher, but everyone calls me Chris."

He is handsome, and I do love the dark chocolate ones, but I already have plans with another guy: my nephew. I ask again about her car. This time, Kim and Chris ignore my question and continue talking about me as if I'm not standing there.

"What about dinner tonight? Where you gonna take her? She loves Japanese and Mexican food."

If looks could kill. I want to slap her. We just had a conversation earlier about me not dating. Now she's putting me out here like I'm some charity case.

Chris looks at me then back at Kim.

"So, dinner tonight? I'll be getting off in a couple of hours. I can freshen up and pick you up."

I take a step back and look at Kim as she continues her conversation with Chris. "You gonna take her for Japanese?" she asks.

I shake my head in disbelief. This situation right here has me embarrassed as hell. I've had enough. I grab one of the business cards off the counter and write down my name and cell phone number.

I slide the card across the counter. Chris reaches for it and his hand grazes mine as I pull away. "I'll call you when I get off work, and I'll pick you up later."

Kim interjects again, "Yes, please. She needs that in her life."

I'm done with this conversation and with Kim.

I turn toward Chris. "No, thank you. I don't know you like that, and it's a dangerous world we live in. People nowadays have stalking tendencies. Plus, I have plans tonight, so maybe another night."

"Don't flake on me and tell me another night then come up with another excuse." He winks.

I smile, say goodbye to Kim, and walk out to my car. I sit in the parking lot until she gets her car then I drive off and head back to my sister's house. I didn't make it to the corner before Kim was calling me. I couldn't get "hello" out all the way before she started ranting.

"You were so rude to that man. Walked out and didn't even say goodbye! He might not be Mr. Right, but he can be Mr. Right Now, if you know what I'm saying. Maybe he can be that someone you can talk to and spend time with. I get that you've had some bad relationships, and I know you are scared of starting a new one. Just start slow. Plus, how long has it been since you had some good dick? Maybe you need one night to relieve some tension instead of that battery-operated thing in your nightstand. Just go out with him and have a good time. You need it and you deserve it."

I hit the "end call" button on my steering wheel and turn up my music. The perfect song is playing on the radio: "Add To Me" by Ledisi.

I don't need a man to take care of me financially or sexually. I got my own money and my battery-operated massager works perfectly well. It always hits the right spot, it's there when I need it, it doesn't complain, and it lasts as long as I need it to. Thank you very much!

While driving back to my sister's house, a vision of Chris standing at the counter comes to my mind. *Should I go to dinner with him tonight?* I promised Jaiden we would watch a movie when I got back to the house. I can't break my promise. Plus, Chris might be all talk.

As soon as I walk through the front door, Jaiden runs up to me. "Auntie, I've been waiting for you! I picked out a movie for us to watch." I don't have much experience with kids, but I think I've been doing a good job with Jaiden. In the short amount of time I've been here, I've learned a lot more about him. He's an inquisitive little guy, always asking questions and pointing out things that I don't pay attention to. And so energetic. I wish I had half the energy he has.

He pulls out the *Monsters University* DVD. "How about some popcorn to go with that movie?" I ask.

I go into the kitchen to pop us some popcorn then put the DVD on in the den. Both of us lie across the couch with our blankets on. We are both into this movie about monsters going to college and trying to get on the scare team.

My phone vibrates on the end table next to me, and I glance at it. I don't recognize the number, so I wouldn't usually answer. But this time something is telling me to pick up, so I do.

"Hello?"

"Hello, Miss Destinee, how are you this evening?"

"Who is this?"

"It's Chris from the shop earlier today."

Didn't I tell him I already had plans for tonight? I walk into the kitchen to continue the conversation. "I was about to ignore your call and send you to voice mail." He has no idea how serious I am.

"Wow, it's like that?"

"Nothing personal. I usually don't answer numbers I don't recognize."

"Well, I need you to save me in your contacts so next time I call, you know it's me and will answer."

I pull the chair out from the kitchen table and take a seat. His voice is so pleasant and calming. I wasn't expecting that. "Don't get it twisted. I don't answer for people in my contacts either." *Put him in my contacts. He thinks he's special.*

"Did I catch you at a bad time?" The tone of his voice changes, like he's sympathetic to interrupting me.

"I was in the middle of watching *Monsters University* with my nephew. It was getting interesting."

"I remember that movie. I took my little cousins to see it in the movie theater. I don't want to cut into your quality time with your nephew but would really love to take you out to dinner tonight."

37

He said "little cousins," so that's a good sign that he doesn't have children.

"I get the feeling if I say no, you will keep calling me until I say yes."

"Look at you, getting to know me already. I'm known to be very persistent."

I bet he's smiling. I can hear the excitement in his voice. I'm not smiling, though. I've had enough of persistent men. I just hope he's not controlling or a stalker. I'm going to try not to let that comment get in the way of me having dinner with a nice man.

"I guess we can go for dinner tonight." The words come out of my mouth before I have a chance to really think about it.

"That's what I'm talkin' 'bout. Now, we are getting somewhere. Kim told me you could use some fun and laughter in your life right now. Hoping I can be that for you this evening. I'm not asking for anything extra. Just have dinner with me, and if you don't enjoy my company at dinner, I won't call you anymore."

"Perfect. What time do you want to meet up?" I laugh because I really don't think I will enjoy dinner and conversation with this man, but I'm going to give it a try. No drinking, just dinner. I learned my lesson with Alan.

I hang up with Chris and finish watching the movie with Jaiden. When it finishes, I run upstairs to rummage through my sister's closet. We may not have a lot in common, but one thing is for sure: We both love clothes. She may be taller than me, but wide hips and long legs run in the family. I need to find something flattering and light. These summer nights are humid, and being hot and uncomfortable is not my style. I find a sleeveless, chiffon romper-short set and some wedge sandals that are perfect for a summer night like this.

I try to sneak out of Michelle's closet without being noticed, but no such luck. She walks into her bedroom and sees me standing at her closet door.

"I thought we were past this stage in our sisterhood. What are you doing in my closet?"

"I'm going out to dinner."

"With who?"

"A guy I met a few days ago."

"So, you're going on a date with a guy you met a few days ago and weren't going to tell me about it?" Michelle can be dramatic sometimes. She always wants to be the first person to know what's going on. "You know it starts with dinner."

She sits down on the cedar chest in front of her bed. Kevin walks into the room and asks what we're talking about. I swear they are the perfect couple. Both nosey as hell. He must have just got home from the gym; his tank top is stained with sweat, and he has a hand towel draped over his shoulder.

"Destinee's going on a date," Michelle tells him.

"Yeah, right," Kevin says sarcastically.

They both look at each other and start laughing.

"All this talk about focusing on yourself, school, and your career, but you're about to go on a date? This must be Kim's doing. Want me to call you at dinner and say there's an emergency and you need to come home?" Kevin asks as he walks out of the room, laughing.

Michelle gets up from the chest, walks over to me, and places her hand on my shoulder. "Are you ready for this, or did Kim put you up to this? I mean, it's only been a couple of months since you and Alan broke up."

Michelle knows Kim all too well. I get that Michelle is concerned, but Kim is right. There's no reason why I can't go out with a man and have a good time. I've turned into a homebody since I've been in Virginia, and maybe it's time I go out, meet new people, and have some fun.

Plus, there is something about Chris's voice that makes me feel like I can trust him.

I take my time getting ready. I jump in the shower, tighten up my curls, and put on some makeup. I'm a little late getting to the restaurant, but when I get there Chris is standing outside, patiently waiting for me, holding a bouquet of red roses. When he sees me walking toward him, he stops fiddling with the roses and smiles. His teeth are as bright as a T-shirt washed in bleach.

I have to compose myself because I did not think he would look as good as he does in regular clothes. Not only do I love chocolate men, but I love 'em well-groomed. He's rocking a fresh cut, he smells good, and he's dressed for the occasion. He's wearing khaki shorts, a polo shirt, and some Vans. It's a different style than what I'm used to seeing, but it's refreshing.

We walk into the restaurant and get on the wait list for a table. We manage to find a bench to sit on while we wait. Usually, I would try to make conversation, but I don't have to with him. He asks a lot of questions. I'm guarded at first because I don't know what to expect, and I'm not sure if I want to share anything about myself with this man. But he certainly doesn't have a problem talking about himself, so I let him.

He's a thoughtful conversationalist. After about fifteen minutes, we get seated at our table. He pulls my seat out for me, waits until

I'm seated, and takes his seat. Once again, this is something I'm not used to, but I can learn to enjoy this kind of attention.

"I probably should've asked before we sat down, but do you have any food allergies?"

I've never been asked that before. "No, I don't. Do you?"

"No, me either."

"Do you drink alcoholic beverages?" Boy, do I. But not tonight. Not falling for the trickery.

"I do, but not tonight."

Once we order our food, he opens up about where he's from, his family, and his military career. He was born in New Jersey and moved to Hampton, Virginia after his mother passed away when he was fifteen. I can't imagine losing my mother as a teenager.

"Do you have any siblings?" I ask.

"I do—a younger sister, Ebony. We are three years apart." He never knew his father and was raised by his maternal uncle Greg and Greg's wife, Regina.

"Do they have any children?"

"Yes. Charles, Dawn, and Sabrina." He tells me that when he graduated from high school, he went straight into the navy. His uncle retired from the navy, so he was a big influence on Chris's decision. Chris has been a mechanical engineer with the navy for twelve years.

Chris abruptly changes the subject. "I'm divorced."

My mouth slowly drops open, but I close it before it becomes noticeable.

"I don't have any children."

I guess he had to make that clear. Now I'm curious to know the cause of his divorce and why he's still single. He doesn't talk about that, though.

"I'm ready for a change. I'm looking for a wife, and I want to start a family. I don't think I can do that and still be in the military."

I almost choke on my food. We just met. It's a little soon to be talking about that kind of stuff.

He continues to tell me about how he helped support his sister through college, and now it's his turn to go to college and get his degree. He has three more semesters to go.

I'm intrigued by the fact that Chris can hold a decent conversation with me without being derogatory. Which makes me question myself and what I saw in the men I've dated.

Finally, he explains where the mechanic overalls come into play. "My uncle, Greg, owns Richardson Auto Repair Shop. I try to help out as much as I can, especially since I'm transitioning out of the navy, and my cousin Charles is too lazy to get his life together to help with the business." It's all coming together now.

I think I'm enjoying myself a little too much at dinner because afterwards he asks if I want to drive down to the beach and continue talking. I haven't mentioned anything about myself yet. I just keep asking questions to keep the conversation going. How does he know how much I love the beach?

We meet back up at the beach and walk along the boardwalk. It's nice to see how we share the same sense of humor and opinions. And how we bounce off each other. I get him. I feel like I can be my true self with him and he will get me. There's something about the tone of his voice when he talks to me and the attention he gives me when he's not talking.

"I love the beach, especially the sunset," Chris says. "The sound of the waves crashing up on the sand makes me feel like no matter what I'm going through, peace is on the other side of it." He looks at me and smiles, and I smile back at him. I can see his soul through his smile. "You've been asking me questions all night, and I've been talking about myself. Can I ask you some questions now?"

We walk over to an empty bench and sit. "Ask away."

"Who is Destinee?"

Oh, no he didn't. Such a loaded question. "One of life's fundamental questions. You sure you're ready for the answer?"

"Yes, I'm sure."

I sit back on the bench and cross my legs. "I am Destinee Clark. I'm a child of God who has been through some rough times, yet I'm always ready for a challenge and refuse to give up. Is that enough, or you want me to keep going?"

"Keep going, please."

I clear my throat and continue. "I like to think of myself as adventurous. I'll try anything once."

"Anything?" Chris asks as he leans in and lifts his hand to touch my shoulder then pulls back. His face lights up in delight like he's pleased with what I just said.

I wink at Chris and continue talking. "I'm kind-hearted and can be sarcastic at times."

When I tell him that I live in D.C. and am only here for a couple of weeks, his smile leaves his face. "What do you do for a living, and what brings you to Virginia Beach?"

"Well, I was born and raised in Virginia Beach. After high school, I couldn't wait for my parents to drop me off at college and drive away. I'm a paralegal and work for a firm in D.C. I'm helping one of the attorneys with a federal case in Norfolk. I have one more semester of law school left. Then I'll pass the bar exam and can practice law, finally."

"Wow, a lawyer."

"Soon-to-be, yes."

I love how Chris looks into my eyes when he talks to me. He's attentive and seems interested in what I have to say. I can get used to this. "What made you decide to go to law school?"

"Funny story. One of my professors recommended that I join the debate team. He said I was always eager to make a point and should think about a career in the legal field. I was sold on being a lawyer by my third debate. So, I stayed in D.C. after undergrad. I interned for a law firm that hired me as a legal secretary. Worked my way up to senior paralegal and enrolled in law school. I wasn't thrilled when I saw the price tag that came with law school, but when my grandparents passed away, they left me a little something to make that happen."

Then he asked about my family. I was honest and told him they were all crazy, except my twin brother, Landon, who is older than me by three minutes. My mother, Eunice, and father, James, have been married for almost thirty-two years, which I still can't believe. My only sister, Michelle, is married with a son. And Landon is in the army, currently stationed in California. Even though they're gone, I can't leave out my maternal grandparents.

"Your face lit up when you started talking about your grandparents," Chris says, smiling.

"They were my favorite people in the world, always looking out for me. I miss them like crazy. I feel like they were the only people who truly understood me."

The more we talk, the more I wonder why he's divorced. Listening to him talk, I can tell he learned some life lessons or had a strong male influence in his life. Maybe both. He says he believes a woman should never chase a man, and that chivalry is not dead in his eyes.

I didn't think it was possible, but I am enjoying myself so much that I don't want to go home. I don't think he does either. I feel something with him that I've never felt before with any other guy. He's different. Someone I wouldn't mind getting to know better and having in my life.

Even though I'll be coming back to Virginia, I'm not sure the time is right for me to get caught up with a new man.

CHAPTER FIVE

I must really be fucked up. Why didn't I realize in the beginning of my relationships that the guys were not good for me? I need to break this down. Here I go trying to analyze shit. Chris could be what I need in my life—the calm after the storm and the man God has sent me. I don't want to ruin a good thing by being scared.

I reach out to Stephanie to see if it's too late to add a plus one to her wedding and reception. She's shocked that I'm even thinking about bringing someone because I'm always a loner when I go to events for my friends. But not this time. It's short notice, but she's excited so she says she'll make it work.

Things have been moving fast with Chris. I've seen him every night since the first night we went out. This is not something I expected, and I can't explain it. He gives me the freedom to be me. No questions asked.

I ask Chris if he'll go with me to Stephanie's wedding. "I must be special if you want me to attend a close friend's wedding with you," he says. Maybe he is special, but I'm not going to tell him that.

I feel comfortable introducing him to my friends, but I'm not so sure about my family just yet. Michelle is dying to meet him. I can tell she's worried about me with all the time I've been spending with Chris. Most nights when I get off work, I go straight to his place. To my surprise, the first time I spent the night, he didn't try to get intimate.

I made it clear that I wasn't ready for a relationship because of what I went through with Alan. I didn't go into detail, but I let him know he's dealing with someone who has been hurt mentally and physically. I need to take things slow. He was understanding about that.

Last night, slow went out the door. After work I met him at his apartment. He got home from work and wanted to take a shower before going to dinner. We never made it to dinner.

The sexual tension between us was building up and I couldn't contain myself any longer. He stopped halfway into it and asked, "Are you sure you want to do this?" *Yes, sir.* I was hot and bothered and ready to see what he was working with. He worked it well, too. Put me out for the count.

I feel the sun creeping in through the blinds from the sliding glass door in his bedroom. I turn over, and Chris is sound asleep. We both took the day off so we didn't have to deal with so much traffic getting to D.C. for Stephanie's wedding this weekend.

I lift my head from the pillow and glance at the clock on his nightstand. It's 8:45 a.m. Almost time to get up so we can hit the road.

I lie in bed for a couple more minutes then slowly pull the

covers off and sit up.

"Where you think you going?" Chris pulls me back onto the bed and wraps his arms around me.

"Going to take a shower so we can get going."

He lets me go and sighs, watching me walk to the bathroom.

I turn on the light and look at myself in the mirror.

"It's okay to let go," I say to myself. It's time for me to stop letting fear of being hurt again get in the way of a good thing.

I take a closer look in the mirror. It's time to get my hair color touched up; I see the gray peeking through and I don't like it. I grab my shower cap and brush my teeth while I run the water in the shower until it gets hot.

As I step into the shower, the room begins to fill with steam. I stand under the water, thinking about last night and what's going to happen next. I'm expecting Chris to walk in the bathroom and join me in the shower, but he doesn't. When I walk out the bathroom, he's still sleeping.

"Chris, time to get up."

"Okay, I'm getting up," he answers with his face smashed in the pillow.

With the towel wrapped around me, I sit on the edge of the bed and start to lotion my body.

Finally, he gets up, kisses me on the neck, and walks toward the bathroom. I watch him as he walks away. He's got a tight ass, and his dick sways from side to side, semi erect. He pushes the bathroom door open, and I can still see the steam from my shower.

"Damn, did you use up all the hot water?"

I laugh and continue putting lotion on my body. By the time he gets out of the bathroom, I'm dressed and, in the kitchen, fixing us something to eat.

I can hear the music playing from his bedroom—R&B from the late '70s and early '80s. You would think he was an old man with the music he plays. A young man with an old soul. Love it.

We eat breakfast and get on the road. Chris is adamant about driving, which doesn't bother me. "I want you to relax and enjoy the ride like you did last night."

So, I sit in the passenger seat and control the music. Some of the songs have me thinking about the time I've been spending with Chris.

It's hard for me to deny there is something special about him. Actually, there's something special about *us*. He knows it too. We can talk all night until the sun comes up. We joke and laugh, and our conversations are intriguing and edifying. It's a turn-on for me. That's why I couldn't hold back any longer last night.

He gently touched me with his fingertips and glided them all over my body. From my face to my neck, all the way down to my feet and in between. And those lips. They are so juicy. I let him use them last night, along with his tongue, focusing on my pleasure. I'm not sure if that's a good thing or a bad thing, but I sure as hell loved it. Every time I think about how he handled me, chills run through my body like I'm having an orgasm. You know the dick must be good when you do that.

I also appreciate the way he treats me. He wants to know more about me—the real me, not just the me in the bedroom. And there are some pretty ugly things about my past that I'm not sure how to share with him. But he's understanding about it all. He keeps telling me he will be here when I'm ready to share.

I glance at Chris as he's driving. He's focused on the road, bopping his head to the beat of the music. He looks over at me as I stare at him. We both smile, and he reaches for the volume button on the radio, slowly turning down the music.

"You okay?" he asks.

"Yeah, I'm okay."

"What's on your mind?"

He thinks he knows me. Of course, there *is* something on my mind. I'm sitting here in the passenger seat, riding in the car with a man I think I'm falling in love with, and it scares me. It's too soon for love. We haven't known each other that long.

"You know you can talk to me about anything, right?"

Pain grips my chest as I try to gather my thoughts and get the nerve to tell him what I'm feeling. "Like how all of this scares me."

"All of what?"

"Us."

"Why?"

I get quiet and the tears start flowing. What if I push him away? I've expressed that I am not ready to be in a relationship, but my actions have shown otherwise. I don't want to play games with this man.

"Destinee, if you don't feel comfortable talking about it right now, that's okay. I see you're getting emotional."

Tears continue to flow and I can't get the words to escape from my mouth. Chris hits the turn signal and exits the interstate. He doesn't say anything, and I don't ask what he's doing or where we're going. I just sit there, watching his every move. He turns into the first gas station we approach and parks the car.

"Now you have my undivided attention. Who hurt you to the point where you are afraid to let me in?" He stares at me with concern and wipes the tears from my face.

"I'm sorry, Chris."

"No need to be sorry. I'm all ears if you're ready to share. If not, we can sit here until you calm down."

I close my eyes and take a deep breath. I'm overcome with panic as I try to get my thoughts together. I can't keep letting my emotions get the best of me. If I really want to give this thing with Chris a try, I need him to know everything I've been through and why I'm so afraid of moving forward with him.

"I've only had two serious relationships, and they both ended in abuse."

Chris glances at me, his eyes tight and worried. He reaches for my hand. "What happened?"

"One reason I was so ready to leave Virginia and never go back is because something that happened my senior year of high school."

I sigh and take another deep breath. He gently squeezes my hand.

"I already told you what happened with Alan and how that ended. But Ricky was worse than that."

Ricky graduated a year before me. He started selling drugs and got involved with some not-so-good people. When I told him I was accepted into Howard University and was leaving, he became controlling. When I got out of school or off work, he would be there, waiting. If I went to a party, the mall, a friend's house ... he was always watching me.

My voice begins to squeak as I tense up. "About three weeks before I was set to leave for college, I found out I was pregnant. I told him about it and let him know I was going to get an abortion. He snapped and punched me in the face. I filed an order of protection against him, and Kim took me a few days later to get the abortion."

"All of this happened before you left for college?"

I nod and continue. "Kim dropped me off at home after the abortion. He was sitting across the street from my house waiting for me to get home and tried to run me over with his car. Missed me by a couple of inches but hit the tree in front of my house. The tree still has the indentation from the car. Another reminder when I go back home of everything I went through with him. When I left for college, I vowed I would never move back to Virginia. Every time I came home from college on break, I felt like he was watching me."

"Wow, I'm sorry, Destinee."

"I pressed charges against him and got a restraining order. But ever since that day, I've been overly suspicious about almost everything and everyone, especially men. I even went into a deep depression and almost flunked out of school."

I feel a little relief telling Chris about my past. I don't know what's going to happen with us, but if we take this thing further, I need him to know how my past still haunts me even when I try not to let it.

"Once I was able to get back into the swing of things, I was committed to myself, finishing school and focusing on my career. Men and relationships were not on my radar. Mentally, I felt like I couldn't handle a relationship. I was afraid men would end up abusing me in some way. The last time I thought I was ready to give a man a try, he abused me. After that, I promised God I would wait for him to bless me with my soul mate."

"I'm not that kind of man. I would never disrespect or abuse you."

"I want to believe that, but a part of me is still scared."

"You may not believe it now, but I'm sure you will soon."

"Believe what?"

"That God sent me to you."

He might be right, but I'm still scared.

We get back on the road, and Chris starts telling me about his ex-wife and why they divorced. He says he's ashamed of his divorce. He realized that he rushed into marriage with a person he really didn't know. Looking back, he recognizes they were on two different levels.

He was twenty-four when he got married, and she was twenty-one. They were both in the Navy, and he thought they were on the same page and wanted the same things, but he started to see that was not the case. He was focused on helping his sister get through college so he could go back to school, and he wanted to travel and enjoy life for a couple of years before starting a family. She, on the other hand, was ready to get out of the Navy, start a family, and be a stay-at-home mother.

"Do you want children?"

"Of course, I want children. I just wasn't ready when I first got married."

The more his wife pushed the issue, the more he distanced himself from her. Plus, she still had some childish ways.

"What do you mean by 'childish'?" I ask.

"Everything had to be her way or no way. There was no compromising. She was disrespectful and never wanted to make time for us."

"Is that being childish or selfish?"

"A little bit of both, I guess."

"Hmm, okay."

"Growing up, I saw how my aunt and uncle were with each other. To me, they were the perfect example of what a commitment looks like, and I wanted the same thing. I didn't mind that she wanted to be a stay-at-home mom. Financially, we weren't ready for that."

I get where he's coming from. Even though my parents have been married for a long time, they didn't always display a positive marriage. But my grandparents showed me what commitment and partnership looked like. Yes, they had disagreements, but they never argued. At least, not in front of the children. My parents, on the other hand, argue like they are about to throw down with each other.

My grandmother always said she and my grandfather would never go to bed angry at each other. They would always make up before closing their eyes to go to sleep. My grandfather showed my grandmother the utmost respect and appreciation. He agreed with not going to bed angry, and he would say they had the best make-up sex. That wasn't something I wanted to hear about my grandparents, but they always gave good advice. I wish my parents would've listened to some of it.

Chris continues, "Things got so bad in our marriage that she told me we needed space and that she was going to Texas to spend time with her family."

"How did you feel about that?"

"I agreed with her and hoped things would get better when she came back home."

"Did they?"

"No. Things got so bad that we both agreed a divorce was for the best. We were only married for a year and a half."

"I guess it's better you guys figured out early things were not going to work before you had children and invested more time and money in the marriage."

"True, but it still felt like failure. I've had time to grow, and now I know what I want. I'm not going to settle."

I feel him with that.

We get into D.C. about two o'clock. He didn't believe me when I told him the traffic and congestion was crazy in D.C. Not to mention the horrible roads. At least in Virginia Beach, they take care of their roads.

Chris is surprised when he sees we have parking at my apartment complex. My apartment is small, but I make the best of it with my decorating. After all, a home is what you make it.

"How much are you paying in rent?" When I tell him, he shakes his head in disbelief. "You can own a whole house in Virginia with what you're paying for this place." He's right about that.

I'm nervous about the wedding tomorrow and how everyone will react to me bringing a date. I told Kim that Chris was my plus one, and she was so excited. "He's the one, Dee," she said. We're supposed to meet up with her and Troy when they get in town later tonight.

After my quick apartment tour, Chris and I head back out to grab something to eat to hold us over until we meet up with them later. The sky is getting dark like it's going to pour down rain, but we make it back to my apartment just in time. I go straight to the bedroom and lie across the bed.

I feel myself starting to drift off to sleep. Faintly, I hear Chris walking toward the bedroom. I feel him standing behind me at the end of the bed. Then I feel the weight of his body as he leans over on the bed behind me.

There he goes with those lips. He nibbles on the rim of my ear then softly kisses my neck. I feel his hands tugging on my shirt, so I slowly lift my arms up so he can pull it off. He unstraps my bra and starts rubbing my back. One of the best feelings in the world is when that bra strap peels away from your back and your man scratches the indentation from the bra strap.

His lips move from the base of my neck down to the dip in my hips. "Turn over," he says.

I oblige and turn over onto my back. He kisses me with intensity then gently grabs my neck, and his hands descend to my breasts. I stare at him, watching as he rubs my breasts. He makes sure to pay special attention to each nipple before making his way down to my pants. Slowly, he lifts up from off of the bed and pulls off his shirt. Then he pulls off my jeans and stands over me, gazing at my body.

"What's wrong?" I ask.

"Nothing. I can stand here all night and stare at you. From head to toe, you are so beautiful. That smile and your curves."

I sit up and scoot toward the end of the bed, closer to him.

I can see the excitement protruding from his pants, so I undo his belt buckle, then his pants button and zipper. Before I can get to his boxers, he stops me.

"Nope. I want you to lie back and let me focus on you."

He doesn't have to tell me twice. With both hands, he pushes my shoulders and I fall back onto the bed. He grabs my hips and pulls me to the edge of the bed.

"Spread your legs and put them on my shoulders," he demands.

Again, I oblige. I feel the warmth of his lips moving up my inner thigh. He starts making love to me with his mouth and tongue. My legs start to close and he quickly pushes them back open. I grab his head as if I want him to stop because I can feel my body start to tremble. I know he can feel it too. Of course, he doesn't stop, and that's when the juices start to flow. I can no longer feel my legs. They are weightless.

"You want me to stop or keep going? Can I keep going?" he asks.

I don't respond. I just lie there as his lips make their way up to my neck. My body twitches from the shock of the pleasure his tongue and lips give me. He doesn't waste any time sliding inside of me, and I welcome him with no resistance. He groans and moans as he pushes my legs together against my chest. I'm not going to last much longer; I feel like I'm going to burst. A tear escapes from my left eye, and I can feel the warm wetness fall down onto my cheek. *What in the world is going on?* This has never happened to me before.

The harder he thrusts, the more I resist.

"Nope, stay right there." He's a man who knows what he wants and lets it be known. He pushes my hands away and starts to go deeper and faster. "Not yet, baby. Just hold on." I don't know if I can.

He must feel that I'm about to explode, so he slows it down just a little bit. *What in the hell is he trying to do to me?* I can't hold it any longer and neither can he. We both let out a moan and my insides begin to flutter. He spreads my legs open and places his head between my breasts. I can still feel the throbbing and wetness between my legs.

Never have I ever had an orgasm like this before. He's got me lying here crying, it's so good.

He wants to continue, but I can't take any more. I can't stop the rhythmic throbbing from down below, and my legs are shaking. I need a few minutes to get it together. He lies beside me and pulls me close to him. I put my head on his chest, and I fall asleep listening to the sound of rain hitting the window.

CHAPTER SIX

I'm woken by the sound of my cell phone ringing in the living room. I'm so comfortable lying on Chris that I don't want to move, but I know it's Kim calling.

I pull myself away from Chris, unwrapping my legs from between his, and get out of bed. Before I can answer, she hangs up. Then there's a knock at the door.

"Open up and let us in! I know you're home. I see your car outside."

Shit. I text her to give me a minute so I can throw some clothes on.

"Oh, y'all nasty," she says loudly at the door.

I run back into the bedroom, throw on some clothes, and tell Chris to do the same.

I can hear Kim and Troy rapping outside the door, "Oh, y'all nasty, so nasty." I open the door without a hello from Kim. She can be so boughetto sometimes. "Where you hiding Chris? Tell him to come on out here."

Chris walks out the bedroom, says hello to Kim, and introduces himself to Troy.

"Y'all ready to go out and have a good time tonight?" Kim asks as she dances around my apartment.

"We are not trying to stay out all night in the club."

"Why not? You ain't got nothing better to do."

Every time Kim comes to D.C., she wants to go clubbing. I don't know if it's because the clubs are better here or if she just needs to let her hair down. I've had enough of clubbing from our college days, though. I'm okay going out to eat, maybe hitting up the casino, and then coming home. But not the club—I can't handle that tonight.

I've always wanted Kim and Troy to get along with whomever I date, but that has never happened. I can tell that this time around, it's gonna be different. Kim is excited about us all hanging out and her and Troy getting to know Chris. Plus, I need to see if Chris can pass the friend test. See how he interacts with my friends and if he's the jealous type.

I know Kim is ready to have a good time, but I don't cave in to her request to go clubbing. The last time we spoke, she was upset because she had another miscarriage—her third one. She's been trying to get pregnant since the day she said, "I do." I'm hoping she will use this weekend to get her mind off everything. Surprisingly, Troy agrees with me about not going out. He's not the clubbing type either.

"We can chill here," I say. "I'll order some food and make some drinks. I have a deck of cards in the kitchen drawer. We can play a hand of spades."

"Damn right!" Troy yells out.

"Let's take this back to our college days," I say.

If we weren't at a party or the club, we were in someone's dorm room or apartment playing spades. I look over at Chris and ask if he plays spades. "That's the card game with all the shapes on the cards?"

I place both hands on my head, looking at Chris like he's lost his mind.

"You've got to be kidding me!" Kim shouts.

"I'm just kidding. I know how to play." He smirks.

I let loose a sigh of relief. Spades is the most popular game with my family and friends. I don't know if Chris would survive them if he didn't know how to play.

"Well, you wouldn't be my partner anyway, so let's get it poppin'. No talking across the board, either." With her eyes scrunched, Kim points two fingers at her eyes then at Chris. "I'm watching you."

I order some wings and pizza, and we get the game started. Troy shuffles the cards and deals them out.

"You misdealing? Or there's not enough cards in the deck?" Chris says.

We all count our cards. Kim turns and looks at Troy. "See, you messing up already, and the game ain't even started." Troy gathers the cards up and deals again.

I look across the table at Chris and observe him sitting back with a confident smirk on his face. I look over at Kim shaking her head, watching Troy deal.

"And y'all were worried about my man not being able to play." *I'm still not sure he can play, but I'm gonna keep talkin' smack like we got this.*

"That's why I don't play with people I don't know," Chris says jokingly.

I don't know if that's a dig at me or them but I keep quiet and watch Troy as he continues dealing. This time we all have the right amount of cards.

Kim starts the game off with an ace of clubs and we all return suit.

"Yo, stop trying to look at my hand," Kim yells at Chris.

"You ain't got nothing anyway," I shout across the table at Kim.

Midway into the game, Chris starts getting aggressive, banging his cards down on the table. It scared me at first. Didn't think he had it in him. Troy gets madder every time Chris slams his card on the table. "Do you have to slam your card down every time you throw a card out?"

"This ain't no game of Uno, my dude, it's called spades. That's how you play."

As the game continues, Chris smacks his king of spades down on the table.

"That's okay, we're still gonna make our books," Kim says.

It's down to the last hand. "What you got, babe?" Chris asks me. "I've got three and a possible. We're going for seven."

I lead with some hearts, and Chris follows with an ace of hearts. We run down with the king, club, and spades from there.

"We're running this whole deck." Chris looks over at Troy, but Troy doesn't respond. "Blaw, look at that." Chris throws down an ace of spades. "You're mighty quiet over there." He looks over at Kim and Troy again. "Last card, Troy, what'cha got?"

Troy throws out a queen of spades.

Kim scoots down in her chair and throws out her last card: a five of spades.

Chris gets up from his chair and smacks his cards down on the table, yelling, "Game over!" It's a king of spades.

"Okay, don't break my table now."

Kim gets up from the table and puts her glass in the sink. "I underestimated you, Chris. Took you for the quiet, shy type. You proved me wrong."

"It's getting late. We need to get back to the hotel and rest up for the wedding tomorrow." As Troy walks toward the door, he extends his hand to Chris. "Good game, man. Next time we need to play Bid Whist."

"Nah, I'll stick with that I know."

"I've never met anyone other than Landon that played the way you did, all aggressive and shit."

Chris walks into the kitchen while I'm putting the cups away. "Did I pass the friend test?"

"With flying colors. Now let's see how this wedding goes."

Stephanie has had her wedding planned since we were in college. She always said she wanted a Cinderella-themed wedding, and that's what she got. Her wedding dress looks like a ballgown. Baby blue with rhinestones. No glass slippers, but her heels are clear, open-toed with a strap around her ankle. I'm so glad the whole service is at one venue. We can watch the couple say their vows and walk across the hall to the reception area. I hold back my tears when Stephanie and Mike say their vows. I try to wipe them away before Chris sees them.

"Are you okay?" he whispers.

I blot the tears off my face before looking at Chris.

"I'm okay. Something about weddings makes me feel mushy inside."

After the ceremony, we make our way to the reception area. The tables are wrapped in baby-blue linen with gold, Cinderella-carriage centerpieces with flowers in them. We take our assigned seats and wait for the wedding party to walk in.

I see a few friends from undergrad that I haven't seen in years. Kim and Troy walk around and talk to a few. I stay seated with Chris.

"You're not going to mingle with your friends?"

"If you haven't noticed already, I am not a social butterfly. That is Kim."

"I'm going to the bar to get a drink. Would you like one?"

"Cranberry and vodka."

I watch as Chris walks over to the bar. I've never seen a man with an ass so round and tight. It's even more noticeable with him wearing that slim-fitting, navy-blue suit.

The music stops, and the DJ introduces the wedding party. Before introducing Stephanie and Mike, he tells everyone to get on their feet. "Ladies and gentlemen, I introduce to you Mr. and Mrs. Michael McKinney!"

Kim taps me on my shoulder. "I knew she wasn't going to keep that ballroom gown on all night." We both laugh. She walks into the reception wearing an off-the-shoulder pantsuit with a lace train. If she had kept that ballroom gown on, she would have probably been uncomfortable all night.

Stephanie makes her way to the guest table, taking pictures and making small talk. She walks over to our table straight toward

Chris.

"You must be someone special for Destinee to ask at the last minute if she can bring a date. It's nice to meet you."

She hugs Chris, then me and everyone else at the table.

Chris looks over at me and says, "I must be special."

"Yes, you are someone special. Thank you for coming with me."

After the couple's first dance, the dance floor opens up to everyone. I watch as Kim pulls Troy out to the dance floor. He looks back at Chris and I like he's looking for us to save him.

"Are we going to sit here at the table all night or are we gonna get out there and dance?"

Chris gets up from the table and stands next to me, holding onto my chair as I slowly get up.

We make our way to the dance floor and the song changes to "Love Riddim" by Rotimi. I was already prepared for the Caribbean music since Michael's family is from the islands. What I was not prepared for was Chris and his dance moves.

Chris pulls my hand as he walks to the middle of the dance floor. He grabs my hips from behind as I sway them from side to side, keeping with the beat of the music.

"The way you move them hips makes me wanna bend you over and do something to you."

I bend my knees a little, arch my back, and grind up against him. I'm trying to keep it tasteful on the dance floor and not reveal my inner freak.

"Stop before you start something you can't finish."

Slowly, I turn around and look up at Chris. I put my arms on his shoulders, and our eyes lock for a few seconds. His head slowly descends and his lips meet mine. Right before the song changes, his thumb brushes up against my cheek as our kiss intensifies.

We walk back to our table where Kim and Troy are seated. I'm grinning from ear to ear like I've won a prize. Before I sit down, Kim gets up from the table. "Let me talk to you for a minute."

I think Troy did something to upset her. He has this habit of flirting with other women. He probably slept with some of the women here from college.

We walk out to the hallway where it's a little quieter.

"What's up with you and Chris?"

"What do you mean?"

"I saw how y'all were grinding up against each other on the dance floor. Like it was only the two of you out there. What's that about?"

I lean against the wall and gaze down the hallway.

"I know you heard me, Destinee."

I shrug my shoulders. "What do you want me to say?"

"There's something different about Chris that I've never seen with the other guys you've dated."

"You think?"

"I think he's good for you, but you think it's too good to be true."

She's right. It feels too good to be true.

"Troy and I were talking last night when we got back to our hotel. We were watching y'all last night playing cards. And tonight, watching you on the dance floor ... the way Chris looks at you."

"How does he look at me?"

"Like he's in love with you."

"Hmph."

"What does that mean?"

I laugh to stop the tears that try to escape my eyes, but it doesn't help.

"Kim, this is different for me. So much so that it's difficult to put into words how I feel."

"That's a good thing, right?"

She reaches down and grabs both of my hands.

"I've seen everything you've been through. I know you are afraid of love, but you deserve it. I see you having that with Chris."

She's right. I deserve love. Chris might just be the one to show me it's okay to let love in.

We walk back into the reception room. Chris and Troy are sitting at the table, laughing.

Kim nudges me and smiles.

When I get closer to the table, Chris stands up and pulls my chair out. I sit down. He sits next to me and stares at me with a flirtatious smile on his face. I close my eyes for a minute and think about what Kim just told me. "You deserve love." I open my eyes, and Chris kisses me on the cheek.

I think we partied a little too much last night. Instead of getting drunk off the liquor, I got drunk off of Chris. We were on the dance floor almost all night. Before we left, Stephanie pulled me to the side. She asked how long Chris and I have been dating. It shocked her that we've only known each other for a few weeks. She said she was watching us from across the room and saw our intense emotional connection. Something she's never seen before.

On our drive back to Virginia, Chris reminds me about dinner with his family. I totally forgot. This will be my first time meeting his family. I was apprehensive at first, but he keeps telling me his family doesn't think I exist because I sound too good to be true. I've never cared too much about meeting the families of the guys I went out with. I thought it was a waste of time, but this time it's different.

We pull up to the house, and Chris turns off the car.

"I want to warn you before we walk in there. My aunt and uncle are very talkative."

"It's okay."

"No, you don't understand. My aunt is nosey, and my uncle will just talk about anything."

"You nervous?"

"I should be asking you that."

He walks around to my door and opens it for me. We get closer to the door and his hand intertwines with mine.

He reaches for the door with his other hand. "Here goes nothing."

His aunt Regina is standing in the kitchen. She's short and petite like Kim. "So, you're Destinee?"

"Yes, ma'am. Nice to meet you."

She walks out of the kitchen and gives me a hug. "Don't call me *ma'am*, and don't call his uncle *sir*. We go by Regina and Greg."

"Do you need help with anything?"

"I got it covered, sweetheart. Thanks for asking."

Greg walks into the living room. "We were starting to believe Chris was telling us lies about you."

"What was he saying about me?"

"You come sit with me in the living room, and I'll tell you all about it."

As I make my way over to the couch, I glance around the living room at all the pictures. My eyes stop at a picture of Chris, Ebony, and their mother. Chris and Ebony look just like their mother.

"So, you're a lawyer?"

"Not yet, but I will be soon. I have one semester left of law school."

The smell from the kitchen reminds me of Sunday dinner with my family. I don't know what Regina is cooking, but I'm ready to eat.

Charles, Dawn, and Sabrina make their way into the living room and introduce themselves.

Greg continues talking as if he doesn't want anyone else talking or asking me questions. "My wife works at the church daycare and is the bookkeeper for the repair shop."

"Yes, Chris told me."

"I've tried to get Charles to help me, but he can't seem to stop running the streets and making babies."

"Are those your grandchildren?" I point to the pictures sitting up on the mantle above the fireplace.

"Yes, all four of them. Has he told you about Dawn? She's home from college. And Sabrina? They'll all be leaving home soon, but I don't see an end in sight with them draining my pockets."

"Unc, let someone else talk," Chris says.

"Boy, this is my house. I can talk all I want."

"I'm sorry," Chris mouths to me.

"I retired from the Navy and wanted to start my own business and still do something I enjoyed doing. Wanted to pass the business down to Charles and Chris." Greg gets up from his recliner, walks into the kitchen to grab a bottle of water, and sits back down. "So, I opened the auto repair shop."

"You went to Howard University?" Sabrina asks me.

"Yes, for undergrad and law school. Have you thought about going there?"

"Of course! I want to major in theater arts."

Greg clears his throat. "No. What you need to do is major in something like law or accounting so you can get a real job."

Sabrina leans back against the couch. "Y'all never listen to what I want."

"Because you're still a child. Now come help me set this table," Regina calls out.

Before Regina calls us to the dinner table, I ask Chris about Ebony. I was looking forward to meeting her.

"Last minute girls' trip. She'll be back tomorrow."

While we're all sitting at the dinner table, Greg tells Chris he better not do anything to mess things up with me because he will never find anyone like me again. The truth is, *I'm* afraid I won't find anyone like *him* again.

Mondays are the worst for me. I'm always too wound up to go to bed on Sunday and too tired to wake up early. Todd won't be back in the Norfolk office until Tuesday afternoon, so hopefully it will be a light day. The case is coming to a close, and I'm not sure I'm ready to go back to D.C. I have been enjoying my time with Chris and my family.

Speaking of family, Michelle is mad at me because Kim met Chris before she did, and his family met me before mine met him. I had to explain to her that I've kept him away from the family for a few good reasons. First, we just met and are still getting to know each other. Second, my family is very judgmental, especially my dad. Third, after everything that happened with Alan, Landon has become overly protective of me. He would want to meet Chris in person and talk to him. Luckily, he will be here this weekend; Mom is insistent that we all be at her house for Sunday dinner, including Chris.

CHAPTER SEVEN

They say times flies when you're having fun. And I've been having my share of it with Chris. Now it's time for him to meet my family. I'm dragging my feet getting ready because I'm nervous about what they are going to say.

"So, who all is going to be at dinner?"

"Just my parents, Landon, Michelle and her family."

"I've never known you to be late for anything. What's taking you so long to get ready?"

"I want my family to like you. I haven't had a good track record when it comes to guys, and they've been the first to point that out."

"Don't worry about your family liking me. They are going to love me." He says that now, but wait until my father gets a hold of him.

"So, you can handle your own."

"Yes, I can."

He sounds a little over confident, but I don't read into it. I just finish putting my makeup on so we can head over there.

We walk through the front door, and it's like everyone was just sitting in the living room waiting for us. I introduce Chris to my dad and he asks, "What's your drink of choice, young man?"

"Well sir, I'm a Hennessy man, but I'll drink anything."

"Damn, right. Come on over here and get a drink."

I watch as they walk away.

"That's different," Michelle says.

"He's never done that before," I say.

Kevin looks over at Michelle. "Yeah, he didn't do that with me."

"That's because you lived down the street your whole life."

It's shocking but reassuring to see my dad interacting with Chris this way. Maybe Chris is a keeper.

Usually for Sunday dinner, my mom is excited to see all of us. But today, she's quieter than normal. Like she has something on her mind. I try not to pry, but I'm curious to know what's going on.

After dinner, we all sit in the living room and she announces that she and my dad have something to tell us. "Are they getting a divorce?" I whisper to Michelle.

"Michelle, take Jaiden upstairs for a minute so we can talk."

"I don't want to miss anything."

"Get him settled and come back down."

While Michelle takes Jaiden upstairs, we sit in silence. I try to prepare myself for whatever it is they have to tell us.

Michelle comes back downstairs and sits next to Kevin. My father leans back in his recliner and places his hands in his lap.

I brace myself because I know if Mom pulled us all together, it must be something serious.

"You're father has been recently diagnosed with stage four

colon cancer. The cancer has spread to some other organs."

"What other organs?" I ask, shocked.

"How long have y'all known this?" Michelle asks.

"We found out last week. His doctor has given him six to eight weeks to live."

I would much rather the news have been them getting a divorce. Although my father and I do not have the closest relationship, he's my father. Who wants to hear their father is dying of cancer? This is a shock to all of us. No matter what differences we've had over the years, he was a good provider. My parents may have argued all the time, but he always made sure his family was taken care of. He was a mean drunk too, but I still love him.

I can't imagine how my mom is feeling. They've had their share of issues, but this is her husband that she'll be losing to cancer. All of her children are grown, and without my father, she will be alone in the house.

While I'm helping Mom clean the kitchen, Dad asks to speak with Chris alone. They stand outside on the porch for about twenty minutes. I try to read Chris's lips, but he isn't doing much talking, just nodding.

On the way back to Chris's apartment, I wait to see if Chris is going to mention the conversation with my father. He's taking too long so I help him out.

"What were you and my dad talking about?"

"I can't tell you. He made me promise not to say anything."

"My dad made you promise not to tell me something?" This is torture, and it's going to eat me up until I find out.

"He said you would be upset, but I reassured him you would be understanding."

I would love to have an in-depth conversation with my dad—talk to him about what's going on in my life or maybe get some advice instead of tiptoeing around in fear of getting a lashing from him.

I expected to get a call or text from Landon or Michelle, but nothing. I guess we all need time to digest what we heard and what's to come.

I toss and turn all night thinking about my father's diagnosis. So many questions run through my mind: Are there any other treatment options? Could it have been caught sooner if he was diligent in going to the doctor? How can the doctors tell he only has a few weeks to live?

I'm hesitant about going back to D.C., but the trial case I assisted with is over, and it's almost time for me to get back to school. I feel like I need to stay here and help out with my dad, so I decide to take a few days off before heading back. I want to clear my mind, plus I want to spend time with my family and get more details about my dad's diagnosis.

Kim invited me to her cousin Keri's cookout. I don't feel like going, but Kim insists. Plus, Chris made plans to go out with his boys, so we're going to meet up later tonight.

Kim and I get to Keri's house a little after 7:00 p.m. It's mostly family there, but the later it gets, the more family starts leaving and friends start showing up. The music blares and everyone is either eating, dancing, drinking, smoking, or playing spades.

I have a couple of drinks and play a few hands of spades before my partner and I get spanked and have to leave the table. Since I am a lightweight when it comes to drinking, it doesn't take long for me to start feeling the buzz. My head starts banging, the room spins, and I'm ready to go to bed.

Kim definitely had too much to drink; she's lying on the sofa, half asleep. I decide to lie down in Keri's room for a little while so I can sober up or just sleep it off a little bit. My head pounds like it's a drum and the drummer is striking his stick on my head. I lie across the bed, hoping the pounding will stop. I hear the bedroom door open then close and someone stumbling across the room to the bed. I don't move. I just lie there, thinking maybe it's Kim. I feel a dip in the bed like someone sat down. The room is dark, so I'm not sure who it is. "Kim, is that you?"

I feel hands slide up my legs and rub on my thighs. The hands are rough, like a man's hands. I push them away but they keep moving higher up my thighs until they reach my panties. I try to lift my leg to kick, but I can't move.

A heavy, sweaty body pins me down into the bed. I try to scream, but he covers my mouth and the music is so loud that no one would hear me anyway. As he penetrates me, he covers my mouth tighter and whispers, "Don't scream." When I try to pull away, he grabs my neck and warns me that if I don't stop pulling away, he'll choke me until I'm unconscious.

Hearing his voice sends me into shock. It's sounds familiar but I'm unsure. I loosen my grip from his hands that are wrapped around my neck, and the pressure of his body slowly eases off me. Still lying in the bed, I hear the clink of his belt buckle and footsteps leaving the room.

After what feels like an eternity, Kim walks into the room.

"What is going on?"

I'm curled up in the bed, shaking and crying. I try to tell her what happened, but the words won't come out of my mouth. Tears stream from my eyes, and Kim keeps asking what's wrong. Still, nothing comes out. She grabs my purse off the nightstand and pulls out my cell phone.

"Call Chris," is all I can get out.

She doesn't leave my side until he gets here. Before I know it, Chris is sitting in front of me. I'm still curled up in the bed, shaking, with tears pouring down my face. He puts his arms around me and says something, but I can't grasp what he's saying.

"Please tell me what happened."

He turns toward Kim and Keri, asking them what happened.

"Move out the way."

He picks me up off the bed and carries me out to his truck. I can smell the stench of that man all over my body—the smell of sweat and liquor. I know Chris can smell it too. He keeps looking at me, pleading with me to tell him what happened.

"Do you want to go to the hospital?"

I don't want to go to the hospital. I just want to take a shower and wash this stench off of me.

We get to his apartment, and he runs me a shower. I stand there, not able to move my hands to wash myself. Chris leaves the bathroom and comes back to find me in the same spot he left me.

He grabs the washcloth from my hand, lathers it with soap, and washes my body. When he gets to my vagina, I push his hand away and grab the washcloth.

He holds both his hands up and closes the shower curtain.

"I'll stand outside and let you finish."

I step out the shower, dry off, and put on the shirt and panties Chris laid on the counter for me. I get right in bed. I can't sleep, though; I keep having flashbacks, and I toss and turn all night. Chris doesn't leave my side.

When I open my eyes in the morning, Chris is sitting up in bed next to me. I want to tell him about last night, but I'm too ashamed to say it. I blame myself. How could I get so drunk and let someone take advantage of me in that way?

Chris doesn't know what to say to me. He makes breakfast and attempts to get me to talk. We are both trying to make sense of what happened last night.

"Can you please take me to get my car from Keri's house?"

He raises his eyebrows at me. "You don't need to get your car right now. Just try to relax."

I want to get the rest of my things from my sister's house and head back home to D.C., but I need my car. "Please Chris, I just want to go home."

"Home to D.C.?"

"Yes."

"You still haven't told me what happened last night."

I sit quietly at the table with my arms folded against my chest. I guess this is going to be our first argument.

"Hello, do you hear me talking to you? What happened last night?" Chris leans forward over the table.

I sit quietly, ignoring him as he apologizes for not being there with me. "If I was there, I would have protected you."

But he wasn't there, and something did happen. I gather the words to reply in my head, but they don't find their way to my lips.

Tears trail down my cheeks.

Chris gets up from the sofa, grabs his keys off the kitchen counter, and puts on his sneakers. "Let's go," he says with an indignant look on his face.

I grab my things from his room and put them in my bag.

When we get to Keri's house, he puts the truck in park and sits there. I wait for him to say something, but he doesn't.

"I'll call you when I make it home." I wait a few more seconds to see if he's going to respond. Again, he doesn't, so I give him a kiss on the cheek, grab my bag from the back seat, and get out of the truck.

When I get into my car, Chris pulls off in a rage, his tires squealing.

The next stop for me is Michelle's house to get the rest of my things. I pray all the way there that Michelle and Kevin will not be home. Prayer answered. I pull up to the house, and both of their cars are gone. I run in, grab all my things from the guest bedroom, and head back out the door. To my surprise, Chris is standing at the trunk of my car.

When he sees me coming out of the house, he walks toward me to grab my bags. He doesn't say a word and neither do I. The silence is awkward.

I pop the trunk and he put my bags in. He closes the trunk and walks toward the driver's side door. I walk over to Chris, but he won't move from in front of my door so I can get in.

He locks his eyes on me. "I don't know what happened last night, but I wish you would tell me. I can't believe you're just going to leave like this. Don't we have something good going on here?"

I should've known there was no way he was going to let me leave without having this conversation. I look at him and try to gather my thoughts.

"I'm not letting you leave," he says.

I'm already emotional, and hearing him say that makes me feel worse.

"I think it's best for both of us if I leave."

My legs start to wobble, and my heart beats unsteadily. I never planned to meet someone while in Virginia. I sure as hell wasn't expecting to fall in love with someone.

Chris grabs a hold of my hands. "I'm going back with you to D.C. until we figure this thing out. I'm not going to lose you over what happened last night. I'm not going to lose you just because we live in two different states. I've known you long enough to know that I want to continue this relationship. We can make this work."

Now I'm really at a loss for words.

"So, you're going to follow me back to my apartment so I can get some of my stuff. I'm going to leave my truck here and drive your car back to your place."

My eyes well up with tears. Chris gently grabs my chin and softly lifts my head. "I got you, Destinee. Don't push me away."

I try to calm myself down so I can drive back to his place. With each blink, tears escape from my eyes and slide down my face. I can't help but think that what I have with Chris is too good to be true. My mind flickers back to last night, and I hope and pray that one day my brain will forget what happened.

When we get back to Chris's apartment, he throws some clothes in his gym bag and we get on the road. I'm not much of a passenger this time. I sit back in silence the whole ride. Chris tries to make conversation, but I'm not in a talking mood. Too much on my mind.

"I'm serious about us figuring out a way to make our relationship work," Chris says, his tone firm.

Relationship? I shrug and stare out my window.

"What do you think about us living together when you move back to Virginia?"

Woah brotha, let's get out of the fast lane and just go with the flow. I take in a deep breath, exhale, and smile at him. "Let's give it some time."

"I respect your decision, but I need you to know that I know I want to be with you." I've heard that before, and I know that people change over time.

I'm back to work in the D.C. office. Working will help take my mind off everything. Plus, Chris is still here with me. I thought he would tell me he was ready to go back to Virginia, but he's here, patiently waiting for me to get home from work.

He has this way of spoiling me. Not with material things, but with his time and attention. Something money can't buy. Somehow, he always knows what I need. We are both anxious to see how this relationship will work out. We compromise and decide to alternate weekends; one weekend, I'll go to Virginia, and the next weekend he will come to D.C. Then there are phone calls, text messages, and FaceTime.

He knows I need to go to Virginia more often to check on my dad, but with school starting back up that might not always be possible.

All the back-and-forth, my dad's health, my mom's sanity,

working, and school have taken a toll on my body. My energy level has been low, making it hard for me to do anything. I told Chris about it, and he suggested I see my doctor and find out what's going on.

I made my appointment for Friday morning, before I head back to Virginia for the weekend. While I sit in the waiting room, it dawns on me that I should have scheduled something earlier to get tested for STDs after what happened at Keri's.

I keep trying to put that night in the back of my mind and focus on the now. It hasn't been easy. I'm ashamed to tell anyone about that night, but I need to tell my doctor so she can run some tests.

I need to make sure I'm okay. She seems a little concerned that I waited so long to get checked out and that I have not spoken to anyone about it. "What happened is not your fault," she says.

She steps out of the exam room and comes back in about five minutes later. "Ms. Clark?" My heart drops down to my feet. I try to brace myself for whatever she's about to share. She leans on the counter and places her laptop down next to her.

"Guess what?" *Oh my God, please don't tell me I have an STD. What if I gave something to Chris?*

I sit up straight on the exam table, waiting for her to continue.

"You're pregnant."

I quiver with indignation and look at her with a flare of annoyance. "What do you mean? I'm on birth control."

"There's always that small percentage."

A chill runs through my body. The thought of being pregnant gnaws at me. *How is this possible?* Chris and I always use protection. My cycle has been out of whack, but I attributed it to school, stress, and everything else I'm worried about.

"Congratulations," the doctor says.

My body feels like lead as she continues to explain the importance of prenatal care. She refers me to a gynecologist.

This is not a moment I want to celebrate. I'm not ready to have a baby. I want to scream, but I just sit on the exam table in disbelief and listen to the doctor's orders.

When the doctor leaves the room, I slowly ease up from the exam table, grab my clothes from the chair, and get dressed. I sit down to slide on my sneakers. How will Chris react when I tell him the news?

I follow the exit signs and stop at the reception desk to make sure I'm all clear to go. "You look like something is weighing heavy on your mind," the receptionist says. I sigh and walk toward the door with the bright red exit sign on it.

Once on the other side of the door, my brain struggles to know which step to take next. I stop for a moment to get it together. Shame washes over me, and I draw a deep shuddering breath as I realize that this might not be Chris's baby.

CHAPTER EIGHT

I feel like I'm on autopilot as I drive down route 301 through the lightly populated rural areas of Virginia. I'm still trying to process the baby news. My stomach is in knots, and my head is pounding. I keep thinking about how I'm going to tell Chris. Do I have to tell him? I'm afraid to see his reaction when I tell him it's a possibility the baby is not his.

I stop at my parents' house before going to see Chris. As I pull up to the house, it feels like a weight settles on my chest. I'm used to seeing my father in the garage sanding or sawing wood for a piece of furniture he's building. Now his days are filled with indescribable pain that flows through his body. I get scared when I see him lying in bed, his body so still it looks like he has passed on. He's adamant about not dying in the hospital; he says he wants to be home and as comfortable as he can be.

When I walk into the house, the living room is empty and quiet. I turn around to close the door and my mother walks out of the dining room. "Hey, you," she says and walks back into the living room. Every time I talk to my mother, she tells me the clock is ticking and my father's time is limited. I can tell she's worn out, but she keeps pushing through—showing her strength while underneath wanting to break down.

I place my keys and purse on the couch and follow her to the dining room. She sits down at the dining room table, picks up her spoon, and stirs the coffee cup sitting in front of her. She must have just poured it because I can see the steam rising from the cup. "Why are you sitting in the dining room?" I ask.

She pulls the spoon from the coffee cup and places it on a napkin. "Just sitting here in my thoughts."

"What's on your mind, Ma?"

"It's happening too fast," she says and takes two small sips of her coffee.

I sit quietly with my head down, trying to think of how to respond. Nothing comes to mind. I look up at her and can no longer see the dimple that sits on her cheek when she smiles. "I'm sorry, Ma," I say.

"I already feel this emptiness in my heart and this heavy feeling on my shoulders. It's killing my soul, and there's nothing I can do about it." Her brows are creased and her face tense.

"Your heart will always be an archive full of memories etched in your brain." As I say that to her, I try to think of a good memory between me and Dad, but nothing comes to mind.

"Ma, can I ask you a question?"

"Sure," she says, giving me her undivided attention.

"I can't recall happy memories of me and Daddy. Why is that? I busted my butt to get good grades and be the perfect student, but he never acknowledged anything I did. Never came to any of my track meets or award ceremonies ..."

"Sweetheart, I wish I could answer that for you."

"I mean, he was always there to show his support for Michelle and Landon. Even when Michelle was constantly getting into trouble and Landon was barely passing and threatening to drop out of school."

"Maybe it was because you were the one child he knew could hold your own."

I scrunch up my face and let what she said marinate. Regardless of whether he felt I could hold my own, I still needed him, and I wish we had a closer relationship.

From the dining room, I can see the pictures on the living room wall. My eyes fixate on Michelle's wedding picture of her and my dad together. I think about how, when I do get married, whenever that will be, my father won't be there to walk me down the aisle and give me away like he did Michelle. He won't get a chance to see Landon's children or my children. My heart hurts thinking about it.

My eyes wander to the rest of the pictures and stop when I see the pensive look on my mother's face.

"Go say hello to your father."

I walk down the hall to my parents' bedroom and see my father lying in the bed. At first glance, it looks like he's sleeping. He opens his eyes just when I'm about to turn around and walk out.

"Come here," he says, his voice frail.

I walk over to the bed and think back to all the times I would get blamed for something and he would call me into the room to spank me. I was never the one causing the problem, yet I was the only one getting in trouble. I sit next to him on the bed. He extends his hand out to me, so I grab it and begin to rub it. He looks so fragile lying in bed. Each time I come to visit, he looks thinner and weaker.

My mother walks in behind me and sits in the chair across from the bed. She nods and smiles at me. I look back at my dad. He's trying to tell me something but can't quite get it out. It takes him a couple of minutes, but he finally says something.

"I'm sorry."

I look over at my mom with confusion.

She whispers, "Listen."

I look back at my dad. "What are you sorry about?"

"I'm sorry I never told you how proud I am of you. I'm sorry I wasn't there when you needed me to be there for you." He takes a deep breath and continues. "You've accomplished so much and achieved every goal you set for yourself. You are the one I never had to worry about because I knew you were the strong one, like me."

Tears well up in my eyes. I can't believe what I'm hearing.

"We've had a distant relationship, and I am so sorry for that, Destinee. Please forgive me."

I sit in awe for a minute that feels like an eternity. I have waited years to hear this from my father. It saddens me that it took him being on his death bed to tell me this.

I wipe the tears from my face and take a couple of deep breaths. I look at my dad and gently squeeze his hand.

"Daddy, I forgive you. Thank you for all that you have done for me."

A tear slowly drops from his eye and lands on his pillow. He turns his head away from me for a moment. "I need you to promise me that you will take care of your mother. She's gonna need you."

"I promise, I will take care of Mom."

He pats his chest with his left hand. He always did that to my sister when she was a little girl crying over something. She would lie on his chest and he would hug her and say, "Everything will be alright, baby girl."

I slowly lay my head on his chest and he whispers to me, "I love you, my baby girl. Everything is going to be alright."

That was it. That was my breaking point. I cry so hard—tears of happiness and sadness. Happy tears because I waited years to hear those words and receive that affection from my father. Sad tears because I know this means he won't be here for much longer.

I sit on the bed next to him until he starts to doze off. Then I walk in the kitchen to talk to my mom a little longer before leaving to meet up with Chris.

She's standing over the kitchen sink, cleaning the chicken and plucking pieces of feather from the wings. When she sees me walk in, she washes her hands, dries them off with a paper towel, and extends her arms out.

"Come give your mama a hug. I'm sorry, baby."

"For what?"

"You shouldn't have had to wait this long to hear those words from your father."

I think back to what I went through with Ricky and how he almost killed me. When Alan was stalking me and almost killed me, my dad didn't seem to care. I expected more of him as my father. I needed him in those moments. To feel protected and loved. Instead, I felt like an abandoned child.

Before I head out to meet Chris at the shop, my mom fills me in on the latest gossip. She wouldn't be Eunice if she didn't have some tea to spill about someone. I get all the info on the neighbors, then on Landon and Michelle. Landon and his girlfriend are trying to come home on leave to see Dad. Michelle is pregnant with baby number two, which I knew already.

What my mother doesn't know is that I am pregnant with baby number one, and I'm not sure who the baby daddy is. I can't tell my mother that. She would have a fit. Plus, I need to talk to Chris first and decide what I want to do.

I head over to meet Chris at the shop before he closes up. It's funny how Chris can read me like a book. Whenever something is bothering me, he senses it. It doesn't matter if we're talking on the phone or in the same room, he just knows.

When I pull up to the shop, he walks over to the door and lets me inside.

"What's wrong?"

Before I can get a word out, I start crying.

"Calm down, catch your breath. It's alright." He grabs my hand and pulls me back into the office. "Have a seat, and start from the beginning."

"I don't know where to begin."

I sit in the chair, silently trying to gather my thoughts. He walks up to me, puts his arms out, pulls me close to him, and squeezes me tight. I slowly begin to calm down. I tell him about the conversation I had with my father. He's thrilled to hear that after all these years, I am finally able gain some closure with my dad.

I so badly want to tell him that I'm pregnant, but the words will not come out of my mouth. I think maybe if I don't tell him, I can just get an abortion and he will never have to know. That's not something I want to do, but I'm not ready to be a mother and I'm not sure I can handle having a baby that might not be his.

But that would be deceiving Chris, and that is the last thing I want for our relationship.

I take a deep breath and speak quickly, like ripping off a Band-Aid. "Chris, I'm pregnant." Here come more tears.

"Are you serious? Why are you crying?"

He balls his fist up and places it over his mouth. I know he's going to be hurt by what I'm about to tell him, but he needs to know.

"I'm not sure if it's your baby."

He takes a step back and plops down in the chair across from me. "What do you mean not mine?"

It's time for me to tell him everything that happened that night at Keri's house. I know he already knows what happened but has been waiting for me to tell him, so I do. He scrunches over in the chair and places his head in his hands.

"Damn, Dee. I'm sorry."

"Look, enough sorries for today. It happened, and now I have to deal with it."

"You don't have to deal with it alone."

I'm thankful to have Chris's support, but I still feel guilt and shame about what happened.

"How far along are you?"

"The doctor said around seven weeks."

"What do you want to do?"

I tell him I'm considering getting an abortion because I can't keep this baby if it's not his.

The room is silent for a few minutes. Chris gets up from his chair, walks out the room for a minute, then returns.

"You know this could very well be my baby. Think about it. You are carrying life inside of you."

"Yes, Chris. I know."

"I'm not going anywhere, if that is something you are worried about. It's your body. Whatever you decide, I support you. But know that I love you and that baby regardless."

Did he say he loves me? This is the first time he's said those words. But is it because I'm pregnant, or does he really love me? I'm glad he's taking my feelings into consideration, and I don't want to regret any decision I make.

School, work, the bar exam, my father, this long-distance relationship, and now a baby thrown in the mix ... it's too much for me to handle. I'm so afraid that it's not Chris's baby. I always try to take every precaution when I have sex, to make sure nothing like this happens. This is not part of my plan.

I can tell Chris is deep in thought, so I leave him to finish closing up the shop. I pick up dinner and wait for him at his apartment. He walks through the door and heads straight to the bathroom to take a shower.

Well, damn! No hello or thank you for picking up dinner. This is going to be a long night. Maybe I should go stay with Michelle. I'm not going to put up with the silent treatment.

I've been sitting here waiting for him to get home so we can eat together. Now I don't even have an appetite. I put my food in the refrigerator and lie down on the couch. I'm fumbling through the channels, trying to find something good to watch, when Chris walks out of the bedroom.

"Did you eat your food yet?"

I don't answer, just ignore him and continue searching for something to watch.

"You hear me talking to you?"

"What?"

"I asked you a question. Why are you ignoring me?"

"You just walked in here, didn't say hello, and went straight to the bathroom."

"I'm tired, dirty, and smelly. Just wanted to wash the day away so I can spend some time with you."

I don't respond, and I'm getting frustrated that I can't find anything good to watch. All these freaking channels, and nothing good is on when I want to relax and watch a good movie.

Chris grabs his food off the table and warms it up in the microwave.

"Want me to warm your food up too?"

"No, thank you. I lost my appetite."

"You need to eat something."

He's right. I haven't had anything since this morning when I stopped for breakfast. So much is on my mind right now. I can tell Chris is upset. So am I, but I'm pretty sure we are not upset about the same things. I feel like I'm always going through some shit. Things are on track for a millisecond, then the bomb drops. I don't know how much more I can take.

Chris finishes his food, walks over to the couch, lifts my feet up, and sits down.

"We need to talk," he says.

"I don't have much to say."

He closes his mouth, then looks at my feet before glancing back up to catch my eyes. "Well, just listen to what I have to say, please."

Here we go. I already know what he's going to say, but I let him talk.

"I'm sorry if I upset you by the way I reacted. That was not my intention. I was excited when you told me you were pregnant. I get why you don't want to go through with the pregnancy, but I want you to have this baby. That's my baby you are carrying. However, it's your body and your decision. Whatever you decide, I will support you."

His voice is void of emotion. I sense he's only saying this because he doesn't want to argue.

"Thank you. I don't know what I am going to do, but when I make my decision I will let you know."

Am I being selfish with my decision? I had an abortion before and I promised myself I would never do it again. Now I'm older, more established, and have the support I need to bring a baby into this world. It just scares me to think this is not Chris's baby.

Saturday morning, I meet Michelle at her salon to get my hair done before heading back to D.C. I've been stretching this relaxer; my new growth is about two inches long, and I can see my natural curl pattern. I'm contemplating whether or not I want to tell her what's going on. I know she can keep a secret and won't tell anyone. She's been so busy opening up her second salon that we barely talk, so I'm eager to catch up with her.

I was excited when she called me last month to share her good news about being pregnant. Kevin was in the background, talking about how he wants seven kids. Michelle's not having that. He'll be lucky if he gets three out of her.

"Hey, sis," I say as I walk through the door. Michelle is standing at the front desk, flipping through receipts. She's always doing something different with her hair. Right now, she has a burgundy red, asymmetrical hairstyle. It's shaved on one side, and hair swoops over the left side of her face, almost covering her eye. Next week it will be something different. Her Louis Vuitton Neverfull tote that she never leaves home without sits on the desk in front of her. She throws everything in that bag.

"Hey, how's everything going?"

I roll my eyes, walk to her chair, and plop down in it. "Well, let's get into it. What's going on?"

She grabs her bag from off the counter and walks toward her chair. "You look like you could use a stiff drink."

"I can't drink."

"Why? You pregnant too?"

I look at her in silence, trying to keep my face blank.

Michelle leans in over my shoulder and whispers, "Dee, are you pregnant?"

We are the only two people in the shop. Why is she whispering? I nod because I can't say it out loud.

"Congratulations, I guess? You don't seem too happy." She gives me a half smile and stares at me like she's waiting for a response.

I spin the chair around and look at her. "I don't know if I want this baby."

She looks at me with concern in her eyes. "Why is that?"

"Because I'm not sure if it's Chris's.'"

Michelle sits down in the chair across from me. "Oh shit! Does he know? Whose baby could it be?"

"Yes, he knows. And I don't want to talk about whose baby it could be."

She gives me this spiel about how I should keep the baby, especially if Chris is okay with everything. "I'm a little upset you won't tell me whose baby it might be," she says.

I don't want to look at this baby and see a face I don't recognize and always think he or she looks like the man that raped me. I can taste the saliva thickening in my throat as I think back to that night.

"You will make a great mom. Take time to think and pray before making your decision."

"If I take time to think, I will end up going through with the pregnancy."

"Don't forget to pray," she says and walks toward the back of the shop.

"I have to do what's best for me."

"You always do," she says as she walks back to my chair.

She begins prepping my hair for a relaxer. As she runs her fingers through my hair, I close my eyes and my mind begins to wander. Michelle told me to think and pray. That's all I've been doing since I found out I'm pregnant. All the reasons why I should go through with the abortion floods my mind. It's not just about the rape. I don't think I'm ready to be a mother.

CHAPTER NINE

I'm not in the mood for coffee this morning, so I fill the teakettle with water and set it on the stove. I pull the chair out from the table and sit down. The pink Post-It note with the clinic phone number is still sitting on the table from when I got back from my weekend in Virginia. I reach over and grab it. I stare blankly at the numbers, then my eyes move to my cell phone sitting on the counter next to the stove. The whistle from the kettle is getting louder. I press the Post-It note down, get up from the table, and remove the kettle from the stove. I glance at the digital clock on the stove, and it feels like time is slowing down.

God, please forgive me. I grab my cell phone from the counter and the Post-It note from the table. My heart races as I dial each number. With the last number keyed in, I press the green button with the phone icon and put the phone to my ear. The phone rings twice and a woman answers. "Hello?" There's a moment of drawn-out silence. "Speak up, please," she says. But I haven't said anything yet. I know there will be consequences to my actions, eternal and fleeting. With resentment and sadness in my heart, I schedule my appointment.

I text Chris to let him know my appointment is scheduled for next Saturday. Three dots appear on my screen, so I wait to see what his response will be. Then the dots disappear. I place my phone on the counter and pour water from the teakettle into my cup. I keep glancing over at my phone, anticipating a response from Chris. I check it to make sure I didn't turn my ringer off.

I grab my phone and my cup and sit down at the table. Again, I glance at the clock on the stove. Emptiness consumes me, and I can't pretend that everything is okay because it's not.

My phone chimes, and Chris's name flashes on my screen. I unlock my phone to read his message. "I'm going to keep my word and be there for you," the message says. I don't respond.

My week has been full of sleepless nights and crying. Chris and I haven't spoke much this week. The silence is better than hearing the sadness in his voice. I'm ready to get this over with and move past it. Not sure how far our relationship will go after this.

Chris texts me when he gets to my apartment. I wasn't expecting him until later this evening, after work. I can't leave work early, but as soon as the clock hits five, I will be on the elevator.

On my way home, I wonder what type of mood Chris will be in. I don't want to stress over this anymore and I don't want him too either. I've been doing that since I found out I was pregnant. I just want to relax and try to enjoy our time together.

I walk through the door, expecting to see Chris sitting in the living room, but he's not there. His bag sits on the floor next to the end table. I walk to the bedroom, and he's lying in bed, sleeping.

Quietly, I open my dresser drawer in search for some lounge clothes so I can get comfortable.

He shifts and yawns, opening his eyes. "Hey, how was your day?"

"I'm sorry. Did I wake you?"

"No, I was about to get up. Was waiting for you to get home."

I pull out a pair of stretch pants and a T-shirt from my drawer.

He sits up, swinging his legs out of bed. "I figure we can order take-out tonight."

I nod, thinking that he read my mind. I'm not in the mood to go out tonight. I just want to relax and sit in my feelings.

After eating dinner, I go straight to my bedroom and get in the bed. Chris follows behind me. "You want to talk about tomorrow?" he asks.

I pull the covers back from the bed and sit down.

"Do *you* want to talk about tomorrow?" I ask in response.

"No, I just want you to change your mind."

I open the top drawer of my nightstand and pull out my head scarf. Chris walks over to the other side of the bed, grabs the remote off the bed, and sits. The last thing I want is for this decision to affect our relationship, but with the silent treatment I've been getting I can tell that has already happened.

"I know you do, but I can't."

Chris kisses me on the cheek and lies back in the bed, flipping through the channels. Sleep comes over me before Chris finds something worth watching.

I'm awakened by the ringing of my cell phone. I glance at the cable box to see what time it is: 3:34 a.m.

When I answer, I hear Michelle's strained voice. "Dee, it's Daddy. You need to make your way home. He doesn't have too much longer."

I jump out of bed and tell Chris we need to get on the road. I grab my weekend bag from the closet and clothes from my dresser drawer, and we get on the road headed for Virginia.

Having Chris with me is a blessing. I wouldn't be able to drive— I'm too emotional. Chris and I pray the whole way that we make it there before Dad takes his last breath. The muscle at the corner of my left eye begins to twitch the closer we get to the house. I tightly fold my arms across my chest and stare out the window as Chris drives. This feels like a bad dream I can't wake up from. I know I can't stop what's coming, but that doesn't mean it hurts any less.

We pull up to my parents' house. Michelle's car and the pastor's car are in the driveway. Chris parks in front of the house. Instead of opening the car door to get out, I just sit there.

"Destinee, come on." Chris grabs my hand, gently rubbing his thumb across my skin.

I can't move. I feel in my spirit that we are too late, and he's already gone. Chris walks around the car and opens my door. My mom is standing at the front door, and I can tell she's been crying.

Forcing my feet to move, I step out of the car. When I'm halfway to the house, Mom says, "He's gone, baby. He's not suffering anymore." I break down before she can finish her sentence.

"Why didn't anyone call me?" I ask, my voice thick with sadness.

"Y'all were on the road, and there was nothing you could do."

We all knew it would be soon, but it's still hard to hear he's gone. I think back to what he said to me last weekend when I was here. He knew he was near the end, and he needed to be at peace before he left. I am so thankful that he opened up his heart to me. Despite the pain of this loss, I know he's at peace, and so am I.

CHAPTER TEN

It shouldn't take death to bring family together, but it's nice to see both my mother's and father's sides of the family. Some family members I meet for the first time, and some I don't mind if I never see again, but right now I'm glad everyone has come together to celebrate the life of my father and be there for one another.

At the repass, my mother can't sit still. She keeps walking around, trying to feed everyone, talking to friends and family. I try to get her to sit down and eat something, but she insists I let her be. I see her shed a tear every now and then, but mostly she tries to console everybody else. I know once everyone leaves and people stop calling and stopping by, my siblings and I will need to be here to help her get through this. We're gonna need to be there for each other.

My father was fifty-four years old; he lived the longest out of the men in his family. My uncle Roger died when he was twenty-two from a drug overdose, and their father died when my father was very young. His mother remarried when he was ten years old. She had two daughters.

They haven't said much to me or my siblings. They never liked how my father would speak his mind no matter who he was talking to, and he didn't care if he hurt your feelings. I think that's why they never called or came around.

My great-aunt Faye, my mom's aunt, finds me sitting in the corner watching friends and family talk about my dad. Some share pleasant memories while others complain about how rude he was. I have lots of memories of him being rude, but for the life of me I can't think of one good time between me and my dad. Aunt Faye is eighty years old and still gets around like she's in her sixties.

"Why are you sitting over here watching everyone? Where's Chris?" she asks.

"He went outside with Landon."

"How you holding up?"

"I'm okay. I just worry about my mom."

"Did you know that your mother met your father her senior year of college?" I nod and she continues talking. "According to your mother, your father was still trying to find himself in this world. Working odd jobs, living at home with his parents, and unsure of what he wanted out of life."

To this day, I'm not sure what my mother saw in my father. I guess it's true that opposites attract. "I don't know how, but he swept her off her feet and they were married after dating for one year." We both laugh. "Before their one-year anniversary, they had Michelle. Two years later came you and Landon."

"Aunt Faye, why are you telling me this story? I already know it."

"Just keeping you company. Sharing memories like everyone else here."

Aunt Faye is known for telling drawn-out stories, so I get comfortable in my chair and continue listening, hoping she will get to the point and her story will come to an end.

"Your dad was not a church goer."

"I know. We called him a chreaster—someone who only goes to church on Easter and Christmas."

She laughs so hard, she farts. I gag. "Eww, Aunt Faye."

She looks around to see if anyone else heard it, but no one is looking. "Whew chil', that one slipped out."

My mother used to have my brother, sister, and me in church all the time. We looked to my father to save us, but his response was, "Listen to your mother." Whether it was a church play, choir performances, or shut-in services, sister Eunice and her three children were there.

I hate to admit that I never wanted to go to those services, but looking back I am thankful for those experiences. When my faith gets weak, I know who to call on.

"I know you had a hard time when your grandfather passed away, and then your grandmother passed away seven months later." Aunt Faye looks at me with sympathy.

That's something I will never forget. My grandmother passed away in her sleep. I was the one who found her. I was on winter break from college and wanted to spend some time with her, so I stayed at her house. That was the hardest thing in the world for me: to find her lifeless in her bed. Every time I think about that day, I get chills.

"You never know when it's going to be the last time you see or talk to someone."

"That's true. Grandma would always say, 'Give me my roses while I'm still living, and love me for who I am because one day I won't be here,'" I say.

"Just like with the passing of your grandparents, it's going to take some time for all of us to adjust to your dad being gone."

"You're right. I'm just glad my parents were able to travel and do some of the things they set out to do once their children were grown."

"I hope your mother continues to travel as often as she can and maybe do some of the things she has always wanted to do. She's been a nurse for over twenty-five years and always talked about being a foster parent or starting her own non-profit organization for children."

"I'll never forget when she told my dad she wanted to do foster care." I smile fondly. "He told her that after he finished raising his children, he was done. He didn't want any more kids running through his house or his pockets."

With the passing of my father, I decide not to go through with the abortion. I don't want to go through with it and regret it. They say everything happens for a reason, and I believe my father's death was a sign that I need to keep this baby.

After the repass, when everyone has left the house, I break the news about my pregnancy to my mother. She says it's the best news she could get after everything with my dad. It gives her something to look forward to. "I'm excited to be having two more grandchildren," she says with a smile.

I refuse to tell her what happened that night at Keri's—that the baby might not be Chris's. Only Michelle and Chris know. As long as I have Chris's support, everything will work itself out. Plus, I'll be moving to Virginia in the next couple of months once I finish my last semester.

This baby is not a part of my plan, and I'm scared of becoming a mother. I still question whether or not I will be able to love this baby the way he or she deserves to be loved. All the "what if" questions run through my mind, but only time will tell.

I'm quickly discovering that pregnancy is no joke. The morning sickness, day sickness, and night sickness ... I am tired all the time. This is it for me ... no more children!

My lease is up in January, so I need to figure out where I am going to live. After being on my own for so long, I know I don't want to move back home with my mother. She has enough room and keeps hinting that she wants me to come live with her, but I need my own space.

Chris only has a one-bedroom apartment. There's no way all of my stuff and a baby will make it there. I've been contemplating whether I should take a leap into homeownership. Might as well, especially since Chris wants us to move in together. I'm trying not to hold back on us. I am okay with taking this leap into buying a home as long as he understands the mortgage and deed will be in my name until, if, and when we say, "I do." I thought he would be offended by me wanting to buy a place by myself. Things are already moving fast enough with us and I don't want to get married just because I'm pregnant. "As long as we are living together, I'm okay with it," he says.

I find a realtor, and she starts sending me listings. On our first day out, I find the perfect place. It's surprising because I am picky and cheap. The condo is a fairly new development in Virginia Beach, not too far from my mother. I fall in love with this spacious three-bedroom condo. It's perfect—not too big or small.

It has a garage, vaulted ceilings, a huge master bedroom, and tons of closet space, and the master bedroom has a little sitting area with a window seat. It's a big step up from my little D.C. apartment. Chris is happy with it too.

We both have fully furnished apartments and have to figure out what we're keeping. I think the most difficult task will be trying to figure out whose stuff stays and whose goes. We decide to pick out new bedroom furniture that we both like. It takes us going to four different furniture stores before we agree on something.

My mother loves to decorate. So, moving into this condo will give her something to do with her extra time. My father still had several pieces of furniture that he built just sitting in the garage. My mother gives me a piece to put in my foyer area, so now I have a piece of my father in my new home.

CHAPTER ELEVEN

I pass the "Welcome to Virginia" sign all the time when I'm driving from D.C., but this last time it feels different. My life is about to change in a big way. The promise that I made to myself back in high school is broken. I'm back in Virginia for good and trying not to trigger any bad memories. Instead, I think about all the good new memories that are to come.

I'm nervous about my transition to the Norfolk office. My due date is just a few months away, and I don't want them to think I'm going to slack on my work just because I'm pregnant. I've worked hard to get to this point in my career. I've expressed to Chris how having this baby scares me. I've seen how my friends changed after giving birth. They were all focused on their careers, had their babies, and decided to give up their careers and everything they worked for to be stay-at-home parents. I don't want this baby to change me like that.

I already get an earful from my mother and Chris about

working full-time. They both want me to stay home, focus on studying for the bar exam, and not work until after the baby is born. I thought about it, and not working does sound nice, but I've come too far to pass up the opportunity of becoming an associate with this firm. Plus, with Chris working part-time with his uncle and going to school full-time, I want to make sure the bills get paid.

I'm thankful that with this move, I don't have to hire movers. Chris, Kevin, and Troy move all the furniture while Kim, Michelle, and I talk. We try to stay out of their way and out of the cold. Michelle's excitement about me being back in Virginia is a little overwhelming. Maybe it's because we are both pregnant. Regardless, it is nice to talk to someone who understands these pregnancy struggles.

I pull three stools from under the kitchen island so we can sit down while the guys unload the truck. Michelle's belly looks like she's going to pop that baby out any day now. She asks me if I will be there in the delivery room when she gives birth to Jasmine.

"I don't know, Michelle. I was there when you delivered Jaiden, and it was horrifying."

"It wasn't that bad."

"Could have fooled me, the way you were moaning and screaming."

"I was determined to have a natural childbirth. No drugs at all."

"Yes, I remember cringing the whole time you were pushing. After seeing Jaiden come out, I told myself that if I ever had children, I did not want to have a natural childbirth. In fact, I questioned whether I wanted to have children at all."

"How was your first appointment with Dr. Johnson?"

"I told her I can't handle pain like you can and want any and every kind of drug she can give me to take away the pain of childbirth. I asked her if she could put me to sleep and wake me up once the baby was out. She looked at me like I was crazy."

I look over at Kim and see pain in her eyes. "You okay, Kim?"

"I don't mean to ruin the mood or sound insensitive, but I would give anything to be able to carry a baby and give birth." She leans back against the kitchen island and glances at the ceiling before forcing her gaze down to the floor.

This is why I'm hesitant about talking about my pregnancy around Kim. I wasn't even trying to get pregnant and she's been trying for years to have a baby.

Michelle reaches over and hugs Kim.

"My mom has this saying that waiting on God's timing is hard, but we have to trust it. It will happen for you soon, and we will be sitting around talking about your delivery, laughing and joking."

"Your mom has a saying about everything." We all laugh, and Kim brushes her hand against her face, wiping away her tears.

As much as I don't want to admit it, it feels good to be back in Virginia and close to my family. My siblings and I are grown, doing well with our lives, and starting families.

I'm excited about Landon moving back to the east coast in April. Just in time for the birth of my baby and my graduation. My graduation is days apart from my due date, but nothing is going to stop me from walking across that stage and accepting my degree. Even if that means me walking across that stage with a big belly or in labor.

Landon proposed to his girlfriend three years ago while they were in Japan, and they set their wedding date for August. Just three months after my due date. They're cutting it close for me to get this body back in shape.

Now that Landon is about to walk down the aisle and say, "I do," my mother keeps hounding me about when I'm getting married. There is no doubt in my mind that marriage is in my future, but I'm not trying to rush it. Things are already moving fast in my life. Having this baby is enough for me to handle at the moment.

Chris and I agree not to find out the sex of the baby until the baby shower, which is right around the corner. My mother, sister, and Kim take charge of planning the baby shower because I suck at planning parties. I let them know that it will be a co-ed baby shower with both my family and Chris's family and friends. My only job is the cake because the filling is going to tell us the sex of the baby.

Michelle insists that I have a gender reveal party so guests will know what to get for the baby shower. I don't want a gender reveal party *and* a baby shower. That's too many parties. I'm all about saving a coin and keeping it simple. I'm excited about the baby shower but nervous because that means I am closer to giving birth. Chris, on the other hand, is ready for it all. Every day, he checks the days off the calendar with a black sharpie. I should be the one counting down. I'm the one carrying the baby.

The house is finally in order, and we've slowly been purchasing stuff for the nursery; I ordered a glider and an ottoman. Every time I walk past the room, I want to sit in it. This morning, I stop at the door, walk in, and slowly lower myself into it. I let out a deep moan from the pain in my back. I frown at my swollen feet as I plop them on the ottoman. Chris has been staying out of my way lately; he says I'm moodier than ever these days, and I'm not surprised since I can barely sleep. Plus, I've been worrying about my due date and graduation. I'm uncertain which is going to occur first, but I'm ready and so is Chris.

After I've been sitting in the glider for a few minutes, Chris walks in the room and reminds me that we need to leave soon for my doctor's appointment. It's my last appointment before the baby shower. I don't understand why they schedule your appointment for a particular time. You end up sitting in the waiting area, waiting to get called back.

I tap my foot on the floor, waiting for the nurse to call my name. Chris patiently sits next to me and plays a game on his phone. He touches my leg with his hand and reassures me that I will be called soon.

Finally, the nurse walks out the door and calls my name. She walks me right to the damn scale every visit, and the number keeps going up. I tell myself it's just baby weight, but I know damn well it's not. I've been eating anything and everything I can, every time hoping it doesn't give me heartburn. No weird cravings, though.

We walk back to the exam room, and I sit on the cold examination table. The nurse walks in behind us with the fetal Doppler. She puts the cold gel on my stomach and begins to move the Doppler around in search of the baby's heartbeat. I always look forward to hearing the whooshing sound of my baby's heartbeat—it's reassurance that the baby is okay. But this time, something is different. I notice the way the nurse is moving the fetal Doppler around my stomach, like she's having a difficult time finding the heartbeat.

As I lie there, trying not to panic, the nurse looks over at me and Chris and says, "No worries, Dr. Johnson will be in shortly." I know sometimes the baby can be in a position that might make it difficult to detect the heartbeat. Chris gives me a small smile and squeezes my hand.

After a few minutes, Dr. Johnson walks into the exam room. She's chipper, as usual. "Good morning. I hear the little one is playing a game of hide and seek with us this morning."

She walks in with the fetal Doppler in her hand and starts moving it around my stomach, slowly. To the left, then to the right. I look over at Chris, who grabs my hand again and tells me to be patient. That everything is okay.

Terrified, I close my eyes and say a prayer. "God, please let everything be okay with my baby, and let Dr. Johnson find the heartbeat." In the midst of the prayer, I wish I knew the sex of the baby or their name so my prayer can be more specific.

Dr. Johnson moves the fetal Doppler away from my stomach.

"When was the last time you felt the baby moving and kicking?"

I can feel my heart pounding against my ribs. I take a deep breath, trying not to panic as I calmly answer her questions.

"I got so used to feeling the baby move and kick that I stopped paying attention to every movement."

It was an early appointment, so I don't remember feeling anything since the night before. She tells me not to worry. She walks toward the door and tells us she wants me to have an ultrasound.

As soon as she walks out of the room, I start thinking the worst. I keep trying to think back to the last time I felt the baby move or kick. For the life of me, I can't be sure when it was. Chris can tell I'm beginning to panic and tries to reassure me that everything is going to be okay.

"The baby is just being stubborn, like his mother."

"*His* mother? What if it's a girl?"

I think to myself that this is my fault. God is punishing me for wanting to have an abortion. Maybe I've been working too hard and studying too much and should have taken time off to rest.

Chris keeps his expression neutral in an effort to keep me calm, but it's not working. I need them to hurry up so I can make sure my baby is okay. I start poking my stomach and praying that I will feel the baby move. Even the slightest movement will suffice, but nothing.

The ultrasound tech walks into the room a couple of minutes later and takes Chris and I down the hall to the ultrasound room. As we walk down the hall, I feel flushed, like I'm going to pass out.

We get to the ultrasound room, and I lie on the table. Dr. Johnson walks in the room to start the ultrasound. She places the ultrasound probe on my stomach and moves it around. Once she figures out how the baby is positioned, she moves the probe around my stomach in search of the baby's heartbeat. She looks up at me and then back at the monitor.

I break down at that point because I know what she's going to say. Dr. Johnson looks back at me and then at Chris.

"I'm so sorry, but there is no heartbeat."

In that moment, I feel my heart leave my body. I shake my head in disbelief and try to scream but nothing comes out. I look over at Chris and see tears falling down his face.

"Please try again," I say, hoping maybe she missed something. But she assures me in the most sympathetic way that the baby is gone and there is nothing either one of us can do. She tries to reassure me that I didn't do anything wrong, and sometimes this happens with pregnancies.

She asks us if we want to know the sex of the baby, but I can't say anything and Chris is trying to console me. Dr. Johnson gives us a couple of minutes and then asks that we come to her office so we can talk.

We sit in the ultrasound room for a couple of minutes in disbelief, crying.

"God is punishing me for something."

"Don't say that, Destinee. That's not true."

"I'm sorry for not listening to you about working. Maybe I wasn't resting enough and doing too much worrying. Maybe it's because the baby isn't yours or because at first, I wanted an abortion."

"Stop blaming yourself."

"I don't understand why God would allow me to lose my baby."

Chris grabs me and holds me close.

"Sometimes we don't understand God's plan, but God is not punishing you."

He helps me off the table and we walk down the hall to Dr. Johnson's office. Still, I'm convinced I'm being punished, and I keep asking God, "Why me?" I was finally getting used to the idea of being a mother. My baby shower is next weekend and my due date a few weeks after that. I anticipated delivering a healthy baby.

Chris and I sit in the chairs directly across from Dr. Johnson's desk. I can see her lips moving but can't hear anything she's saying.

Chris grabs my hand and asks, "Do you understand what the doctor just said?" I say no and ask her to repeat it.

"You will need to go over to Labor and Delivery so you can be induced and deliver the baby."

Chris rests his hands on mine. I look at Dr. Johnson like she has lost her damn mind.

"You mean to tell me I still have to deliver this baby? Why not just put me to sleep and take the baby?"

I beg her not to make me go through the pain of delivering a baby that I can't take home with me.

I don't think I will survive that. No one ever envisions delivering a lifeless baby or giving birth to a baby that will never leave the hospital with them.

She gives me instructions to go to the hospital to start inducing labor. Chris calls my mother and his aunt, and they meet us at the hospital. My mother called Michelle and Kim, and they make their way up to the hospital too.

We get to the hospital and head straight to Labor and Delivery. There's a woman seated directly across from the nurses' station, and she looks like she's about to give birth right there. I walk up to the nurses' desk and give the nurse my name. She looks up at me and says, "Hmmph, give me one minute." Then walks down the hall. When she comes back, she has another nurse with her.

"Hi, Ms. Clark, I'm Nurse Nikki. Let me get you checked in and to your room."

I lean on the counter with my head in my hand, answer some questions, sign some papers, and she puts a wristband on my arm.

We walk down the hall to the delivery room. "Here's a gown for you. The bathroom is right there." She points to the door on the left. "I will be back in a minute to get things started."

I walk in the bathroom and remove my clothing. I fold my bra and panties up in my pants, place my shirt over it, and walk out of the bathroom.

Chris gets up from the chair and helps me into the bed. He lifts the covers over my legs. "Do you need anything?"

"Yes, I need to get out of this hospital."

"Well, that's not possible."

"Nothing I want is possible, so why ask?"

He throws his hands up and steps back. "I'll let you be."

Nurse Nikki walks into the room and places a small cup on the counter.

"What's in the cup?" I ask.

"We need to soften your cervix so you can begin labor, but first I'm going to get you hooked up to an IV and get some fluids in you."

I lie in the bed and watch her as she gets everything together. I see the fetal monitor next to the IV pole.

"I guess you won't be hooking me up to that?" I ask and point to the monitor.

"No, we won't be using that today."

I let her continue, and there's a knock on the door. My mom walks in and stands in the corner until the nurse finishes with the IV and placing the pill in my vagina. Shortly after the nurse leaves the room, Michelle and Regina walk in.

I don't want them here. I can feel them staring at me with sorrow written all over their faces. I don't need anyone to feel sorry for me. I have enough sorrow for myself. Kim walks into the room and over to my bed.

"I'm so sorry, Destinee. I left work as soon as I heard." She takes a deep breath in and releases it as she glances around the room.

"You didn't have to come." They all try to get me to talk, but I don't have anything to say. I can't understand why this is happening. I'm a good person. I always try to live my life right. I'll help anyone in need. Why is this happening to me?

My mother moves her chair up to my bed and prays over me.

"Ma, please don't."

I squint at her with my hardened eyes and turn my face away from her. I don't want to hear anything about God, scriptures, or prayers. I'm mad at God for letting this happen.

The nurse walks in and starts me on the Pitocin. I'm unable to give her my undivided attention while she explains what the medicine is and what it does. She might as well be talking to a brick wall. Everyone watches my every move, and my mind is racing. When she walks out of the room, I tell everyone to leave.

Chris gets up from his chair, walks over to my bed, and asks, "You want everyone to leave?"

"Yes. I don't want everyone sitting in here watching me and feeling sorry for me. I just want you here. Everyone else can go."

One by one, Michelle, Kim, Regina, and my mom walk out of the room. My mom peeks back in the room and asks, "Chris, can I talk to you for a minute?"

When Chris walks out of the room, I take both hands and place them over my stomach. *I'm sorry, baby.* I wish we were here under different circumstances and could celebrate this moment instead of being full of sadness and hopelessness.

Chris walks back in and closes the door behind him.

"They all are going home, but your mom wants to be here when the baby comes so she asked that I call her when you are close to delivering." I remain silent and look up at the television.

I remember when Michelle gave birth and how the baby monitors were on her stomach. Everyone was laughing and joking, anticipating the baby's arrival. This is nothing like that.

After a few hours, Dr. Johnson comes in to break my water. The contractions get stronger, and I beg for drugs.

"I can't do it. I just can't do it." The physical and emotional pain combined is too much to handle.

"It will be over soon. If you want an epidural now, I can have the anesthesiologist come up."

"Yes, please!" My eyes are watery, and I'm squinting through the pain. I breathe in and out, but it feels like the air won't enter my lungs.

Chris is standing next to me, unsure of what to do or say. His eyes have this haunted look as he glances down at his phone and then looks back up at me. "Your mother is on her way back up here."

I put my hand over my face and let out a moan.

"You don't want your mom here?"

"I just want this baby out of me. I'm tired of lying up in this hospital hearing the damn baby bell ring every time a baby is born. All those women get to take their babies home. I don't."

"I don't know how to respond to that."

"Of course, you don't."

"I know you're dealing with a lot right now, so I'm not going to take that to heart."

I turn over on my left side and curl up like a ball. My contractions are getting stronger and closer. About three minutes apart now. Chris stands in front of me, mimicking my breathing, trying to keep me on track and rubbing my back.

"You got this, Dee. Keep breathing. Don't hold your breath."

"Help me, please. Call the nurse. I need that epidural."

Chris hits the nurse call button on the bed, and I hear a voice coming from the speaker.

"How can I help you?"

Chris responds, "Her contractions are getting closer and stronger. She's ready for her epidural."

"I'll be in there shortly," the nurse says.

I take a minute to catch my breath before the next contraction starts. "Chris?"

"Yes?"

"I'm so sorry." I let out a loud cry. I'd been holding it in all day.

"Sorry for what?"

"The baby."

"Stop it! It's not your fault." He reaches over me and wraps his arms around me.

Another contraction hits me, and I curl up into a ball again.

Dr. Johnson steps in the room like she's ready to run a race. "Your nurse just told me your contractions are getting stronger and closer. I'm going to check to see how dilated you are."

"I feel tingling and pressure down there."

"That's normal," she says as she lifts my blanket and places her hand on my leg.

"Nothing about this is normal," I say as she inserts her fingers into my vagina.

"Your labor is progressing fast. You've been here for almost seven hours, and you're almost ready to push."

"What?"

"You are almost ten centimeters dilated."

"What about my epidural?"

"Might not have time for that."

"I don't even care at this point. Just get it out."

"Why is she shaking?" Chris asks Dr. Johnson.

"She's transitioning into active labor. Her contractions are lasting longer and are more frequent."

Another contraction hits me, and Dr. Johnson tells me to look at Chris and breathe though the contraction. My mom walks in. "You are right on time. She's almost ready to start pushing," Dr. Johnson says.

"I feel like I gotta shit."

My mom laughs as she walks across the room and places her purse on the couch. "I'm just going to sit over here, out of the way."

I let out another moan as another contraction comes on. She walks over and stands at the foot of the bed. "You are so strong and brave. You got this, Destinee."

In too much pain to speak, I shake my head in disbelief.

The moment I've been dreading is here. Two nurses walk in the room and start pulling stuff out of cabinets and drawers. Nurse Nikki looks at me and says, "Time to push. Tuck your chin in your chest and give it all you got." My mom holds my right leg while nurse Nikki holds my other leg. Chris stands on my left side, coaching me through my breathing with each contraction.

"I see a head," Dr. Johnson says.

"Why is it burning?" I yell out.

"That's normal. Just the baby stretching you out a little bit. You're doing good."

With the next contraction, I bear down and push and I feel like the pressure is easing up. I look up and see my lifeless chocolate baby in Dr. Johnson's hands. "It's a boy." I pray that I will hear him scream, but there's just silence.

Chris looks at me with tears in his eyes. "I knew it was a boy."

I can't see straight, I'm crying so hard. They clean my baby boy up, wrap him in a blanket, and ask me if I want to hold him. A part of me wants to say no, but I know I need to see and hold him. I don't want to regret not doing so.

I nod and the nurse places him in my arms. Here I am, lying in the bed, holding my baby boy with his head full of curly black hair. Chris decided if it was a boy, his name would be Christopher Marcus Richardson, Jr. We would call him CJ.

At my first appointment with Dr. Johnson, I mentioned that I wanted a paternity test once the baby was born. Chris was against it the whole time. He said he knew it was his baby the moment I told him I was pregnant.

After looking at CJ, I no longer need a test to confirm anything. He is a spitting image of Chris.

My mom pulls the blanket back to look at CJ's hands. I see the tracks of tears on her face, smearing her makeup. "I'll give you two some time alone." She grabs her purse and slowly walks out of the room. Chris sits down on the bed next to me. I rest my head back on the bed and we sit and cry as we stare at CJ.

This beautiful, innocent, little baby boy that I will never get the opportunity to mother, breast feed, and see grow up. Chris will miss out on watching his son play sports, will never get to teach him how to work on cars. My lips quiver as I hold my baby boy, wondering how we will ever recover from this loss.

CHAPTER TWELVE

I get home from the hospital and notice that Chris put away everything baby-related. The nursery door is closed, and all the sonogram pictures are no longer pinned to the refrigerator with magnets. Even the framed sonogram over the fireplace has been removed.

I place CJ's clothing from the hospital in a Ziploc bag and put it in the closet in a baby-blue box with his ashes. I find myself opening the bag to get a whiff of his smell from his hospital blanket. I'd give anything, I mean *anything,* to have my son home with me. To be able to kiss his little fingers and toes and watch him sleep in his crib. Or to sit in the rocking chair and stare into his eyes.

The days since his birth have been unbearable. My breast milk has come in, so my breasts are leaking and hurting. The shock of losing CJ has not subsided, and I don't think it ever will. Guilt still weighs heavy on my heart. I thought I couldn't sleep during the pregnancy, but it's even harder now. All I want to do is lie in bed. I don't want to see anyone or talk to anyone at all. I wouldn't wish this pain and loss on my worst enemy. A piece of me has left, and I am so lost without it—without him.

I can tell Chris is trying hard to hold it together and take care of me at the same time. We are both hurting, grieving, and as the days pass, we become more and more disconnected. I feel like he blames me for losing CJ. I blame my damn self, constantly questioning what I could've done differently. Maybe if I was paying attention to the kicks and flutters, I would have noticed when he stopped moving and could've done something to help him.

My maternity time is coming to an end, but I am in no condition to return to work. I am so thankful that my boss has been understanding. Most employers don't care about the employee and just want them back in the office to get work done. I've received calls, flowers, and text messages from almost everyone I work with, but everyone's calls have gone unanswered. My voice mailbox is full. I am tired of hearing "I'm sorry for your loss" or "I'm here if you need me." No one understands this grief. I feel the love, but it's not enough to get me through this.

Graduation comes and goes. My mother tries to get me to go, but the thought of walking across that stage and having to face friends and classmates who knew I was expecting depresses me even more. I'm not ready for all of that.

Chris went back to work at the shop a couple of days after I got home. When he leaves the house in the morning, I'm in bed, and when he gets home I'm on the couch lying down. I can't find the strength to do anything. Television and food have become my addiction. I never realized there were so many ratchet television shows, but for some reason these are the shows that keep my attention. I binge watch shows on demand and order food with Grub Hub.

The doorbell rings. I'm glued to the couch as usual. I just got hooked on *Love & Hip Hop*, and it's getting good. Chris left for work hours ago, and I didn't order any food, so I have no clue who it is. Maybe if I keep quiet, they will go away.

As my luck would have it, the doorbell rings again. I pull myself up from the couch and walk over to the door. It's Chris's aunt, Regina. Damn. All she does is talk, and I can't handle that right now. She's peeping through the glass window next to the door, waving, gesturing me to come open the door. She can probably see that I am not too thrilled to see her since I haven't opened the door yet.

I open the door, say hello, walk back to the couch, and plop down. I'm wearing pajamas, and there are junk food wrappers sitting on the coffee table in front of me.

"Destinee, what are you doing? I spoke to your mom and Chris, and they tell me you barely leave the house. You even missed your graduation."

If she already spoke to my mom and Chris, then she knows I am not in the mood to talk or listen to her. When I don't respond, she gets up from the couch, picks up the remote, and turns the television off. I look at her like she's crazy.

"Come with me," she says. She grabs my hand and pulls me up the steps to my bedroom.

She points to the bed and tells me to sit, which I do. I feel like I don't have an option, really. She walks into the bathroom and I hear water running.

"Get in that bathroom, take a hot shower, then come downstairs."

She has a serious tone I've never heard from her before. I don't want to take a shower. I would rather sit in my filth and sulk on my couch, but I listen, hoping she'll leave.

I get out the shower, dry off, and reach in my drawer for another set of pajamas. The drawer is empty. With the towel wrapped around me, I walk over to the door and yell out, "What did you do with my pajamas?"

"You won't be needing those today. Find something else to put on." I grit my teeth and open the other drawer to grab my sweatpants. She yells, "Don't you think about putting on sweatpants, either. Hurry it up, and come downstairs."

She's playing with my comfort zone, and I don't appreciate it.

I sit on the bed for a moment to gather my thoughts. When I look up, I catch a glimpse of someone in the mirror, and it takes a few seconds to recognize that it's me. I look horrible—my hair knotted up, my face all fat and droopy.

I stand up, remove my towel, and look at my body in the mirror. I place my hand over the empty pouch on my stomach and stand there crying and moaning softly. I fall to my knees and hear Regina walking up the stairs.

She appears in the doorway, her forehead wrinkled in concern. "Are you okay?"

"No, I'm not okay. God took my baby. Why did he take my baby from me?"

"I'm so sorry, sweetheart." She gets down on her knees next to me and wraps the towel over me.

"I don't get it," I whisper.

We sit on the floor for a few minutes, and she holds me close while I let the tears fall and the screams bellow from deep down inside me.

"Why don't you put some clothes on and come back downstairs with me. It's a statement, not a question."

I get up from the floor, walk into my closet, and pull out a pair of comfortable jeans and a short-sleeve shirt. Then I make my way back into the bathroom to tackle my hair the best way I know how. When I get downstairs, Regina is sitting on the sofa, waiting patiently.

"Come sit next to me," she says as she reaches into her purse and pulls out an envelope. She slowly opens the envelope and pulls out a picture. She shows me the picture of Chris and I holding CJ. I forgot Chris took that picture when it was just us in the hospital room with CJ.

I look away. "How did you get that?"

"Chris gave it to me."

"Why would you show me that?"

"Destinee, I need you to look at this picture."

I look in the opposite direction and push her hand away. "No, this is disrespectful of you to do this."

She flips the picture over. "By no means do I intend to be disrespectful. Chris gave me this photo the other day. He wanted to show you but said you just sit around the house all day and won't talk to him or anyone else."

I don't want to see that picture. "What is there to talk about?" I turn my body so I can get up, and Regina reaches for my hand.

"I know it's hard, but you have to keep moving. Keep living. CJ may not be here in the flesh, but he will always be with you in spirit."

"I don't want to hear this." I get up and walk into the kitchen.

She follows behind me. "I know you are still grieving but at some point, baby, you have to push forward. Every time I talk to Chris, he tells me you are not getting any better."

"I will never be better. How can anyone expect me to be better? I lost my baby, my son. I carried him for thirty-four weeks. I pushed a lifeless baby out of my vagina and came home from the hospital empty-handed. Who in the hell can ever get over something like that? Please, tell me?"

"You will never be the same. A part of you will always be missing. You will never be able to get over losing your baby, but you need to learn how to continue living your life. Look at all that you accomplished with law school and the law firm. You missed walking across that stage to accept your law degree. You will regret it, and you're letting life pass you by."

"I regret that I am not a mother."

"You will always be a mother." She holds up the picture again. "This will always be your baby. He will always be rooting for his mother."

I lean over on the kitchen island and Regina places her hand on my back and prays, "Father God, I pray that you grant Destinee the serenity to accept the things she cannot change, the courage to change the things she can, and the wisdom to know the difference. I know you have a plan and purpose for her life and that the loss of CJ was not in vain. Release her from this depression, isolation, and weakness. Help her understand that sometimes things happen to us that we have no control over, but it's all a part of life's journey and your plan. Please give her the strength she needs to get through each day. Bless her with more faith and hope. In Jesus's name, I pray, amen!"

"Amen!"

She wraps her arms around me and holds on to me until there are no more tears left for me to cry. In that moment, I realize I need to get it together. Chris and I have become so distant. It's time for me to be there to support him. I also need to get rid of all this weight I gained. Time to start running in the morning again. Maybe Chris will join me, and we can do it together. It might help clear both our minds and help us get focused.

I know things will never go back to the way they were. I lost a part of myself that I will never get back, but CJ will always remain in my heart. Chris has been so focused on taking care of me and putting himself and his feelings on the back burner. I need to show him how much I appreciate everything he has done for me.

After Regina leaves, I run to the supermarket to pick up some food. I decide to make Chris's favorite meal: meatloaf, macaroni and cheese, cabbage, and corn bread. Sounds like a Sunday dinner with the family, not a Friday-night dinner for two. But this is what he loves and I'm sure it will be a good surprise for him to come home to a clean, well-dressed girlfriend and his favorite meal.

CHAPTER THIRTEEN

I flip through the magazines while I wait for Michelle's last client to leave the salon. The other two ladies in the salon have already left for the day, so it's just us. These stylists don't play around on Saturday. They want to get in and get out.

I had to stop through and get my hair done before I go back to the office on Monday. Michelle and I haven't talked much since CJ's birth. She walks her client to the door and locks it then twirls around and walks toward me.

"Hey, sis! Come on back."

We walk toward the back of the shop to her chair. Before I sit down, she pulls me in for a hug and squeezes me tightly.

"I miss you."

"I miss you, too. I've been neglecting everyone, including myself, but I am slowly coming around."

"Glad to hear that. Mom told me what happened with Regina." She grabs the broom and starts sweeping the hair on the floor around my chair.

"Yeah, I needed that, though. Did Mom tell you about Kim?"

"You know she told me. Everybody probably knows now."

"She found out the week after CJ was born. She was worried that telling me about the baby would upset me."

"I told her it would happen soon."

Although I'm still grieving the loss of CJ, I'm happy for Kim and Troy. They've been trying for a baby for a while but had so many disappointments. This is the perfect opportunity for me to box up the nursery and give some baby stuff to her.

"I'm praying this pregnancy will be different for her. She's been through enough."

"Me too." Michelle wraps the salon cape around my neck and snaps it closed. Then she swings me around in the chair.

"Whew, this right here is a hot mess."

"That's why I'm here. Work your magic."

"It's going to take a lot of magic to fix this mess." We both laugh as we walk toward the sink bowl.

I lean my head back into the sink and she begins shampooing my hair. I feel my body slowly releasing tension and my muscles relax. My scalp is thankful for this special attention.

After conditioning my hair, Michelle leaves me sitting at the sink bowl.

"Let this conditioner sit for a few minutes. I'll be right back."

I hear the door unlock, open, and close. *Did she just leave me in here by myself?*

The door opens again and I hear a click when she locks the door back.

"Alright, let's rinse this conditioner out so you can get under the dryer."

"Landon will be back on the east coast soon. I'm excited about him being closer but wish they weren't getting married so soon. I gotta get my body right."

I'm a little shocked that Landon is about to settle down and start a family. I'll never forget when he called and told me he was starting to catch feelings for Erica. I'd never heard him talk about a woman that way.

"August will be here before you know it."

Michelle wraps the towel around my head and walks over to her station.

"Where did those come from?"

It's The Million Roses black "LOVE" box with magenta roses. I always wanted one of those.

"So, what's the occasion?"

"They're not for me. They're yours."

"Stop playing."

"Chris just dropped them off. He told me to give you this, too."

She hands me an envelope with "My Love" written on the front. My chin quivers and I stagger backward into the chair.

"I can't believe he got these for me."

"Don't cry, Destinee. You haven't even read his note. Open the envelope."

She walks away to grab me some tissues, and I open the envelope to read Chris's note.

"I love you with all my heart and soul. It has been a rough couple of months, but we're making it. It's time we get back to us. Keep loving on each other and building each other up. You and me, we are made for each other. Can't let what we have dissipate.

Instead, we have to continue to grow. That's why tonight we're going to do something we haven't done in a while. Go out on a date. So be ready. Love, Chris."

Michelle reaches around my shoulder and hands me some tissue.

"I can't believe he did this."

"Why not? He loves his woman, and that's you."

This man has touched my soul and changed my life in so many ways. In such a short amount of time, he has shown me what it means to love someone and truly mean it. I had my doubts, but he has overshadowed them all.

Michelle squeezes foam lotion on my head and uses the comb to mold my hair. After placing the wrap strip on my head, she sits me under the dryer. I watch her as she talks to Kevin on the phone and straightens up the shop. I think back to when they first started dating. Michelle was not trying to give him a chance, but look at them now.

When Michelle is done with my hair, I look in the mirror and see my edges are laid and my curls are tight. Just the way I like it.

"You need to let me wax those eyebrows before you go."

"Really, Chelle, you got jokes."

"Nah, just trying to make sure you're straight for your date."

"Yeah, my date."

I leave Michelle's shop and head straight to the house. When I get there Chris is already there, showered and looking good as always.

"Change into something comfortable and casual," he says. So, I shower and change into an olive shirt-dress with a brown belt and some open-toe sandals.

I'm glad we are spending some time together outside of the house. Most nights he closes up the shop, so he gets home late. We pull up to the restaurant we went to on our first date.

"It's been a while since we've been here," I say.

"Yes, it has."

We walk in, get seated right away, and order our food.

"You ready for the bar exam?"

"As ready as I'm going to be."

"I see you're not stressing over it like you used to."

"No, I'm not. All I can do is try my best."

Chris keeps glancing down at his watch and then looking up at me.

"Are you waiting for someone else to join us, or do you have some place to go?'"

"Why do you ask?"

"Because you keep glancing at your watch."

"No, I'm good," he says, nervously. I don't question him. I continue eating and making small talk.

When the waitress brings the check to the table, he glances at his watch again. I glance down at mine too, and it reads 7:32 p.m. "Don't go yet," he says to the waitress as he quickly pulls out his credit card. I take my phone out of my purse and look down at it while I observe his movement through the corners of my eyes. "Why are you so jittery?"

"I'm not jittery. I'm waiting for my card so we can leave."

"Okay," I say, giving him the side-eye.

The waitress brings his card back. He signs the receipt and pushes himself away from the table. "Okay, let's go."

We get in his truck, and the first thing he does is start it and turn on the radio. "Are you waiting for something?" I ask. He's sitting in the driver's seat, looking out the front windshield. "Just give me a minute."

I reach for my seat belt and fasten it. Maybe this will get him to start driving.

"Stop rushing me, and be patient."

The song on the radio stops playing and Clint, a local DJ and friend of Chris's, starts talking. Chris turns up the volume, and I raise an eyebrow at him. *Why are we still sitting here*? I open the sun visor and the mirror to fix my makeup.

"I have a special request from a longtime friend. It's a special message for his lady, Destinee Clark."

I stop and look at Chris. "What's going on?"

"Just be quiet, and listen."

I hear Chris's voice come over the radio. "Destinee, when I first saw you at that gas station on St. Paul's Boulevard, I knew you were the woman for me. I just felt it, like I was drawn to you. I prayed that I would see you again and have the opportunity to get to know you. I feel so blessed to have you in my life. We have been through a lot in such a short period of time, but through it all we have always been there to support each other. You have made me a better person—a better man—and I want us to continue strengthening each other and building a life together. I need you in my life forever, Destinee Clark. Will you marry me?"

Clint comes back on the radio. "Chris and Destinee, ya'll better hit me up and fill me in. This song is for you." He plays "She" by Stokley Williams.

I sit there with my mouth wide open. Chris grabs my hand, pulls out a black box, and opens it. He picked out the ring I wanted. A one-carat, princess-cut, halo ring in white gold. "Oh my goodness. I love it."

"I'm glad you love the ring, but all I want to know is: Will you marry me?"

He reaches for my hand, looks me in the eyes, and puts the ring on my finger. "So, will you marry me?"

"Yes, yes, yes! Of course, I'll marry you."

I've been through so much over the years. I doubted whether or not I would ever find the man for me. Turns out I needed to let the right man find me, and he did.

I hold my hand up in front of my face so I can get a better look at the ring. I wipe tears from my face with my other hand.

"Did anyone else know about this?"

Before he can answer, both our phones ring.

"I hope you said yes," my mom yells out before I can even say hello.

"Yes, Ma. I said yes."

"Listen, I don't want you to get too emotional, but Chris asked your dad for his blessing to marry you. You remember when you all found out about his diagnosis?"

"Yes. That was the first time everyone met Chris."

"Well, while they were outside talking, he asked your father."

"What did Dad say?"

"You know he gave him an earful. Told him it was a little too soon for him to be thinking about marriage but that he better do right by you or he will have Landon to answer to."

"So that's what they were out there talking about."

"He asked me to go with him to pick out your ring. I hope you like it."

Tears stream down my cheeks, and I squeeze my eyes closed. It feels good to know my father had the opportunity to meet the man I will marry. I'm ready to be Mrs. Christopher Richardson and continue building a life with Chris.

CHAPTER FOURTEEN

Three years later.

It's been quiet in the office today, which is good because it's Friday. I reach for my cell phone sitting on the corner of my desk. No notifications. I place the phone back down, and my eyes drift and focus on my engagement ring. A reminder that it's been three years since Chris proposed and no wedding date has been set. A lot has been going on since Greg passed. I understand a lot of responsibility has fallen upon Chris with the shop and making sure his aunt and cousins are taken care of, but don't put me on the back burner.

My cell phone vibrates on the table, and I pick it up to see who's calling. It's Michelle. I get up from my desk and close the door.

"Hey, are we still on for lunch tomorrow?"

"I guess so," I say in a sarcastic tone.

"What's wrong with you?"

I lean back in my chair and swing around so my back is facing the glass window in my office.

"Ever since Greg's passing, things have been different with me and Chris."

"Different how?"

"We don't spend any time together. He works during the day and is at the repair shop most nights and on the weekend."

"I thought his cousin …"

"Charles."

"Yeah, Charles. I thought he was working there now?"

"He is, but Chris doesn't trust him enough to let him do everything."

"He still be on that shady shit?"

"I guess."

"Have you told Chris how you feel?"

"Yes, on more than one occasion."

"Hold on, I gotta answer this call." I grab my earpiece from my desk drawer and connect it while she has me on hold. "Okay, I'm back."

"I just want us to do some of the stuff we used to do like go to the beach, take weekend trips, go out to dinner and to the movies. I don't bother cooking dinner anymore because when I get off from work, he's either at the shop or his aunt's house."

One of the reasons I changed jobs was because I was getting burned out from working at the firm. Too many late nights, early mornings, and meeting with clients. I didn't like going to court all the time. I wasn't able to focus on my relationship with Chris and give him the time and attention he needed. So, I made the decision to remove myself from the firm and find something else.

"You have to talk to him again."

"Are you driving?

"Don't try to change the subject."

"Enough about my life. I know you didn't just call me to ask about lunch. What's up?"

"Nothing important."

"You sure?"

"Yeah, I gotta run. I'll see you tomorrow."

Before I can say goodbye, the phone beeps three times and I see my screensaver on the screen.

I swipe the screen, open up my note app, and make a short grocery list. If I leave work early, I can stop by the store and be home in time to cook dinner before Chris gets home.

I pull up to the house and see Chris's truck parked in front of the house. I guess he got off early, too. I catch a glimpse of my smile in the rearview mirror as I turn into the driveway. It excites me when I get home from work and Chris is already home. The anticipation of us spending time together comes over me.

I pull into the garage and walk into the house. Chris meets me at the door and grabs the shopping bags from my hands. I kick off my shoes and start taking the food out of the bags and putting it away.

"Are you going to the shop tonight?" I ask.

Chris kisses me on my neck and walks over to the refrigerator to grab a bottle of water. "Yeah, I have to go check up on Charles and close out for today so I can finish the books for this month."

Same shit, different day. I walk over to the cabinet and put the cereal away. "What time do you think you'll be back? I was going to cook dinner, but maybe we can go out or do something."

"Don't feel like going out."

I turn my head over my shoulder and look back at Chris. "What do you feel like doing? When it comes to spending time with me, you're always busy with the shop."

"Not true. I just don't feel like being out in the crowd."

I walk over to Chris and stand between him and the refrigerator. "Listen, we need to talk."

He turns away and walks into the living room. "Here you go with that *we need to talk* crap. What do we need to talk about?"

What kind of question is that? I walk into the living room and lean against the couch. "I understand you've had a lot on your plate since your uncle passed away. But things have been slowing down lately. You're not in school anymore, you got a new job, and Charles has stepped up and has been doing more at the shop. Lately I've been feeling like I am no longer a priority in your life. It might help if we take some time away from work and all these other distractions so we can focus on us and get back to the way things used to be."

"So now you feel like you are not a priority because I'd rather sit at home and relax?"

"You are missing the point, as usual. Either you are blind to the fact that our relationship has changed, or you just don't care."

I walk back in the kitchen and finish putting the food away. "Oh, I care," he says as he walks toward the front door.

"You care, but you're just going to leave when I am trying to have an important conversation with you?"

"Yup, I don't want to argue. I'll talk to you later."

Chris walks out the door, gets in his truck, and pulls off. I pull out a bottle of wine and sit at the table by myself. If he doesn't want to put effort into this relationship, then maybe I should quit trying too.

This is why women stay single—so they don't expect something from a man, only to be let down. Maybe I need to be about that single life again. No strings attached, you do your thing, I'll do my thing.

As I reach in the pantry to grab a wine glass, my cell phone rings in my purse. I run and grab it before whoever is calling hangs up.

I'm hesitant to answer when I see Kim's name flashing across the screen. Lately, her phone calls have been nothing but drama and male bashing. I get tired of hearing about her divorce with Troy and being asked a million questions about the custody of Jordan. That's why she has a lawyer. She almost caught a charge last year when she found out Troy was cheating on her with someone from their church.

I try not to say much to Kim about her divorce situation. I just let her vent when she needs to. With everything she's been going through, she swears up and down that Chris is cheating. I'm not going to lie, it has crossed my mind, but I try to give him the benefit of the doubt.

I take a deep breath and answer the phone, reminding myself to support my best friend.

"It's Troy's weekend to get Jordan. Let's go hang out," Kim says instead of hello.

"I'm down. I refuse to spend another night home alone."

"Why would you be alone when Chris is there?"

I fill her in on the one-sided conversation I had with Chris before he walked out on me. "Oh, hell no," she says and questions why I'm still wasting my time with someone who doesn't value my time or the relationship.

"Let's go out to dinner," I say, trying to get her off the topic of Chris.

"I refuse to go to another boring restaurant just to come back home alone and be bored for the rest of the night. Let's do something we haven't done in a while, like go to the club?"

It has been a while since we've had a ladies' night out in the club, so I agree.

I'm tempted to call Chris and let him know I'm going out with Kim. That thought comes and goes quick. He obviously doesn't want to spend time with me, so I'm gonna do what I gotta do.

The mall is calling my name. I need something to wear tonight. All I have in my closet is suits and jeans. Might as well grab something to eat while I'm out, too.

It's been a while since I've been shopping for myself. I need to get back in the habit of treating myself to something new every now and then.

As I walk through the mall, I see Regina and Sabrina.

"Destinee!" Regina calls and waves.

I give her and Sabrina a hug and ask what brings them to this side of town since they live across the water in Hampton. "Trying to find Sabrina a graduation dress and some accessories for her prom dress."

"Oh, that's right. I forgot prom and graduation are right around the corner."

"Are you stopping by with Chris later tonight?"

Chris never mentioned anything about going over there. I try not to sound too concerned with my response. "No, I'm not. Didn't know he was stopping by. I made plans to go out with my friend Kim."

"Can we talk for a minute?"

I'm hesitant about saying yes because she can be long-winded, and I still need to find something to eat.

Regina and I sit down on the bench across from the fountain, and Sabrina walks into Macy's.

Regina looks at the fountain as she speaks. "I've noticed a change in Chris. He's been distant lately."

This is a surprise coming from her, considering Chris has been spending so much extra time over there. "I've noticed the same thing." I hesitate, wondering if I should tell her more. "We really don't spend any time together and barely communicate because he's hardly ever home."

She brings up a wedding date, which is something I don't want to talk about. I've been trying to talk to Chris about it, but he seems uninterested.

After a moment of awkward silence, I switch the topic to Sabrina's graduation. Regina's face lights up when she talks about her youngest graduating high school and going off to college. She asks if I will help out with the graduation party she's planning to have at the house. "Of course, I'd love to help."

We talk for a few more minutes until Sabrina walks out of the store. Our conversation has me thinking something else is going on with Chris, but Regina's not going to come out and tell me.

I find an outfit to wear to the club before leaving the mall. And I have the perfect shoes to go with it. I pick up some other stuff, too, on the clearance rack. My mother always taught me to never pass up a deal if you can help it. I saw some stuff that Chris would like but left that shit at the store.

Kim is always late whenever we make plans to meet up. She's only on time if I pick her up and she rides with me. So, I'm not expecting her to be at the club when I arrive. I grab a seat at the bar, order a drink, and wait. I'm sitting, watching the room, thinking at some point in life you grow out of clubbing and partying. Maybe, maybe not. But tonight, I'm going to enjoy myself, have some drinks, and dance the night away until my curls fall out.

Kim walks into the club like she's a supermodel with her spandex dress and stiletto heels. I don't know how she does it. She looks surprised that I'm even here. I think she thought I wasn't going to show up, but I refuse to spend another night in the house by myself.

"What are you drinking?" she asks, sauntering over to me.

"A jolly rancher."

"What kind of liquor is it? I need something strong."

"Vodka, I think."

"Well, order me one while I find us a table."

I don't know why she's worried about what's in the drink. She's gonna be drinking all night anyway.

"I think the best part of coming to the club is watching people get all dressed up to come out and knowing they shouldn't be caught outside the house with what they be wearing." Kim looks around the room and laughs. "I'm just saying. Don't be in the club sucking it in and trying to balance. Not sexy."

"You make it sound like you're perfect."

"I'm nowhere near perfect, but I refuse to wear anything that is too tight and uncomfortable."

"Well, my mama taught me that I don't need to be out here showing all my goodies."

I grab Kim's drink, and we walk over and sit at a table. She doesn't waste any time, chatting it up with some guys at the table across from us. I glance at the door and see a guy walk in. He heads straight to the bar where a group of guys are standing. He looks familiar, but for the life of me I can't remember his name. Then it clicks.

"Is that Sean?" I ask Kim.

She follows my gaze, squints, and nods. "I knew he looked familiar. That's Troy's friend from college."

"He still looks good, though."

"If he's here, I wonder if Troy is going to show up. They always hang out when he's in town."

We went out one time in college, and I realized we didn't mesh well. I love a man that is into looking good, but we can't compete. Plus, I prefer dark chocolate and not caramel.

Kim catches me staring at him. "Stop staring before he sees us and walks over here."

"Opps, too late. Here he comes."

Let me not get myself into trouble. I came out of the house tonight to have some drinks with my girl, dance, and have a good time. Kim walks over to the dance floor when she notices him walking over to our table.

"Hello there, Miss Destinee." His voice is much deeper than I remember.

"Hello, Mr. Sean. How are you?"

"I'm am well, how about yourself?"

Looks like he's been spending some time in the gym. I can see his muscles protruding through his shirt.

"I'm well but surprised to see you here. Last I heard, you were married with a daughter living in Atlanta."

"Yeah, well, now I'm divorced, living in Norfolk. I'm relocating back home to be closer to family."

I remember Troy mentioning something about Sean getting a divorce.

"Sorry to hear that, but it's always nice to be surrounded by family."

"It is nice to be back home. If I remember correctly, back in the day you hated going to clubs."

"Still do. Just wanted to come out, have some drinks, and dance a little."

"I got you. I'm not the clubbing type either. Just catching up with the fellas."

He takes a seat next to me and asks if Kim will come back if she sees him sitting at our table. "As long as Troy is not going to make an appearance, she will be alright." He reassures me that Troy is not coming out tonight because he has Jordan this weekend. I already knew that, but if Troy really wanted to come out he would get his mother or sister to watch Jordan.

"I see you have that rock on your finger. Who is the lucky man?"

That is not a conversation I want to have, so I brush it off and start another conversation. "Aren't you out with the fellas?"

"Yeah, but they can wait?"

He grabs my hand and pulls me onto the dance floor. We dance to a few songs, and then I have to sit down. I'm not built for this club life anymore.

I love good music, but only R&B or old school '90s music. I don't understand what I hear on the radio nowadays. My parents used to complain about the music I listened to in the '90s, but this music today is worse.

The later it gets, the more my body shuts down. Kim is still going hard on the dance floor. I don't want to leave her here alone, but I am done for the night. She makes her way back to the table, and I let her know its time for me to go.

"Give me a minute, and I'll be right behind you."

Sean walks me out to my car. He asks if I'm going to wait for Kim or just leave. We both know how she can get when she goes to the club, especially when she's had a couple of drinks. I lean against my car and listen to Sean reminisce about our college days. I admire how he's changed over the years. He seems more laid back, and his wave game finally got strong. He used to walk around campus, always brushing his hair, trying hard to get it to wave up.

Fifteen minutes later, Kim walks out. She looks like she had a good time tonight. Her hair is all sweated out and she's carrying her shoes in her hand.

"What are y'all out here talking about?"

"Nothing," we both say and laugh.

Sean and I exchange business cards and say goodnight.

As Sean walks away, Kim shakes her head in disbelief. "What's up with you and Sean?"

I shrug my shoulders and remain silent.

"You should call him and go out. You know he's single now."

"He's recently divorced, and I'm already in a relationship."

"With who?" Wow, shots fired.

I narrow my eyes at her. "You be going hard about people who cheat, and now you're encouraging me to cheat on Chris?"

"Listen, you are not married. All you have is a ring on your finger and a man that is obviously cheating. Girl, look at the signs. No booty, no quality time, no communication. What else do you need? For the girl to drop on his lap in front of your face? The signs are there, sweetie, and I am only telling you this because I've been through it and don't want to see you hurt like me. When you love someone, sometimes it's hard to see the truth, but it's all there right in front of you."

I have a sinking feeling in my stomach. I don't want to assume the worst, but Kim could be right.

CHAPTER FIFTEEN

Chris's truck is parked in front of the house when I get home from the club. I pull into the garage, walk in the house, and see him lying across the couch, sleeping. I can't believe he didn't bother to call or text to check on me. I head straight upstairs, change into my night clothes, and plop right in the bed. I'm drained from all the dancing. I start to doze off and hear Chris walking up the steps. He comes into the room, pulls off his gym shorts, and joins me under the blankets.

Now I'm wide awake, and it's bothering me that he doesn't seem to care where I was, who I was with, or that I came home so late. I turn over and he's lying on his back. "What's your problem?" I ask. He doesn't respond.

"I don't know if you've noticed, or if you even care, that this relationship is falling apart. You don't talk to me anymore, you never want to spend time together, you walk away when I'm trying to have a conversation with you, and you give the excuse that you don't want to argue." My voice grows louder as I speak. "I can't do too much more of this. I asked you earlier if we could do something tonight, and you said you'd rather stay home. Your aunt told me you had other plans. Then I go out and come home late, and you act like you don't give a damn where I was, who I was with, or what I was doing. What if something happened to me?"

Chris rolls toward me and sighs. "Destinee, relax. I knew you were out with Kim because my aunt told me. You know it's been a rough couple of months for me. It's been a lot of responsibility placed on me with my family and the shop, and on top of that work." He rolls back over onto his back.

"Rough couple of months? Try a rough couple of years. You've lost all perception of time!"

I lie back down and turn my back on him. After a few minutes of lying there, he turns over and pulls up my T-shirt. My body tenses up as he gently massages my back. I'm mad as hell at Chris, but it feels too damn good to tell him to stop.

My body slowly begins to calm, and I cave in with each touch. With both hands, he firmly grabs my panties by the waistband, pulls them down around my ankles, and tosses them across the room. Before flipping me over and spreading my legs apart, he removes his form-fitting, ribbed tank top. He lowers himself onto my body and I can feel the heat escape from his mouth as he caresses my body with his lips.

He spreads my legs open and let's his tongue pleasure my clit. I gasp and sway my hips as his tongue induces an orgasm out of me. His tongue slithers up my body, making sure he gives my breasts the attention they both deserve.

"Are you still mad at me?" he asks.

I'm too absorbed in my pleasure to respond. My hands grip the bed sheets and he laughs as he lifts my left leg up to rest it on his shoulder. He does the same with my right leg and takes his time entering me. The deeper he gets, the harder I squeeze and the louder I moan. This is not make-up sex. I'm still mad, but I'm not going to pass on some dick.

As his strokes begin to shorten I slide my legs off his shoulder and wrap them around his waist, then push him onto the bed. "I can't let you have all the fun." I lower my body and straddle him with my hips. His hands make their way to my waist as he slides his shaft into my core. I look down at him and see him staring back at me. Ecstasy is written all over his face. I know it's good. I'm in control of the speed of my grinding as Chris reaches for my hips. I reach down to kiss him and he meets me halfway.

"We're not done yet." He wraps his arms around me and tosses me onto my back.

Our eyes lock as he slides inside me again. I lie there, silently studying his every move. *It feels so good.*

He lowers his body onto mine and his thrusts begin to get more erratic. "That's it, baby." I feel him pulsating inside and I tremble from the intensity of our orgasm.

With his body pressed against mine, we lie there in our sexual afterglow.

On Saturday mornings, Chris usually gets up early to open the shop with Charles and is gone before I wake up. So, I'm surprised that he's still lying in bed, asleep. Maybe he's tired from all the work he put in last night.

I don't attempt to wake him; I just go for my morning run. When

I get back home, he's in the kitchen cooking breakfast. Eggs, grits, and bacon. I'm a little shocked because it's been a while since he cooked me anything. I lean over the stove to see if he put cheese in the grits. Yup, he did.

"Good morning. How was your run?"

He sounds chipper. I raise my eyebrow and give him the side-eye as I walk toward the refrigerator to grab a bottle of water. *Is he talking to me?* I'm not sure whether I should engage in conversation or keep to myself. It's been a while since I've seen this side of Chris. Caring, calm, and talkative. I pull the kitchen island counter stool out and sit down.

Chris places a cup of coffee in front of me, lays out the creamer and sugar, and takes two plates out of the cabinet. He makes our plates, sets mine in front of me, and sets his down next to mine. We enjoy our breakfast.

"Destinee, I'm sorry for the way I've been acting, and I promise I will do better."

It feels good to hear him acknowledge his behavior and apologize, but actions speak louder than words.

"I need you to show me that you want me in your life. Pay me some attention. Communicate with me. It's going to take more than booty and breakfast for me to believe you are going to do better."

"Do you have plans for this afternoon? I was thinking we could spend the day together."

I take a sip of my coffee and think about his question. I already have an appointment to get my nails done today, then I have lunch with Michelle and my mom. I'm not rescheduling my lunch. It's bad enough we don't get to spend a lot of girl time together because we're all so busy.

"How about dinner and a movie tonight?" I ask. I've been trying to tell him about a job opportunity in Atlanta. I leave next week for the interview. I tried to tell him last week, but he's always busy with either the shop or stuff with his aunt. Hopefully I can tell him tonight.

He gets up and walks into the kitchen. He places his plate in the sink. "I look forward to it."

After our talk, he makes his way to the shop, and I call my mother to make sure we're still on for lunch. As soon as I hang up the phone with my mom, I continue with my Saturday routine: cleaning, changing sheets, and washing clothes. All while blasting music through the house.

I remember when I was younger how my mother made sure everyone in the house got up early on Saturdays to do their chores. If we weren't up by a certain time, she would wake us up and assign us chores to do before we could go anywhere or do what we wanted to do. Both my parents would tell us there was no reason for them to bust their butts cleaning the house when they worked hard and paid the bills. "That's what we have kids for," they would say. I hated it, but I have to admit it taught me and my siblings how to be responsible and take care of ourselves.

On the way to my nail appointment, I open the sunroof to let the sun shine down on me. There's a slight chill in the air, but the heat from the sun balances it all out. I love it when I'm out and about and the radio is in rotation with songs I can jam to. After I'm done with my nails, I head over to my mom's house. Michelle's car is in the driveway. The front door is open, and the glass is down on the screen door. I walk up to the door and hear my mother fussing, which she normally doesn't do unless someone pisses her off.

I slowly open the screen door, unsure of what I'm walking into. Michelle is sitting on the couch. It looks like she's been crying. I don't say anything. I walk in and sit in the chair across from her.

My mother walks in the living room and looks at me. "Give me a couple of minutes, and I'll be ready to go." Then she walks back into her bedroom.

I learned at a very young age that if Mother has a certain tone in her voice, don't say anything unless she asks you a question.

I lean over toward Michelle and whisper, "Is everything okay?" She doesn't say anything but looks up at me.

"Destinee, I've come to the realization that I have always been the problem child."

I throw my hands in the air and turn my head. "What are you talking about?"

She points her finger at me. "You heard me. Every time something goes wrong in my life and I try to talk to Mommy about it, she always brings you into it somehow. Like you're so perfect. Always telling me that I act more like the baby sister than the big sister and should be more like you."

I shake my head in disbelief. "Bullshit!"

"No, it's the truth."

"I don't know what I walked in on, but I was just trying to make sure you were okay. Just being a concerned sister."

"Whatever, Destinee."

"You should know by now that you can't tell Mommy everything."

My mother walks down the hallway and we both get silent and sit back in the chair. "If you two ladies are done bickering, we can go now because I'm ready to eat."

She stops when she gets to Michelle. "I've said all I need to say about that situation."

What situation? Why are they being so secretive?

My mother can't keep anything to herself, so I know she will spill the tea sooner or later. I'm hoping it's sooner and not later.

They both walk out of the house and stand at my car, waiting for me to unlock the door. "Do I have to drive?" I roll my eyes and unlock the car, and we all get in. The awkward silence is killing me.

"Okay ladies, where are we eating?"

Utter silence. They both sit there with a sullen look on their faces.

"Going once, going twice ... Okay then, I'm picking."

They still don't say anything, so I drive to this new Mexican restaurant where I've been wanting to take Chris.

We sit down, and I moan in delight when the waitress brings the chips and salsa to our table. She asks what we are drinking. I immediately ask for a margarita. It's early in the afternoon, but I need a little something to get through this awkward silence. Maybe we should've rescheduled lunch.

"I'll have what she ordered," my mom tells the waitress.

Michelle asks for water.

"Just a water? You sure you don't want a drink?" my mother asks.

"No, Ma. Just water," Michelle responds.

I'm too scared of my mother snapping at me to say anything. I just sit there, looking at the menu, trying to figure out what I'm going to order.

My mother reaches for a chip and dips it in the salsa. Before putting it in her mouth, she says, "I've been seeing someone, and I want y'all to meet him."

Michelle and I look at each other. I chuckle and take a sip of my drink.

"Ma, stop joking," Michelle says.

I wonder if this is what they were arguing about. Michelle has always been a daddy's girl. Maybe she feels some kind of way about Mommy dating.

"I invited him to Sunday dinner tomorrow, so both of you need to be there."

Oh, I will definitely be there. I have to see who this guy is. Not missing this dinner for anything. I knew my mother wasn't going to be alone forever but it's awkward hearing her says she's been dating when all we've known is her and my dad.

I figured since she had some news to share, I would share some news of my own. "I may be relocating to Atlanta."

"Atlanta?" They both stare at me with their eyes wide with surprise.

"Yes, Atlanta. My mentor, Mr. Dan, asked me if I would consider joining his firm in Atlanta, Georgia. I'm going next week for an in-person interview with him and his partners."

My mother's mouth twitches and she gives me an uneasy look.

"Why didn't you tell me about this yesterday when we talked? Better yet, why do you want to move to Atlanta? And how does Chris feel about it?" Michelle asks.

I've been trying to tell Chris about it but he hasn't had the time to sit and listen to what's been going on with me. "I plan on telling him later tonight." My interview is next Thursday. I plan on flying out Wednesday and coming back home Sunday. Figured I'd stay a few extra days to check out the area while I'm there.

I see the sadness creep into my mother's eyes. "If this is something you want and it will further your career, go for it. Atlanta is a lot farther than D.C., but I support whatever decision you make."

I miss litigating cases, but I'm not thrilled about moving to Atlanta. If Mr. Dan thinks it's a good fit, I'll give it a try. Plus, nothing is happening here in Virginia.

Michelle wipes her mouth with her napkin and clears her throat. "Since everyone is in such a sharing mood this afternoon, let me share my news. I'm pregnant, but I don't want it."

So that's what they were talking about.

"I told Kevin I wanted to get my tubes tied after I had Jasmine, but he wanted me to wait a few years. So, I did." I remember when Kevin and Michelle started dating. He told her he wanted a large family. I guess he thought if she didn't get her tubes tied after having Jasmine, she was on board with having more children.

"So, baby number three?"

"I told Kevin that I feel like the more children we have, the less time I will have to focus on my businesses. I want to get an abortion."

Although I don't have any children, I understand where Michelle is coming from. Children are a blessing, but the weight of caring for them always falls on the mother. We carry them, birth them, breastfeed them, and when they get sick we have to take time from work to take care of them. It doesn't stop there; the list goes on.

My mother bangs her fist on the table. It's so loud that I look around the restaurant to see if anyone is staring at us. I can tell from my mother's body language that she's extremely agitated by this conversation. She points her finger at Michelle and in an authoritative tone, says, "This is the last time I am going to say it. Another baby is a blessing, not a curse. Abortion is not the answer."

Babies are a blessing, but this is Michelle's life, her decision, and her body. Sometimes my mother has a difficult time listening to Michelle's perspective. I think Michelle just wants to hear comforting words from my mother, not a scolding.

"I support whatever decision you make, sis."

I quickly change the subject because everyone is starting to get tense. Plus, I want to hear more about this person Mom's been talking to. How long have they been seeing each other? How serious are they? Where did they meet? No matter how hard I try to get it out of her, she won't tell us.

All she'll tell us is that he is a nice guy and we will like him. I guess we'll find out tomorrow because she is surely tight-lipped about him. She's quick to tell everyone else's business, but she's like a vault when it comes to her business.

After lunch, I drop my mom and sister off and run a couple of errands before going home. Between the food and conversation with my mom and sister, I'm burned out. I lie across the couch and fall asleep, still fully dressed.

Chris walks through the door shortly after. I open my eyes, and he's standing over me. "Do you still feel like going out?" I don't but he seems excited and sounds like he still wants to go.

"Can we stay in tonight and go out another night?"

"If that's what you want to do. We can order something." He walks upstairs and jumps in the shower.

Chris comes back downstairs wearing some gym shorts and a T-shirt with the sleeves cut off. "Let's order some sushi and hibachi?" He reaches in his pocket for his phone before he collapses on the couch next to me.

"Who's going to pick it up?"

We look at each other and both say, "Grub Hub."

It feels good to be in a happy space with him.

"I promise, I will be better than I was before," he says. He lays his head in my lap and grabs my hand.

I nod. "Actions speak louder than words." I fill him in on lunch with Mom and Michelle. The pregnancy and the new man. "I will be there for dinner. I want to see who this mystery guy is."

I don't want to ruin a perfect evening with an argument, but I need to tell him about Atlanta.

"So, I got a call last week from Mr. Dan. He asked me to come interview for a position at his firm in Atlanta."

"Atlanta?"

The doorbell rings before I can respond. Chris lifts his head from my lap and gets up to answer the door. *Saved by the bell.*

He places the food on the coffee table and sits down. "I support whatever decision you make. It's just an interview, right?" I don't read that much into his response. I eat my sushi and turn my focus toward the television.

I try my best to get up on Sundays to go to church. But this Sunday, I sleep a little longer than usual and miss the early morning and late morning service. My stomach is turned upside down, and everything I ate has made its way out of me. My stomach muscles hurt from throwing up all morning.

I find the energy to jump in the shower, and Chris walks in to tell me he's leaving to check on Ebony and the baby. She's a new mom and her fiancé is out to sea, so he's been checking in on her. He could have asked if I wanted to go with him. It would be nice to see Ebony and the baby. But it's all good. I'm gonna lie around the house, relax, and watch movies until it's time to go to my mother's house. Plus, the way I'm feeling I don't need to be around her and the baby.

I throw on a pair of leggings and a cami and head downstairs to the couch.

Stretched out across the couch I feel something vibrating beneath me. I reach between the cushions and pull out Chris's cell phone. I flip the phone over and it shows a missed call and voice mail from Izabelle. *I don't know an Izabelle.* I unlock his phone and see text messages from her.

Curious, I open up the messages and start reading the text. I notice other messages from earlier in the week. The most recent one from her reads, "I just got back home, see you soon!"

I'm leaning over the couch reading the messages, and it feels like I'm having an out-of-body experience. I keep scrolling through the messages, and it's evident that whatever this is has been going on for a while.

In the back of my mind, I can hear Kim telling me, "I told you so." I decide to call Izabelle from his phone to see what she has to say. She answers on the first ring.

"Hey there, did you get my message?"

"Yeah, I got it. How do you know Chris?"

She gets quiet for a minute and then asks, "Who is this?"

When I say my name, she hangs up. Chris walks through the

door as I put the phone down on the coffee table.

"Seems as though Izabelle is waiting for you. Don't keep her waiting too much longer."

He replies with silence, which I should have expected. Maybe he's gotta get his lie straight. "You should be more careful where you leave your belongings." I toss him his phone and watch the expression on his face. There's no need for him to explain anything to me. The messages on his phone speak for themselves.

I get up from the couch and walk toward the stairs. I push him out of my way, and he follows me upstairs.

"Destinee, please don't jump to conclusions and start assuming stuff. I know how you are."

I sit down at the foot of the bed. My hands are shaking, and I want to take a swing at Chris's face. Instead, I take deep breaths and try to calm myself down.

"It's okay, Chris. I get it. I saw the messages. It's just sad that you weren't man enough to tell me the truth. I think the worst part is that I trusted you more than I trusted any other man, and I never thought you would do something like this to me." I roll my neck, plant my bare feet on the carpet, and stand up.

"No, you don't get it."

"Those messages were pretty clear that something has been going on between the two of you. What else is there to get?"

His hands drop to his sides. "That's not true."

I walk over to Chris and get up close to his face. "So, what is it then?"

"A friend ..."

I lift my hand up to his forehead and mush him in the face. "Bullshit!" His body falls back, but he catches himself before he falls.

"Liar!"

He stands in silence for a minute and then responds, "Why can't you believe me when I say it's nothing? Trust me."

"Trust? You want me to trust you after reading those sexual text messages? You are not the man I thought you were."

"After all we've been through, you gonna do me like this and not even listen to what I have to say?"

Tears stream down my face and my voice cracks. "Chris, you need to leave before I snap."

"Can we please talk?" Chris walks toward me with his arms out. I push him away and sit back down on the bed.

"What is there to talk about, Chris?"

"What did she say?"

"Call and ask Izabelle."

He scowls, his body trembling. "No, we need to talk. All those sexual text messages were her, not me."

"Yes, but you never told her to stop sending them. I just need you to leave. I don't have anything else to say to you, Chris."

He walks over to the bed and sits beside me. "I'm not leaving!"

"Chris, please …"

"I'm not leaving until you talk to me."

I wipe the tears from my eyes so I can see clearly. If he's not going to leave, I need to. If I don't, one or both of us will be in jail. I get up, open the closet, grab a T-shirt, and put on my pink Baby Phat slides. I am beyond frustrated with this man right now, and I feel so stupid.

He grabs my arm and tries to pull me back from leaving. I break free, grab my bag and keys, and run for the garage. I look back to see if he's still behind me but he's not. I get in my car and take off.

As I'm driving, I reach in my bag for my cell phone, but I can't find it. I realize I left it at the house on the end table in the living room, charging. I hit the wheel with the palm of my hand in frustration. *Damn it.*

I can't believe it. I knew from the beginning that my relationship with Chris was too good to be true, but I put my trust in him anyway. *Why do I always end up hurt in the end?*

I'm driving with tears and snot rolling down my face, wiping them away as they fall so I can see the road, and praying that my mother is home from church. I know this is something I shouldn't be talking to her about, but I need her words of encouragement right now.

I pull up to my mother's house. The front door is open and her car is in the driveway. *Thank God.*

Whatever she is cooking, I can smell it as soon as I walk up to the door.

"What are you doing here so early?" she calls out from the kitchen.

The tears continue to fall and I can barely say anything. Finally, I manage to tell her that Chris has been cheating on me.

"Lord have mercy, child. Calm down, and talk to me. How do you know he's cheating?"

I catch my breath and tell her about the phone call and text messages from Izabelle.

"Have you suspected that he's been cheating?"

"I was giving him the benefit of the doubt. Trying not to believe he was that type of man." We had such a good time last night. It's been so long since we spent real time together, and it felt good. Kim knew it all along. I should've believed her, but I had to see it for myself.

"Maybe Izabelle is just a friend, and he is telling the truth."

"You didn't see those text messages and pictures."

"Yeah, keep that to yourself. I don't need all those details. I can't tell you what to do in this situation, but I will say this. Everyone makes mistakes. No one is exempt, and we are all human. Maybe you should hear him out."

Hear him out? There is nothing else that needs to be said. It was all in his phone. This shit hurts so bad. Makes me wanna bust the windows out of his truck and slash a hole in all four of his tires. Or maybe have someone steal his rims and have his shit sitting on bricks. We've been through a lot together. But this is something I don't think we can recover from.

I know my mother is always there to listen and help me get through hard times. If she only knew what Chris and I endured in the beginning of our relationship. I want to tell her, but I don't want her to be upset that I didn't come talk to her like I do about everything else. She might judge me like she did Michelle.

I don't want to stay too long at my mother's house just in case Chris comes by looking for me. I use my mother's phone to call Kim to see what she's up to, but she doesn't answer. Knowing her, she's probably still sleeping. Or maybe she went to pick up Jordan. I have nothing but time to kill, so I take a ride over there.

I bang on the door until she answers.

"Why are you knocking on my door so damn hard? Where is the fire?" Kim asks when she opens the door.

I walk in and lie across the chaise longue in her living room. I sink into it and don't want to get up.

"Something is wrong. Tell me what happened," Kim says, standing at my feet.

Once again, I try to hold back the tears.

"No crying, just spill it. What's going on?"

"You were right. He's been cheating on me."

She kneels down on the floor next to the chaise. "I am so sorry, Destinee. How did you find out?"

"His cell phone."

"Damn!"

I don't want to hear, "I told you so." I already feel bad enough.

Kim grabs my hand and says, " Everything happens for a reason." She's right about that.

"Maybe this opportunity in Atlanta is what I need, and with Chris out of the picture I don't have anything holding me back."

Kim jolts up from the floor and looks down at me. "Atlanta? What the hell are you talking about?"

"I got a call from Mr. Dan asking if I was interested in joining his firm in Atlanta."

She sits down on the arm of the chaise and leans on me. "I just got you back, and now you're going to leave me?"

With a lopsided grin on my face I say, "Maybe, if this is a good opportunity for me."

She pulls away from me and walks into the kitchen then back in the living room and sits on the sofa across from me. "But Atlanta, though? You're really going to leave me and Jordan?"

This is why I was hesitant to tell anyone about Atlanta. Nothing is set in stone. I don't know what I'm going to do. I'm confused about everything right now.

"You hungry? Cause I'm hungry, and think we should grab a bite to eat," Kim says as she rises up from the sofa.

"I'm down as long as you're driving and we don't talk about relationships and men."

"Deal. Let's go!"

This situation right here is more ammunition for Kim's hatred toward men, and there is nothing Chris can say that will change the way I feel. I just want him gone.

When we get to the restaurant, we both order mimosas. I don't have an appetite for more than that. As the waitress walks away, Kim's cell phone rings. She's rummaging through her bag trying to find it before it stops ringing. She pulls it out and shows me who's calling. It's Chris.

He calls back and Kim shows me the phone again. "Do you want me to answer it?"

"Hell no, let that shit go to voice mail!"

CHAPTER SIXTEEN

I need to get my cell phone before heading back to my mother's house, but I don't want to take the chance of running into Chris. I sigh in relief as I turn the corner and don't see his truck. I leave the car on and run in the house to grab my phone. I remember putting it on the charger and laying it on the end table, but it's not there. It's sitting on the kitchen island.

Chris must have been snooping through my phone, or at least trying to. I'm smart enough to use a passcode he doesn't know.

As I'm walking toward the door, Chris walks in. "I'm glad you're home."

I shake my head and continue walking toward the door.

"Destinee, please wait. Can we talk?"

I stop and turn toward Chris. "There's nothing to talk about. I just need time and space from you right now."

The corners of his mouth are turned upwards in a grimace. "I am so sorry, Destinee."

"That's what they all say."

"I was wrong; I know I was wrong." My heart begins to race, and I'm beginning to feel lightheaded.

"Please, leave me alone."

"Oh, so it's like that?"

"Well, how else would it be?"

"What do you want me to do?"

I point my finger at the front door and tell him to leave and stay gone.

He looks at me, surprised by my gesture. "So, you're kicking me out now? This is our house."

Chris is still standing in the same spot. I walk toward the front door and say, "Technically, this is *my* house, remember? I used *my* money to buy it and it's in *my* name."

He stands in front of the door, blocking me from leaving. "Wow, I can't believe you."

"Please, get out of my way and let me leave. When I get back, please be gone."

"I'm not leaving."

"Okay, Chris, I meant what I said. Please be gone before I get back."

I don't have time for these games. We're both grown. I'm not going to argue because we can't change the past. He steps to the side and holds the screen door open. I walk out and get in my car.

I pull up to my mother's house, and Landon's car is parked in the driveway. He didn't mention anything to me about coming into town.

He's standing at the door, waiting for me to get out of the car.

He looks behind me and asks where Chris is. "He's not coming. We're not on good terms right now." I walk through the door, and Jasmine and Jaiden run up to me and give me a hug. Jasmine's hair is braided with beads on the ends. I can hear them clacking as she runs back into the kitchen with Michelle. I don't see Kevin, who never misses my mom's Sunday dinners, but I don't say anything about that. I'll wait until Michelle says something.

"What's this I hear about you moving to Atlanta?"

Mom strikes again. I thought she was turning over a new leaf. It's not a secret; I just didn't want anyone to know until I decide what I'm going to do.

"I'm going for an interview. Nothing is set in stone. Where's Erica?"

I pray their relationship is not on the rocks.

"I'm not going back tonight, and she has class in the morning. With exams coming up, she didn't want to miss class."

I breathe a sigh of relief.

The house phone rings, and I reach to answer it since I am close to it.

"Hey, it's Kevin."

"Hey, Kevin. You coming for dinner?"

"No, not this time. Please tell Michelle I will be picking the kids up from daycare tomorrow." He hangs up before I can respond. Something's not right. That's not like Kevin to be so abrupt. Why he calling my mama's house when he could've called Michelle's cell phone?

I look across the room at Michelle and mouth, "What's going on?"

She walks toward the stairs and asks if we can go upstairs to

169

talk.

This baby situation must be worse than I thought. We walk upstairs to my old bedroom. Michelle sits in the chair at my desk, and I close the door.

"Kevin and I need some space, so I'm gonna stay with Mom for a couple of days." She leans over in the chair, her elbows digging in her legs and her hands gripping her head. I'm a little confused as to why she would leave with the kids. If anything, *he* should've left.

"Does this need for space have anything to do with the B-A-B-Y?"

She nods, and I see her eyes fill with tears.

"What about what I want? It's my body. I'm the one who has to carry this baby, give birth to it, wake up in the middle of the night every two hours so this thing can suck on my breast and never be satisfied. I'll be starting all over, and I am just starting to get in the rhythm of being a mother of two. Jaiden can almost do everything by himself, and Jasmine is learning. Now I would have to train another one. I'm content with my boy and girl."

I walk over to the bed and sit down. "Wow, Michelle. That was a lot. I guess you were really serious about not having any more children."

"Yes, drop-dead serious. Everything is going to be on me. Kevin will be helpful in the beginning, but that will wear off after a few weeks."

"I know I'm not a mom, but I get what you are saying."

"Oh Dee, I am so sorry."

"Don't be, it's okay."

The doorbell rings and Landon runs upstairs.

"Promise me you won't tell Landon about this."

"I'm not Mommy."

Landon peeks his head around the door. "Y'all need to come downstairs. You will never guess who this dude is." *Please don't be a relative.*

I walk downstairs into the living room, and Mr. Evans is sitting in the recliner. Mr. Evans was one of my dad's close friends from work. He loves my mother's cooking. When his wife passed away a couple of years ago, my dad started inviting him over for Sunday dinner. I haven't seen him since my dad's funeral. I think it's a little weird that Mom would want to date a friend of my dad's, but whatever floats your boat. Michelle stands at the doorway in a shocked silence. Landon looks over at me and shakes his head.

"That's your mama," he mouths.

Landon, Michelle, and I sit and talk with Mr. Evans.

"I started calling and stopping by to check in on your mom after your dad passed away. Then one day I asked her out to dinner, and she said yes."

"And we've been going out ever since," my mom adds.

"Funny, my mother never mentioned this to us," Michelle says before getting up and walking into the kitchen.

Michelle was a daddy's girl, so I can understand why she's reacting the way she is. Mom is a grown woman. She was a good wife and mother and deserves to live her life and be happy.

My mom and Mr. Evans walk into the dining room. Landon and I stay put in the living room. "Can you believe this?"

"I'm just glad the guy turned out to be a decent dude."

I walk into the kitchen to check on Michelle, and Landon follows behind me. "Are you okay? You look a little shocked by all of this."

"I'm stunned by the fact that our mother, the woman who gossips all the time, did not let this one slip out. Not a peep." We all laugh and walk into the dining room. Mom and Mr. Evans are sitting at the table talking to each other as if we aren't sitting there.

"Ma, you could have told us over the phone that you and Mr. Evans were dating," Landon says.

"He has been a huge support for me after your father died."

I'm just glad she is happy and not lonely.

After Sunday dinner, we follow the same ritual we've had since we were little. Mom cooks the meal, and the kids clean up. Jasmine runs into the kitchen and brings me my phone. "Auntie, Auntie, your phone is ringing."

I look at it and realize she answered it. It's Chris. I want to hit "end" and hang up on him, but my mother is staring at me from the dining room. So, I put the phone to my ear and say, "Hello?"

"We're too grown not to be able to talk about our situation. When are you coming home?" I stay silent. "Hello? I know you're still there," Chris says.

I hit the end button and slide the phone in my pants pocket. I don't want to see his face or hear his voice right now. I wish he would stop calling and texting me. It's like I'm reliving some of what I went through with Alan.

"You gonna tell us what that's all about?" Landon asks.

"The long version or short version?"

"Short version, please," Michelle responds as she continues loading the dishwasher.

"He cheated. End of story."

My mom walks into the kitchen places her left hand on

Michelle's shoulder and her right hand on my shoulder.

"Listen here, girls. There are always going to be things that happen in your life that you may question. You have to learn to pray about it and give it to God. If you spend all your time worrying and questioning every little thing in your life, you will be in a crazy house. Take time for yourself, pray about the situation, and I promise that you will find peace in whatever decision you make."

She turns toward Michelle. "You have those babies to worry about, all three. What's done is done. You can't change it."

Landon's eyes widen. "Damn, I come home to visit and find out everybody's business."

Leave it to Eunice.

I make it home from Mom's and try to prepare myself for the work week. The house is quiet and dark. No sign of Chris. I go upstairs and run a hot bath. I just want to soak the day away and clear my head so I can get some rest tonight. Or at least try to.

I step out of the tub and wrap a towel around my body. As I'm walking toward the bathroom door, the reflection of myself in the mirror catches my attention. I stop at the mirror, place both hands on the counter, and gaze at myself.

"Everything is going to work itself out. It always does." Sounds good coming out of my mouth. Now I just need to believe it.

I walk out of the bathroom and see Chris standing at the bedroom door. I ignore him and reach for my underwear and a nightie.

I grab the cocoa butter from my dresser and sit on the bench in front of the bed. One leg at a time, I slowly rub the cocoa butter on.

"I know you see me standing here," Chris says.

I don't respond. He's watching my every move. I place the cocoa butter back on the dresser and walk into the bathroom to brush my teeth. I hear his footsteps as he follows me into the bathroom.

"Destinee, I know you see me standing here. Don't be childish."

Childish? My mother always told me if you don't have nothing nice to say, don't say anything at all. So, I remain silent.

"Tell me how I can make it better. *Us* better."

I walk out of the bathroom toward my dresser.

"I'm sorry for breaking your trust."

"Chris, there is nothing you can do to make us better. What's done is done!"

He walks over and leans on the dresser. "Come on, Dee, I love you so much. I don't want to lose you."

"Too late and too bad."

I walk back into the bathroom and he follows behind me. "The last thing I wanted was to hurt you."

I close the bathroom door and put on my underwear and nightie. When I walk out the bathroom, he's still standing by the door. "Well you did, and it hurts like hell. When we first met, I told you I didn't want a relationship, but I gave in because you said you were different. I've wasted over three years of my life for us to end like this. Understand that I didn't need you in my life, but I wanted you because I thought you were different. I love what we had, but I'm hurting like hell right now. Just pack your shit and get out!"

"I'm not leaving."

"Look, we can do this the easy way or the hard way."

"Are you threatening me now?" He clenches his jaw and remains standing at the bathroom door.

"Take it how you want. Just get the hell out!"

He pulls back his shoulders and walks toward the bedroom door. He looks back at me and says, "I tell you what. I'll go stay with my aunt tonight and give you some space. We can talk tomorrow."

He walks out the room, down the stairs, and out the house. I hear his tires screech as he pulls off. In that moment, I am immensely grateful we didn't get married.

I run down the stairs to lock the deadbolt then grab a couple of trash bags from the kitchen and head back upstairs to the bedroom. I open Chris's dresser drawers one by one and toss everything in the trash bags. I remember that I have some extra Rubbermaid bins in the garage. So, I grab them and bring them upstairs too.

I throw his shoes in the bins, and I empty his dresser drawers and all his stuff from the drawers in the bathroom.

I carry everything downstairs to the back door, grab my phone off the counter in the kitchen, and search for a locksmith. I always tell Chris that actions speak louder than words. Let this be a lesson.

I finish putting all the bags and bins in the backyard by the fence door. I'll text Chris in the morning once I leave for work and let him know he can come get his shit from the backyard. I call a locksmith to change the locks and change the code for the alarm.

I toss and turn all night. I keep hearing noises downstairs like Chris is trying to get in the house. I turn my thoughts toward the opportunity in Atlanta—it might be what I need. A fresh start somewhere other than Virginia. I shouldn't have come back to begin with.

I get up earlier than usual and skip my morning run. I don't want to take the chance of Chris coming here while I'm still home. I make a stop for my morning coffee: dark roast, caramel swirl, and cream. I get to the office, find a parking spot, and type a text message to Chris:

"No hard feelings. I'm thankful for the time we had, but we've come to an end. There's no coming back after what you did. Your belongings are in the backyard by the gate. You can make arrangements to come get your tools from the garage. Don't bother using your key or codes. The locks have been changed and so have the alarm codes."

I hit "send," put my phone on silent, and walk into the office.

I try to make the best of the day by keeping busy. I keep my personal life personal and leave it at home. I don't even have pictures of myself or my family in my office. It's better that way.

I need these hours and the next two days to go by fast so I can get on that plane to Atlanta. I'd much rather be going to an island, but I'll take this much-needed time away and possibly an opportunity for a new beginning.

It could be a good thing. It might be a little scary at first, but focusing on something new will help take my mind away from my broken heart. There's no reason for me to stay in Virginia. I'm not married, and I don't have any children holding me back. So, why not take this opportunity and run with it?

All morning, it's been back-to-back phone calls and text messages from Chris. He sounds pissed off on all the voice mails he left. "I don't appreciate you putting my stuff outside. You could've handled this situation differently. Why you gotta be so heartless?" I scoff when I read that text. He could've handled his dick a different way and not fucked another woman.

I usually don't go out for lunch, but since I didn't make my lunch this morning, I decide to go out and grab something. Plus, I could use some fresh air. I get back to my office and see the red light flashing on my desk phone. I pick up the receiver and check my voice mail. One message is from the receptionist, letting me know I have something at the front desk. The other voice mail is Chris. That makes seven calls, and it's only 1:45 p.m.

I walk downstairs to the reception area and see flowers sitting on the desk. Those must be my "something." I approach the reception desk and the receptionist lets me know a gentleman dropped them off about an hour ago. I thank her and head back upstairs to my office.

I open the envelope and read the card: "All the sorries in the world won't make up for what I did. Please talk to me. I love you!" He must've sent these before he found out all his stuff was outside and the locks were changed.

I place the card on my desk, close my office door, and sit in my chair with my back facing the glass door and windows, willing the tears not to fall.

I put the flowers in the trash can because they are a reminder of how Chris did me wrong. I bury myself in work until about 7:00 p.m. then clear off my desk and make my way to the parking lot. I see Chris's truck parked across from my car.

I continue walking toward my car, not paying him any attention. He gets out of his truck and stands behind it with his arms folded across his chest. I look at him and still don't say a word. I'm not fazed, nor am I playing games with him.

I click the unlock button on my key fob, lift the door handle, and open my door. Chris walks over to my side of the car and stands there. "Why do you keep ignoring me? I just want to talk. Let's figure this thing out."

I pull my door open and plop my ass down in the driver's seat. I close my door, lock it, and start the car. He knocks on the window as if I don't see him standing there. I look at him and raise my hand to push the button to crack the sunroof open.

"Please move out of the way before I roll over your feet," I say.

"Destinee, this is some bullshit."

I put the car in drive and pull forward from the parking spot, smiling. I know that pisses him off even more. I'm not sure what he was expecting since I have not answered any of his calls or responded to his text messages.

Flowers are not going to make me want to talk. Showing up at my job doesn't help anything, either. He's working on my last nerve.

As I drive toward the interstate entrance ramp, I see Chris following behind me in my rearview mirror. He's a few cars back, but I can still see him. I continue driving, listening to my music. Every turn or stop I make, he's still right there behind me. When I get to the house, I pull into the garage as usual.

As the garage door closes, Chris pulls up to the house. I walk in the house through the door in the garage and can hear him knocking on the screen door and ringing the doorbell. I take my heels off. With my keys still in my hand, I run up the stairs to my bedroom closet, reach up on the top shelf for my locked case, and pull out my pistol.

I refuse to be abused or hurt by another man. I will kill him before I let him put his hands on me. I walk down the steps and place the magazine in the gun, but I keep the safety on. I can still hear him banging on the door and yelling for me to open it.

I walk over to the front door and open it but keep the screen door locked. I stand there with the gun in my hand, pointed to the floor. Chris looks at me, then down at my hand.

"Really? You gonna shoot me?"

I refuse to be the victim again. All of this feels to familiar and I don't like it. With fear written over my face, I stand there for a moment, staring at Chris.

"I need you to listen, and this time really hear what I am saying to you. It's over. I do not want to see you. I do not want to hear your voice. What I need is for you to leave me alone. Give me some time and space. You got me in a real bad headspace right now. If and when I'm ready to talk to you, I will call you. I've been real calm about this situation even though I'm hurting like hell. Just honor my request. If there is anything else of yours that you need out of the house, text me and I will drop it off at the shop or at your aunt's house. This is the last time I am going to tell you to *leave me alone.*"

I stand there for a minute, waiting for him to respond. He shakes his head and walks away. I close the door, go back upstairs, and put the gun back in the safe.

My hands are shaking. I never thought I would have to pull my gun out on him. I'm just tired of being hurt by the men in my life. When I think they are going to be different, they all end up doing me wrong.

CHAPTER SEVENTEEN

It's seven in the morning, and my flight leaves at eleven. I'm still not packed. I was hoping I could sleep in a little longer, but I need to get up and pack. I reach over to grab my phone off my night table, and there is one new message from Chris.

"Hey, I don't blame you for acting the way you did the other night, although I'm pissed you took it there with the gun. I should have respected you enough to honor your request and give you space instead of pushing you to talk. I hope you know I would never put my hands on you. I just want us to get everything out in the open so maybe we can work things out."

I take my time to respond, trying to gather my thoughts. I'm not ready to see him or talk. Maybe we can talk when I get back from Atlanta, but I'm going to put him out of my mind for now.

I fumble through my closet and pull out a suit dress and some heels. I grab a brooch from my jewelry box to wear on the collar of my dress. Everything else just has to be comfortable and has to fit in my suitcase. I'm not paying a baggage fee.

I throw my luggage in the trunk and make my way to the airport. I hate flying, but I should be used to it with all the traveling I've done for work. This is my second time going to Atlanta. The last time was for a business trip, and I was only there for a conference. I didn't get to see much of the city. This time around, it's still business, but I will definitely make time for pleasure.

As I'm boarding the plane, I hear someone call my name. *Please don't let that be Chris.* I keep walking and make my way to my seat. I stand with my back turned toward the passengers, waiting for them to walk by so I can put my bag in the overhead compartment.

"I know you heard me calling you."

I turn around and look over my shoulder. "Sean? That was you calling my name?" I try to hide the excitement in my voice.

"I see some things haven't changed with you. Still ignoring people."

I laugh and turn away. "I know, right? Where are you headed?"

"Atlanta. What about you?"

Sean helps me place my bag in the overhead bin and sits down in the aisle seat across from me.

"Me too. I have an interview tomorrow morning."

"Well, I wish you the best. I'm flying back to see my daughter and finalize my divorce."

My attention is drawn to his lips. He has this way of seductively licking them when he talks.

Out of all the people I know, it's ironic how we are on the same flight, headed to the same city. I don't know what he's been doing since college, but it's working in his favor. His skin is clear and his body is tight.

181

When we land, we both walk toward the escalator to the Sky Train to pick up a rental car. Before parting ways at the car rental center, Sean reaches for my hand.

"You think we can meet up for dinner while we're both in town?" he asks.

"Sure, but not tonight. Maybe tomorrow?"

"I'll give you a call tomorrow."

"How are you going to call me? I never gave you my phone number."

"You gave me your business card, remember?"

I grab my phone from my pocket and hand it to him so he can put his number in. "I'll text you from my personal phone," I tell him.

"I feel special." Still the same Sean. Cocky.

I get my rental car and head to my hotel. The bed is calling my name. I text my mom once I get to the hotel to let her know I made it safely. After checking in, I head straight to my room, turn the T.V. on, and lie across the sofa.

I wake to the sound of an infomercial program playing on T.V. I glance at the clock on the nightstand next to the bed. It's 2:00 a.m. I grab my phone from under me and read yet another text message from Chris. "I know you don't want to be bothered by me right now. Just wanted to make sure you made it to Atlanta safely. If you could just text me and let me know." I hit delete, walk over to the bed, and go back to sleep.

Thank God I set my phone alarm. I would've overslept if I didn't. I have just enough time to get ready and grab breakfast before heading to my interview.

I contemplate whether I should walk or drive. I don't want to sweat my hair out before I have my interview. The office is an eight-minute walk from my hotel, just west on Peachtree Street. I think I'll be okay.

My phone vibrates in my hand as I exit the hotel.

"Good morning! Wanted to wish you luck on your interview and check to see if we are still on for dinner tonight?"

"Thank you. We are still on for tonight. Just let me know what time."

"I was thinking seven, if that's not too late. Gonna pick my daughter up after school and spend some time with her."

I never asked him how old his daughter is. It must be difficult living in a different state than your child. I put my phone on silent, throw it in my bag, and give myself a little pep talk before walking into the building.

I've haven't seen Mr. Dan since my second semester of law school. I was shocked to hear he was moving to Atlanta and even more shocked when he called me about this position. I just hope I make a good enough impression on the other partners.

I check in at the front desk, get a visitor's badge, and wait for them to call my name. A few minutes later, a woman walks down the hall to get me and escorts me to the fifth floor.

She takes me to an empty conference room and tells me to have a seat. My stomach is in knots; I hate the pressure of panel interviews.

I see three men and a woman turn the corner and walk in with Mr. Dan leading the way. "Hi, Destinee! So good to see you," he says when he walks into the room. And so, it begins.

They fake-smile like they are amused by what I'm saying. I can tell they're fascinated by some of my responses to their questions, like they doubt my intelligence and experience. I try not to judge a book by its cover, but I get the feeling this firm is not big on diversity. Mr. Dan is white, but he is the blackest white man I have ever met. He reminds me of that comedian, Gary Owen.

About forty-five minutes later, I'm done with the interview, which felt like an interrogation. Everyone but Mr. Dan leaves the conference room.

"You haven't changed at all," he says. Why do people keep telling me that?

"Mr. Dan, you know I'm always going to speak my mind. I just have to change my delivery depending on the audience."

I'm privileged enough to get a tour of the office before heading out to lunch with Mr. Dan.

"I was going to ask the partners to join us, but they act like they've got sticks up their asses." He's right about that. But I don't mind—I'd rather have lunch with just him and catch up on what's been going on.

He brags about his wife, which he always does. I tell him what's going on with Chris and I—that we are taking a break. Mr. Dan keeps reiterating that he knows I would be excellent for this position. It does sound like something I would be interested in, but I'm not sure if I'll fit in.

After lunch, Mr. Dan drops me off at my hotel. This heat got me sweating in all my cracks and crevasses. I take a shower and text Sean my hotel information so he can pick me up later for dinner.

I nearly jump out of my skin when I hear knocking at my door. Feeling flustered, I open the door.

Sean stands there, staring at me. I follow his eyes as he looks my body up and down. "I am so sorry I'm not ready. I got back from my interview, took a shower, and fell asleep." He walks in and I let the door close behind him.

"No worries. We got time."

I grab my cosmetic bag off the desk and my clothes off the chair.

"Have a seat while I get ready."

I escape to the bathroom and get myself together. I leave the door cracked so we can talk. "How was court?"

"I'm officially a free man and a single father. I got full custody of my baby girl."

"Congratulations!"

"How did your interview go?"

I tell him about my panel interview and lunch with Mr. Dan.

"I can't believe after all these years, you still keep in touch with him."

"He's my mentor. He's helped me out a lot in my career."

"I can't remember what class we were in, but he was the professor and you had a comeback for everything."

I laugh and walk out of the bathroom. "He was the one who convinced me to go to law school." I finish getting ready and grab my sweater from my suitcase. "Are you ready to go?"

Traffic on the way to the restaurant is a little hectic. Sean seems used to it, though. I can see why he wanted to move back to Virginia. This is worse than D.C. traffic. We make it to the restaurant and I contemplate whether or not I will order a cocktail. As I peruse the menu, Sean orders an appetizer and a Long Island ice tea.

I'm curious to know why his daughter isn't with him now since he has full custody of her now. He explains that she has school tomorrow, and her mom agreed with him that he would pick her up from school Friday and she would spend the weekend with him until he leaves on Sunday.

The conversation starts to get interesting as he opens up about his ex-wife and the divorce.

"About two years after Najah was born, my ex-wife told me she didn't want to be married anymore and didn't want to be a mother." He takes a sip of his drink then sets it back down on the table. "She was still young and wanted to experience life."

"Maybe she was overwhelmed with being a wife and mother," I say.

He nods his head in agreement. "I thought that at first. That's why I started helping her more around the house and with the baby."

He stops mid-sentence as the waiter brings our food to the table. He reaches across the table, grabs my hand, and bows his head. I mirror his posture and sit silently.

"Father, we thank you for this food we are about to receive, for the nourishment and strength of our bodies. Thank you for this opportunity to reconnect with a friend. In Jesus's name I pray, amen!"

My eyes widen and I say, "Amen." I cut up my steak and start eating.

Sean takes a bite of his salmon and continues talking. "She would leave for a couple of weeks at a time then want to come home and work it out. I dealt with it for a couple of years because I loved her and wanted the marriage to work and to be a family for Najah."

I dig my fork into a piece of steak, look up at Sean, and say, "You mean *love* her?" I don't get how people divorce and all of a sudden don't love each other anymore.

He laughs, grabs his drink, and takes a sip. As he places it back on the table, he says, "I will always have love for her. She is the mother of my child, but I am not *in love* with her anymore."

I shake my head and say, "Okay."

"After that, I filed for divorce and started making my plan to move back home to Virginia."

We sit in an awkward silence. Then Sean asks, "When's the wedding date?"

"The wedding is off." I pick up my glass of sangria and sip until there's no more left.

"I was wondering why you weren't wearing your ring. I hope everything works itself out."

He gives me a long gaze and has a devilish look on his face. "I don't want to come off as being offensive, but I never thought you would be in a serious relationship or get married. You were always slick with the tongue, strong-minded, and autonomous."

"Not offensive. I was very standoffish when I started college. I was dealing with a lot at the time."

"So, why is the wedding off?"

I decide to be blunt. "He cheated."

"It's unfortunate when your significant other, whether married or in a serious relationship, takes your heart for granted."

"I agree."

After we finish our entrées, we sit at the table for a couple of hours talking and laughing. Reminiscing about college. I stop him in his tracks when he starts talking about Kim and Troy. I am not the type of friend that's gonna let someone gossip behind their back.

While he's talking, I think, *Am I wrong for having dinner with Sean?* But I remind myself that Chris and I are over. And Sean is just a college friend.

After dinner, we head back to my hotel. While driving down I-85, Sean notices a Ford Mustang speeding toward us in the rearview mirror.

"He's going too fast and going to lose control of his car."

I look back over my shoulder to see what Sean's talking about. Just as I do, the Mustang passes us and tries to change lanes two cars in front of us.

"Looks like he's trying to get off the interstate," Sean says as he tries to control his speed; the cars in front of him are braking hard.

"We're gonna crash," I say. The Mustang loses control and flips over three times. I watch as the two vehicles in front of us collide. Sean turns the steering wheel, but not in time to avoid hitting the car in front of us. We are vehicle number three in a five-car accident.

The crash happened so fast. My ears are ringing and my head is killing me. Fire and Rescue has to use the jaws of life to get the driver out of the Mustang; he's air lifted to the hospital. Sean is relatively unharmed, but I'm transported to the hospital, with three other people, even though I insist I don't want to go. I can't stand hospitals.

"You're so stubborn," he says, shaking his head. "Just go get checked out. I'll go with you."

After being examined, having test done, and a couple of hours of waiting, the doctor walks into the room.

"Ms. Clark, everything looks good except for one thing."

My heart drops. "Oh my God. What is it?"

Sean stands up and walks over to my bed.

"Your pregnancy test came back positive. You're pregnant."

I sit paralyzed for a moment, trying to take in what she said. "Are you sure you are looking at Destinee Clark's information?"

"Yes, ma'am. These are your results." She looks at Sean and says, "Congratulations." Sean looks at me and laughs.

I frown. "How did this happen?"

Sean puts his hand on my shoulder. "I think you know how. Sounds like this is unexpected."

"Sure is."

The doctor tells me to follow up with my obstetrician when I get back home. The nurse walks in a few minutes later to give me my discharge papers. "Congratulations!" she says.

"No congratulations. This is totally unexpected. A baby changes everything."

"You had no idea you might be pregnant?" Sean asks.

"No idea at all! I mean, I've been tired lately, but I figured it was because of stress."

"Maybe this is the right time."

"Why? With everything going on, I can't believe this."

Sean nods sympathetically.

Enough of this conversation. I need my discharge papers so I can get out of here.

We get an Uber to bring us back to my hotel. Sean doesn't want me to be by myself after the accident, and I'm glad for the company. Maybe he'll take my mind off of this baby situation. I haven't been on birth control, but I also wasn't trying to get pregnant. Chris already wants us to get back together. If I tell him I'm pregnant, that will make things worse.

Sean keeps asking me if I'm okay. *No, I'm not okay. I am petrified to know that I am carrying another life inside of me.* "Come lie down in the bed," Sean says. "I'll lie over here on the sofa." After a couple of minutes, he continues, "Are you going to tell Chris about the baby, considering what y'all are going through right now?"

I'm not sure how to answer.

"You need to tell him. Don't keep this from him."

"If I tell him, he's going to think we're getting back together."

"You still love him, right?"

I consider my feelings in that moment. How can I not love him? Look at how long we've been together, and what we've been through.

"Yes, I love him. You still love your wife, right?"

"Yes, but that's different." He pulls his phone out of his pocket and starts fumbling with it.

"How is that different? Love is love."

"I tried to make it work with her, and she didn't want the same things as me. You and Chris want the same things."

I lift my chin toward Sean. "No, we used to want the same things, but he messed that up."

"We all make mistakes Destinee—"

I snap off before he can say another word. I point my finger at him. "Bullshit!"

"I'm a man, I know."

"So, you cheated before and that made you realize that you had a good thing?"

"No, but I know a couple of men who have, and they ended up losing the best thing they ever had. Troy is a perfect example."

"He should have known he had a good thing before he did what he did."

"You're going to have to forgive him at some point."

Maybe, maybe not. Only time will tell. I crawl under the covers, and Sean walks over from the couch and lies across the end of the bed.

I have a crazy dream that I tell Chris I'm pregnant, and he tells me he doesn't want anything to do with me anymore, that he doesn't think it's his baby. When I wake up, Sean is back on the couch, sleeping. I get up to use the bathroom, and when I walk out he's sitting up.

"I was forced to get on the couch because someone kept kicking in their sleep."

"I'm sorry about that. Had a bad dream."

"Tell me about it so it doesn't come true."

"I'll pass. That's the stupidest thing I ever heard."

Sean laughs then gives me a pensive look. "Would you like to spend Saturday with me and my daughter? We're gonna do lunch and go to the aquarium."

I don't want to intrude, but he seems earnest. "I would love to meet little Miss Najah."

I need to shower and get dressed so I can take Sean back to his hotel and then to the car rental center at the airport.

I lay my clothes on the bed as I pull them out of my suitcase. Once I have everything out, I walk into the bathroom, hang my clothes on the towel rack, and turn on the shower. "Don't forget to brush your teeth. I can smell your breath from here."

"That's your ass you're smelling."

191

Since Sean is in the main room, when I get out the shower, I push the toilet lid down and sit on it so I can moisturize my body then put on my clothes.

"You okay in there?" Sean asks.

"Yup, just getting dressed." I know I take a long time getting ready. I don't need a reminder.

When I walk out of the bathroom, he's lying across the bed, flipping through the channels. "Finally. Thought I was going to have to come in there and make sure you were okay."

"Not finished yet. Still have to comb out my hair and put some makeup on."

"You know damn well you don't need no makeup."

"Flattery will get you nowhere with me, sir."

I leave the bathroom door open and start putting on my makeup. I sense Sean staring at me. I turn and look in the mirror on the wall facing the bathroom and see him watching me.

He grins. "Yes, I am watching you put your makeup on."

"Why?"

"I just like watching you."

"Whatever, it's just makeup." He's making me uncomfortable, so I hurry and finish.

The accident from yesterday has me feeling nervous about driving these Atlanta streets, but I can't let that stop me. Before heading to his hotel, we stop and pick up some breakfast, which is good because I am in desperate need of some food. My stomach feels like it's on my back.

We get to Sean's hotel and he flashes the key card in front of the door and holds it open. "Ladies first."

I walk in and sit on his bed. "Make yourself comfortable while I get cleaned up." He opens his closet and pulls out two hangers—one with a polo shirt on it and the other with a pair of shorts. He has always been very particular about his wardrobe, and he's stylish. He lays his clothes on the bed and walks into the bathroom. I hear the water running then the shower door close. I hope he doesn't expect to get dressed in front of me.

I patiently wait for him to finish showering. The hotel might run out of hot water, he's taking so long in there. It's been almost thirty minutes. He had some nerve, questioning how long I took to get dressed.

Sean walks out of the bathroom with his towel wrapped around his waist.

Jesus take the wheel. Water glistens and drips from his chest and tight abs.

"Sir, why are you walking out here like that?"

"Like what? You like what you see?"

Damn right, I like what I see. He's playing with my emotions. I try not to watch as he reaches down to his waist to take his towel off.

"Wait a minute, don't do that in front of me," I say, holding up my hand.

He laughs. "Don't do what? Take my towel off?"

"Yes."

"Why not? Don't you want to see what's under the towel?"

I do want to see what's under the towel. That's the problem.

He reaches for the towel and pulls it off. I turn my head and put my hands over my face.

"It's okay. You can look. I have boxers on, relax."

I can still see what he's working with, and it's got me excited. I should not be feeling this way about another man.

"Do you usually get dressed in front of your female friends?"

"No, I don't, but I feel so comfortable around you."

"But you're making me feel uncomfortable." My hands are getting sweaty.

"Is that because you like what you see?"

"Stop playing, Sean. Put on some clothes before you start something you can't finish."

"Rest assured, I finish everything I start."

"We are not going there." I scrunch up my lips as I consider letting him show me how he starts and finishes.

"Why not?"

"Because we are just friends."

"Just friends, that's it?"

"Yes, Sean. Just friends."

While Sean is getting dressed, I can't help but think about this baby and Chris. Would I be able to take care of this baby by myself if I moved to Atlanta? I wouldn't be the first woman to raise a child in another state away from the father and family. If this job is meant to be, everything will work itself out.

I drop Sean off at the airport to figure out his car rental situation and drive around some neighborhoods I looked up before heading back to my hotel. I try to get all my running around out today so I can spend Saturday with Sean and Najah. I'm excited to meet his daughter. I pray she's not one of the smart-mouthed little girls.

Sean texts me when he gets to my hotel. I walk outside and see

Najah in the back seat of the car, bopping her head. She has a head full of hair and looks just like Sean. There's no denying that one. What is he going to do with all of that hair when she moves to Virginia?

Najah is a little shy at first, then she starts opening up to me and talking more. She is for sure a daddy's little girl. At lunch, she talks about all her friends and how she'll miss them when she moves to Virginia, but she's glad she'll be living with her dad. She's not nervous about going to the first grade and starting over at a new school. She says she's ready to meet new friends.

We have a blast at the aquarium. They don't call it the magical aquarium for nothing. We get to watch the sea lion show. I see the excitement come over Najah. I can tell she enjoys the show. There's so much to learn in that place, and Sean takes his time explaining the animals to Najah. He's so patient with her and tries to make everything exciting.

I tell Sean about running around the Atlanta streets yesterday after I dropped him off at the car rental place. He promises to show me some places he's sure I missed and need to see before I leave. But first, Najah and I do a little shopping.

Spending the weekend with Sean and seeing him interact with his daughter makes me realize how much I do want a baby. This baby is a blessing and my second chance at motherhood. I pray things will work out in my favor this time.

It made me feel good when Najah asked if she could come visit me when she gets to Virginia. I would love that. I really enjoyed getting to know her.

I make it back home in time for Sunday dinner at my mother's house; I go there straight from the airport. I contemplate sharing the news about my pregnancy with her, but if I tell her, the whole family will know before I get a chance to tell Chris. *If* I tell Chris.

Tears escape my eyes when I think about how CJ would be four years old and a big brother. There's not a day that goes by that I don't think about him. What would he be like if he was still here? Who would he look like? I know he would be happy to be a big brother.

When I pull up to my mother's house, Michelle is sitting on the steps looking stressed.

"Are you okay?"

I sit down on the steps next to her. "I had an argument with Kevin."

"About what?"

"He's still giving me a hard time about the baby." She has bags under her eyes, and she's not the spunky Michelle I'm used to seeing.

"Did you explain to him how you feel?"

"He said he's tired of me pushing him away and making him feel like all I have time for is my businesses."

"What did he say when you told him you were going to stay with Ma?"

She lets her head fall down, her chin resting on her chest. "He was upset and told me he's not bringing the kids back to Mom's house."

I reach for her hand, but before I can she moves it and brushes the hair out of her face. "He told me if I need space, I can stay with Mommy, but he's not going to make the kids go through all the back-and-forth."

I know Michelle is hurt over the situation, but she doesn't need to stay with my mother. She needs to be home with her husband and children, trying to work things out. When Michelle doesn't get her way, she likes to make everyone else around her miserable.

I get that she worked hard to get to where she is now, and I am so proud of her. I get why she is so focused, but she needs to remember that she is a wife and mother.

"Is all of this separation and arguing worth possibly losing your husband?"

"Yes, if that means he wants me to keep on having babies."

"Really? Y'all can't compromise and call this the last one?"

"Yes, really. I don't want any more children. I have a boy and a girl. That's all I need. If he feels like I don't have time for him now, how is he going to feel if we get to baby number four or five?"

"Wow. Didn't you guys talk about this kind of stuff before you got married?"

"Yes, but I was just starting my career. I never knew I would be where I am right now."

"Well, at the end of the day, you have to do what's best for you and what makes you happy. But think about what you might lose in the long run. Kevin is a good man. He's a good provider, and he loves you."

"I envy you, Destinee. You have worked hard for everything you have. You have always lived your life the way you wanted. You planned and set goals since you were little. I remember you telling me you were going to leave and go away to college and never come back. I never really thought you would leave, but you did, and now look at you."

I look at her in admiration because I remember where she started from and I see what she has achieved as a business owner, wife, and mother. I don't want her to envy me.

"Thank you, Sis, for listening."

"Anytime, Sis."

"Why didn't you give me all the details about what's going on with Chris?"

"What details?"

"The pictures and text messages. Mommy told me."

"Figures."

"Seriously, I see how Chris looks at you and how he talks about you. He loves you. You just have to decide if you still love him and can forgive him. Tell him how you feel."

There's no doubt in my mind that Chris loves me. It's the respect that I have an issue with.

We go inside the house, and Mr. Evans is sitting on the couch. I guess this is the new normal. Seeing him sitting in the living room makes me feel like my dad is in another room and will walk out at any minute. Seeing him with my mother is something that will take some time getting used to.

My mother is in the kitchen, finishing dinner. I stand at the kitchen door and observe her happiness. She smiles, and that dimple that was once hidden from her sadness is now visible.

I hug my mom before going to use the bathroom. When I walk back into the kitchen, she's no longer smiling. She's standing there with the phone in her hand.

"Please talk to this man."

"I don't want to talk to Chris."

I shake my head and gesture quietly for her to tell him I'm not here. She lifts the phone up to her ear and tells Chris that I'm there but don't want to talk to him. "Chris, I love you like a son, but don't call or come over to my house with no drama. We got enough going on over here." She hangs up the phone, and all I can do is laugh.

Chris texts me right after my mother hangs up on him. "I'm on my way to your mother's house so we can talk." My whole mood changes. I want to get in my car and leave, but wherever I go, he won't be too far behind. So, I sit in the kitchen with my sister and mother while I wait for Chris.

"How did your interview go with Mr. Dan?"

"It went okay. Not sure if I'll mesh well with the other attorneys, though." I don't go into too much detail. It will be a little while before a decision is made.

"Tell Mom about your weekend with Sean and his daughter."

"Really, Chelle?"

"You be careful. Don't open that door with another man until the other one is completely closed."

I get where she's coming from, but Sean is just a friend. A friend I would let take a dip in my honeypot, but I'm not trying to take it there with him. He's just getting out of his own situation, and his focus right now is on his daughter. I respect that.

Chris sends me a text message letting me know he's outside. I walk out to the truck and sit in the passenger seat with the door open. I don't want him to drive off with me in the truck. I just want to listen to what he has to say and go back inside the house.

"Something wrong with your phone? I was worried about you. You couldn't respond and let me know you were okay?"

"I know you want to talk, but I'm not sure I am ready to hear anything you have to say."

"Let me come back home?"

"Not gonna happen."

The fact that I'm pregnant sits in the front of my mind. I know once I tell him, he's going put more pressure on me to work things out.

He was ready to have a baby about a year after CJ was born. He begged me to, but I wasn't ready to go through another pregnancy. Being pregnant now is frightening. It scares me that I might experience what I went through with CJ.

Finally, after sitting in the truck with Chris for a couple of minutes, I agree to meet him one night for dinner so we can talk. He practically begs me to let him come home because he doesn't want to go back to his aunt's house.

I'm surprised to hear he's staying there. "Figured you might be staying with Izabelle."

Chris looks at me like he wants to say more, but I guess the expression on my face makes him think twice.

I walk back in the house, and my mother and Michelle stare at me like they're waiting for me to say something.

"I told him we could have dinner one night this week to talk."

I don't stay much longer at Mom's house after dinner. I'm tired from my weekend and my flight, and I need to get ready for work in the morning. Before I leave, I convince Michelle to go home and talk to her husband. I think once they get their true feelings out in the open, they will be on better terms. I have faith that they will work things out. Chris and I are another story.

CHAPTER EIGHTEEN

"What took you so long to agree to have dinner with me?" Chris stares at me from across the table.

I know we eventually needed to talk. But I'm still unsure of what he thinks he can say that will change how I feel about him. I'm glad I drove, so when he starts up with bullshit I can leave.

"I'm only here because you keep telling me you want to talk. I'm here to listen."

"Why haven't you been home lately?"

"How do you know when I'm home and when I'm not home? You stalking me?"

"No ... I'm not," he responds in a nervous tone.

I can't stand it when people lie to me. "Just so you know, I went out with an old friend from college that recently moved back to Virginia."

Chris clears his throat. "What friend?"

I sit quietly for a moment before responding. "We are just

friends and nothing more."

He flicks the silverware wrapped in cloth across the table. I don't have anything to hide other than the fact that I'm pregnant. I place my hands under the table and touch my stomach.

"I see you're still wearing your ring."

I lift up my left hand, pull the ring off my finger, and place it in the middle of the table. "I've been wearing it for almost four years. Was expecting to marry the man that gave it to me."

"Why are you taking it off?"

I close my eyes and think back to the night Chris asked me to marry him.

Chris picks the ring up from the table, looks at it, and swirls it around the tip of his pointer finger. "Put it back on, please." He places the ring down on the table and gently slides it in front of me. I look down at it and then up at him.

I never thought I would have a baby daddy. The goal has always been to get married first then have children and raise them together. I've seen the baby mama and baby daddy drama, and I don't want anything to do with it. I wouldn't be the type of mother to keep my child away from his father. I want my child to see and know that his or her parents have a thriving relationship, preferably in the same household. But if that doesn't happen, Chris and I will need to work together and do what's in the best interest of the child.

I reach down, pick up the ring, and look him in his eyes. "This ring came with a promise, and that promise has been broken. Makes no sense to put it back on."

I place the ring back down on the table and push back my chair.

"Where are you going? Please don't leave."

I sigh and pull my chair back to the table. "Maybe you will have an opportunity to put that ring back on my finger."

Chris picks up the ring and puts it in his pants pocket.

"Are you going to take the job if they offer it to you?"

"I'm not sure. I have a lot to consider."

"Like us?"

"Don't get beside yourself."

Our food comes out and Chris sits quietly like he no longer has an appetite. I pay him no mind and dive into my pasta.

"I've thought about the pain I caused you. I made some bad choices. Choices that hurt the one woman I love. Someone who I should've never hurt. You've always been there for me, and I appreciate you more than you know. I pray it's not too late for us and that you will give me another chance."

"Why should I give you a second chance? I don't trust you."

"Let me come back home, and you can start to regain trust in me."

I try to keep my voice down so I don't bring on unwanted attention. "No, not happening. You're walking around like I'm the bad person when all I was trying to do was be there for you. You were constantly pushing me away. In the back of my mind, I thought you might be cheating but, in my heart, I felt like you wouldn't do that to me. If you wouldn't have left your phone at home that morning, I probably still wouldn't have found out you were cheating, and you would still be doing the same things."

"What happened with Izabelle was a one-time thing."

"You expect me to believe you? She was waiting for you!"

"I'm telling you the truth. She wanted something she couldn't have. We had sex once."

"I don't believe you."

"I fucked up, Destinee."

I slam my hands down on the table before getting up and walking out of the restaurant. "Damn right you fucked up."

I don't have time for nonsense and foolishness. I have other things that require my attention, like scheduling my appointment with an obstetrician.

When I walk in the house, I glance at my phone. There's a missed call from Sean. I sit down on the third step and return his call.

"Hey there! I hope I didn't catch you at a bad time."

I laugh and lean back against the stairs. "I just walked in the house."

"Oh, okay. Hot date?"

I let out a deep sigh. "Dinner with Chris, and it didn't go so well."

"Want to talk about it?"

"No, I'd rather forget it happened."

"That bad, huh?"

"It could've been worse."

"Would I be overstepping my boundaries by asking you out to lunch or dinner?"

I sit silently in my thoughts, thinking about the time we spent together in Atlanta and watching him with Najah.

"Hello? You still there?"

I forgot I was still on the phone. "Yeah, sorry. Just thinking."

"How about you let me take your mind off of things and focus on something else."

"Sean, you are so nasty."

"Get your mind out the gutter. I need your help getting Najah's room ready."

If Kim finds out I'm spending time with Sean, I will never hear the end of it. I'm not doing anything wrong. Although some nasty things have crossed my mind. The good thing is I haven't acted on it.

I keep my promise to Sean and schedule my appointment with Dr. Johnson. "Congratulations! Is this a surprise or a plan?" she asks. *Not a plan, for sure.* I was just here a few months ago having my pap smear. "Almost into your second trimester." I didn't think I was that far along. I haven't been as sick as I was with CJ. Just tired all the time.

"I'm surprised Chris is not here with you today."

"We are going through something right now. Plus, he doesn't know about the baby yet." I need to get over the shock of this baby and process my emotions first.

"You need to tell him soon. You're gonna need his support."

I will tell him in my own time. For now, I'm going to focus on what I have to do to take care of myself and not stress.

As I'm leaving Dr. Johnson's office, I run into Kim. "What are you doing here?" I ask.

"I was just about to text you." She flips her hair back off her shoulders and swings her head around.

I shrug and lower the tone of my voice. "My first prenatal appointment."

"What? Oh my God! Congratulations! Wait, please tell me it's not Sean's baby. I heard you two have been spending a lot of time together." *How does she know we've been spending time together?*

For her and Troy to be going through a divorce, they still do a lot of talking. The only way she would know what's going on is if Sean told Troy and Troy said something to her.

"No, it's not Sean's."

"So, it's Chris's? I don't know which one is worse."

Sean and I have been seeing each other almost every day since I went with him to pick out some stuff to decorate Najah's room. It doesn't help that he lives close to my office, so most nights when I get off work, I just go over there.

"I'm a little disappointed you didn't tell me."

I hope Sean didn't say anything about me being pregnant. "Didn't tell you what?"

"That you've been spending time with Sean?"

I'm glad Sean can keep some things to himself. Kim would be devastated to learn Sean knew about my pregnancy before she did.

"Be careful. He might have a hidden agenda and want more than your time."

I look down at my feet and mumble, "I'm okay with that." I get the feeling that sometimes he's trying to move past the friend zone.

"Girl, I can't with you." She swings her hand in the air. "Let me get in here for my annual. I'll call you later."

When I get back to my office, I think about what Dr. Johnson said at my appointment.

I thought Atlanta might be an opportunity for me to move away and start fresh. Especially after everything that happened with Chris. I open my desk drawer, pull my cell phone out of my purse, and call Mr. Dan.

I share my pregnancy news with him and tell him how it was a major factor in my decision to remove myself as a candidate for the position. As much as I want to take this job and advance in my career, I need to think about my child and our wellbeing.

He assures me that more and better opportunities will present themselves because he knows how passionate and driven I am when it comes to my career. A wave of relief rushes over me as I hang up the phone. Now I have to figure out how to tell Chris about the baby.

I get home from work and respond to a message Chris sent me earlier asking if I'm still going to Sabrina's graduation.

"I wouldn't miss her graduation ceremony just because we are not on the best of terms."

"Can I pick you up for the graduation?"

"Sure, Chris. Good night." I toss the phone on the bed and plop down next to it.

CHAPTER NINETEEN

I'm starting to notice a bulge in my stomach. Every time I get out of the shower, I glance in the mirror and get a little emotional. My growing belly makes this pregnancy feel real, and it's getting harder for me to hide. I can't believe I have another life growing inside of me. God has blessed me with another gift.

As much as I want to support Sabrina at her graduation ceremony and party, I do not want to be questioned by Chris's family about why we haven't got back together. They probably don't even know we're not together anymore. He's not going to tell them what he did. He's too ashamed, which he should be. If Greg was still alive, he would be so furious with Chris. He always told him I was the best part of his life and that Chris needed to cherish that.

When Chris arrives to pick me up for Sabrina's graduation ceremony, I can hear the excitement in his voice. "You look nice and comfortable." If he only knew how many outfits I had to try on to hide this baby bump. It's hot outside, so I can't wear a sweater. I settled for a floral maxi dress that flows from my waist.

"Is there something wrong with what I'm wearing?"

"No, you look good."

I lock the door and walk behind Chris to the truck. He opens the door and stands there until I'm seated, then he closes the door.

After the ceremony, the family gathers outside of the Coliseum to take pictures and talk. His aunt stands across from Chris and I, and she keeps smiling at us. *Awkward.*

She walks over and asks, "Are you still helping with Sabrina's graduation party on Saturday?"

"Absolutely! I'm excited for her to be going off to college and to my alma mater."

Chris walks over to talk to Ebony, and as soon as he does Regina takes the opportunity to bring up our relationship.

"Chris always looks so happy when you are around."

"Does he?"

"Yes, he does. I really hope you two can work things out."

Before I can say a word, Chris walks back over.

"Okay, time to go."

Either she doesn't know the real reason we are not together or she knows and was about to ask questions she has no business asking.

On the drive back to the house, Chris is silent. He doesn't sing along to any songs or look my direction. That is, until he pulls up to the house.

"Can I come inside for a little while?"

"You can come in, but don't expect too much out of me because

I'm tired."

"I understand. Just want to spend some time with you."

I walk in the house, and he stands at the door until I tell him to come in and have a seat.

"I put the gun back in the safe." I laugh.

"I don't find that funny."

He sits down on the couch, and I run upstairs to change my clothes. I'm still trying to hide my bump, so I find an oversized T-shirt in my drawer that will do the trick.

When I get back downstairs, he starts talking about when we first started dating and how we used to talk to each other about everything. We were so in sync with each other.

"Destinee, I just want you back. I love you and want you in my life. This distance is driving me crazy. There is nothing else out there for me—no one better than you. You are the best thing that has happened to me, and I'm the fool that messed everything up."

"I don't know where things went wrong." I sit back on the couch and fold my arms across my chest.

"I was dealing with a lot when my uncle died. It was so unexpected. He was like my dad, my best friend. I went to him about everything."

"I know the loss of your uncle was a lot, and I tried my best to be there for you, but you wouldn't let me in."

He rubs his hand over his head and slouches down on the couch. "You're right. And I did something I should've never done; I slept with another woman. We were both dealing with a lot. You lost your dad, we lost CJ, then my uncle passed away. I stopped thinking about our future. Having to help my family get their shit together was a lot. But I forgot to make sure you were taken care of."

"Finally, the truth." I press my lips together, annoyed that it has taken him this long to talk about what was really going on.

"Yes, the truth. I was wrong for hurting you." I look down at his hands, which have fallen into his lap.

"I never thought we would be dealing with something like this in our relationship. I trusted you more than I've trusted anyone."

"Please let me show you. I promise you, I will never abuse your heart again. You asked for time, and I gave it you. You asked for space, and I gave it to you. Baby, I just want to come back home and be with you."

"I'm scared to let you back in."

Why does he think it's so easy to forgive? I lie down on the couch, my feet touching his leg. He lifts my feet and places them on his lap. I don't want him touching me, so I move them back on the couch.

I must have dozed off, because I open my eyes and Chris is staring at me. "Get up and get in bed. I'm getting ready to leave." He kisses me on the cheek then my neck and whispers in my ear, "I'm going to get you back, and I'm coming home soon."

My morning routine has changed significantly. I no longer go for my morning run. Instead, I use the extra time to get more sleep. I go to bed tired and nauseated and wake up feeling the same way. I've been working from home a lot more, which is something I don't usually do.

Sean has been spoiling me by cooking me dinner almost every night. He throws down in the kitchen, and I'm right there to eat it all up. It's been nice, helping him prepare for Najah's arrival. He has turned her bedroom into a princess-themed room with a castle bed. She's going to love it.

He helps keep my mind off work and everything else that might cause me stress, which I need. But my feelings for Sean have exceeded the friend level. I find myself wanting to spend more time with him. I can tell he wants to spend more time with me too, because he's always calling me.

For some reason when I pull up to his house tonight, I sit in the car for a few minutes, contemplating whether I should go in his house or go back home. Part of me wants to go home and call Chris. The other part wants to go inside with Sean. I take my time walking to the door, still unsure if I'm making the right decision.

Before my finger taps the doorbell, Sean opens the door.

"What's taking you so long?"

I stand frozen in the doorway. My eyes focus on his chest and the gray sweatpants he's wearing.

He grabs my arm and pulls me into the house.

"You out there daydreaming?"

"If you want to call it that."

He's got the house smelling like a Mexican restaurant. I turn the corner and walk into the kitchen to see what he's cooking up. Chicken quesadillas, black beans, and rice. Oh, and he got the table set up with guacamole, salsa, and chips.

"This food gon' tear my stomach up."

"Go ahead and sit down. I'll make your plate."

I have a seat at the kitchen table and help myself to the chips and guacamole. He places my plate of food on the table in front of me and pours me a glass of water. He grabs himself a beer out of the refrigerator and sits across from me.

"How was work today?"

"Another work-from-home day. My mornings have been brutal. Always too exhausted to get up."

"Heard anything about Atlanta yet?"

"I turned it down. I told you this baby was going to change everything."

"Maybe it's for the best." I'm not too sure I agree with him on that. "Have you told Chris about the baby yet?"

"Nope."

He sets his fork down on his plate and looks up at me. "What are you waiting for? You need to tell him. He needs to know you are carrying his baby, and he's going to be a father."

"I will tell him when I'm ready."

"Well, you're running out of time because you are starting to show."

Damn it! If he notices, I wonder if Chris noticed. And if he did, why hasn't he said anything? Time is ticking, and I know Sean is right. I hate that he's right.

After dinner, I offer to help wash dishes. It's only fair since he cooked.

"No, all I want you to do is sit back and relax."

"You don't have to tell me twice."

I use the bathroom before going into the living room. Upon relieving my bladder, I stay seated on the toilet for a few minutes, thinking about how I need to stop hiding this pregnancy and deal with my issues head on. But when I'm with Sean, I don't think about anything or anyone else.

I walk out to the living room, and Sean is seated on the sofa next to the sliding glass doors. "You finished quickly,"

"That's why I have a dishwasher, and I clean as I cook so it won't be so much work afterwards."

I have a seat on the other sofa facing the television.

"You don't want to sit next to me?"

I get up, walk over, and sit next to him.

"I don't bite. Unless you want me to." He laughs as he reaches down to my feet, takes my sandals off, grabs my legs, and sets them in his lap. He begins rubbing my feet, and I moan with each press of his thumb into my foot.

"Does that feel good?" Before I can answer, he stops rubbing my feet. "Can I ask you a question?"

I want to say, "No, keep rubbing my feet," but I give him my full attention. "Sure, go ahead."

"What's going on with you and Chris?"

"What do you mean? Nothing is going on with Chris."

"I mean, you still talk to him but haven't told him about the baby. You gave up a career opportunity to stay here. I mean, why is it so hard for you to forgive him or make a decision on whether or not you want to be with him?"

"Because I'm still hurt over the situation."

"Do you want to get back together with him?"

"I don't know. Why are you asking?"

"Why is that such a hard question for you to answer?"

"It's complicated. I still love him, of course. Look how long we've been together and what we've been through. I just don't know if I can live with the fact that he cheated."

He resumes the foot rub and the questions stop. I sink into the sofa as the tension leaves my body and my eyes begin to droop. That's my queue to leave and go home, but I'm so comfortable. Sean flips through the channels until he comes across a movie worth watching: *The Best Man Holiday*. I love Lance and Mia's love story. And the love Mia had for her friends. My favorite part is when the guys dance for the ladies.

Feet still in Sean's lap, I sink deeper into the sofa. Halfway through the movie, I glance up at Sean. He's dozing off and his head rests on the back of the sofa. Looks like we are both ready to call it a night. I slowly lift my feet up, trying not to startle him. No such luck. Before my feet make it to the floor, he lifts his head and opens his eyes.

"Where you going?"

"It's time for me to go home."

"No, please don't leave. You look so peaceful sleeping."

"*You* were the one sleeping."

"It's been a busy week."

"Sean, I appreciate dinner and the time we've been spending together, but I think it's best if I go home."

"Why? Are you afraid something might happen?"

"Something like what?"

He scoots closer to me and wraps his arm around my neck.

"What are you doing?"

He bites his bottom lip. "I'm gonna kiss you."

Damn, his lips are so soft and thick. I can't help but give in and kiss him back. He pulls me close to him. Part of me wants to pull away, but I've kind of been waiting for this moment for a while. Maybe we both have.

His kisses start to get more intense as he reaches up my shirt to grab my breast then slowly pulls away. "I'm sorry. I don't want you to do something you don't want to do."

"It's too late for that."

He leads me down the hallway toward his bedroom while kissing me and pulling my shirt off. We stop halfway down the hallway, and he firmly kisses my body from neck to down to my stomach as I stand against the wall. He stops and I watch as he slowly unbuttons my pants and pulls them down, lifting one leg up at a time to pull them off.

I pull his shirt over his head and can finally rub my hands across his chest. His sweatpants fall down to the floor.

He lifts me up against the wall, and my legs sit on his forearms. His hands press against the wall. *Please don't drop me.* He slowly slides inside me, penetrating deeper and deeper with each thrust. I wrap my arms around his neck to help keep me balanced. I'm about to reach my peak when he lifts me off the wall and carries me to the bedroom.

"Ah, why did you stop?"

"You gotta wait for me."

"I don't think I can."

He lays me on his bed and flips me over. Kind of rough, but I like it. He grabs my waist as he slowly slides inside me from behind. We both gasp with each thrust. He loses it when I match his rhythm, which is good because I am ready to blow. And boy, do I. My body is pressed against the bed, stretched out, and Sean rests against my back.

The next morning, I wake up with this creepy sensation like someone is staring at me. I open my eyes to see Sean gawking at me, smiling.

"Am I drooling or something?" I lift my head and look down on the pillow case.

"I could watch you sleep all day."

"Oh, stop it." I roll my eyes and sit up on the bed.

"Can I be honest with you about something?"

"Of course."

"I've had a crush on you since college. I always thought you were beautiful, smart, and ambitious. But you wouldn't give me the time of day."

I laugh and nudge his shoulder. "Because you were a player back then and a pretty boy."

"No, I really wasn't. The guys I hung around with were players, but I was always sincere."

"I'm here right now. You finally got me."

"Yeah, but can I have you forever?"

I stop smiling and let my body fall back onto the bed, gripping the covers against my body. "Forever? That's deep. Is it because of last night? It was so good, even though I was a little upset you told me to wait for you. These past couple of weeks with you have been amazing. The last thing I want to do is confuse things. You are getting out of a situation. I don't know what's going on with my situation. I don't want to hurt you or lead you on."

"We are both grown. I understand what you are saying, and I am sorry if I put you in awkward position last night. Just know that if you want to take this to another level, I am willing to go with you. I really care about you, and I love spending time with you, if you haven't already noticed. I love how you interact with my daughter. And the baby situation does not scare me at all, if that's what you're worried about. I want a family. I want a wife. I want to make a relationship work with you. I know what I want."

"I'm glad you know what you want. Now I need to take the time to figure out what *I* want."

I kiss him on the lips, get up from the bed, and gather my clothes from the hallway and put them on. "I'll call you later, Sean."

"Please think about what I said."

I walk out to my car, muttering, "Damn, damn, damn." What did I get myself into? Why did it have to be that good? Not just the sex. I mean, it felt good every time I was with Sean. I should've got some of that in Atlanta.

CHAPTER TWENTY

Confusion plagues my mind as I make my way home. Was last night a mistake? I hope we didn't ruin a great friendship with sex. Should I even consider a relationship with Sean? Would I be able to look at Sean the same if Chris and I got back together? Would he be able to look at me the same? Do I tell Chris what happened?

Sean is more laid back than Chris. He's more of a homebody— a true cancer who would rather stay at home in his shell, surrounded by people he loves. But he also enjoys an occasional day out and about. He loves music and art, which is something we have in common. We could be in the house listening to music, and on a whim, he would stand up, grab my hands, and pull me up from the sofa to dance with him.

I heard him loud and clear when he said he knows what he wants. Although we've had deep conversations about relationships, we've never claimed to be in one with each other. We were just friends who were at a place in our life where we needed someone to talk to and take our minds off the hurt from previous relationships.

Got to admit, the sex was better than I expected. If I knew it was that good, I would have got some a long time ago. Deep down, we both knew it would happen eventually with all the time we were spending with each other.

I hear my phone chime as I'm driving. I stop at a stop light and check it. It's a message from Sean: "I apologize if I over-stepped my boundaries last night. I understand you are trying to figure things out. I just need you to know that I value our friendship, and I am here whenever you need me."

That means a lot, but what happened last night makes it even more difficult to decide what to do about my relationship with Chris. I've invested a lot of time with Chris, so a part of me feels obligated to continue the relationship. I was afraid to give Chris a chance at first because of the pain from my previous relationships, but he broke his way through to my heart and I felt like I could trust him. I fell in love. Now I feel like I wasted four years of my life with a man who stole my heart and all my dreams of a happily-ever-after.

A child is no reason to stay in a relationship, but it makes my decision so much harder. It hurts knowing he was willing to risk everything we built for a piece of ass.

When I get home, Chris's truck sits in front of the house. It's just after 9:00 a.m. Why is he sitting in front of the house so early, and how long has he been sitting there waiting? I pull into the driveway, get out of the car, and walk to the front door. He walks up to the house to meet me.

"Is everything okay?" I ask slowly.

"You tell me. You're the one who's been out all night."

"What?"

"Where have you been?"

I look at him like he has lost his mind. "How dare you question my whereabouts?"

Quickly, he changes his tone. "I drove by the house last night about seven and saw you leaving. You have on the same thing you had on last night when you left. Where have you been?"

"Why do you keep stalking me?"

"I'm not, I just drove by to check on you. When I got to the corner, you were getting into your car, so I kept on going. I drive by every now and then to check on the house."

"No, you're stalking me! What are you doing here now?"

I open the door and walk in the house so we can continue talking. I already have nosey neighbors.

"I wanted to take you out for breakfast since you were too busy yesterday. And I wanted you to go with me to pick up the rest of the stuff for Sabrina's graduation party. Was hoping we could go together."

"Why didn't you just call me?"

"Would you have answered?"

"Yes, and I would've been ready for you when you got here this morning."

"I'll just see you later, Destinee. That's if you are still coming to the party. I don't know who this dude is, but you need to figure out what you want."

I stand at the front door and watch as he pulls off. *Figure out what I want?* He's the reason I'm in this situation.

I try calling Kim to fill her in on what went down last night and

221

this morning, but it goes to voice mail. It's weird that I haven't seen her or spoken to her lately. It's not like her to go more than a day without calling me. I feel like she's been distant since that day we ran into each other at the doctor's office. I'm not sure if it's because of Sean or what's she's going through with Troy.

I dial Kim's number again, and this time she answers.

"Were you sleeping?" I ask.

"No," she responds sharply.

"Are you okay?"

"Yes," she says in the same tone.

She doesn't sound too convincing.

"You sure you okay?"

"Yes. What's going on? I'm listening."

"I was calling to tell you about what happened last night."

"What?"

I pause for a minute, surprised by how short she's being with me on the phone. "I spent the night with Sean last night."

"I knew it would happen eventually because it was all a part of Sean's plan."

"What's with the attitude?" I ask.

"Have you told Chris about the baby?"

I take a moment before responding.

"Hello?" Kim calls out.

"No, I haven't told him about the baby."

"You need to tell him soon."

I hang up with Kim and take a nice hot shower. I can't help but think about what happened last night with Sean. I need to stop and focus on getting ready for this graduation party.

I try to find something in my closet that will flatten this baby bump. It's getting harder to hide it, and now that I'm into my second trimester I feel a little more comfortable sharing my secret.

I promised Regina I would be there early to help her set up, plus I have to pick up the balloons and the rest of the decorations. I'm anxious to see how this day plays out. Especially after how Chris reacted this morning.

When I pull up to Regina's house, Chris is standing outside talking to his uncle Mack. He smiles and walks over to my car.

I feel like I'm going to throw up the toast and eggs I ate for breakfast, so I sit in the car for a minute, hoping the feeling will pass. He walks over to the driver's side and opens the door.

"Are you okay?"

"I'm feeling lightheaded." I play it off and step out of the car. He grabs the balloons and bags from the back seat and walks with me to the house.

"Maybe you need to eat something." I wonder if he's still mad at me from this morning.

Regina is happy to see me, which is no surprise. "Come on in here and give me a hug." She pulls me into the hallway, away from the kitchen and the rest of the family that has already arrived.

"Are you okay? You look a little flushed."

I reassure her that everything is okay, and she walks back into the kitchen. I almost let it slip that I've been dealing with morning sickness but caught myself. Family is around. I don't want to make a scene, and I still haven't told Chris.

Regina, her sister, and her niece are in the kitchen, cooking and putting food on party trays. I help them finish putting food in the serving trays before starting the decorations. I have to keep sneaking outside to get some fresh air because there are too many smells in the house.

As much as I can't take the smell of the food, I hate being outside in all the heat and humidity. I need some shade, and there's a lack of it in this yard.

The little kids run through the house as they arrive, and Regina yells at all of them. "Get out my house with all that running! Go outside." She can't stand it when the kids run through her house, especially her kitchen. I'm surprised all four of Charles's baby mamas let the kids come over for the cookout. He must be making those child support payments. It's nice to see all the little cousins playing together. CJ would be out there running around with them.

Finally, the decorating is finished. The graduate arrives, and the DJ is setting up. Chris and Charles are manning the grill.

Uncle Mack walks toward them. "Y'all know what y'all doing with that grill?" He pulls his flask from his front pocket and takes a few sips. When he gets to drinking, he says anything that comes to his mind and gets a little frisky with the ladies. Especially the young ones. "Y'all make sure that chicken is cooked all the way. I don't want to bite into the chicken and see blood. That ain't cool." We all laugh as he walks inside the house.

I walk past Chris to go back inside the house, and he winks at me. He hasn't said much to me since I showed up. Every time he looks at me, I feel like he wants to say something, but he doesn't. He must know what happened last night. It's not like I cheated. *He* did that. I know I can't let what happened last night happen again. I don't want my feelings for Sean getting any deeper than they already are.

Everyone is gathered outside. The food is ready and everyone is in a rush to make a plate. Charles puts two fingers in his mouth and whistles.

"Yo, listen up. Mama gonna say a prayer, then we can eat."

Everyone gathers together and holds hands while Regina says a prayer. Chris reaches down for my hand and interlocks his fingers with mine. We bow our heads as Regina leads us in prayer and say "amen" in unison.

"Go sit down. I'll make you a plate." Chris releases my hand, and I go sit back down. I look around at all the family gathered to celebrate Sabrina. This is nothing new for them. They are used to cooking out and gathering together—something my family used to do but hasn't done in a long time. I'm thankful that Chris's family has embraced me from day one; they make me feel like part of the family, especially Regina.

Being outside in the heat, surrounded by food, is starting to get the best of me. I feel like everything I just ate is about to come up. I get up from the table and make my way inside the house, trying to avoid causing a scene. Chris notices and rushes inside the house behind me. I manage to make it to the bathroom and let everything out. It's coming out my mouth and my nose, and my eyes are tearing up from the pressure.

Chris knocks on the door twice then walks right in. "Are you okay?"

I flush the toilet, put the toilet seat down, and sit on it. He closes the door behind him, grabs a wash cloth out of the cabinet behind the toilet, wets it, and starts wiping my face.

"What's going on? Are you okay?"

There's not going to be a better time than this to tell him. I hold my head up and look him dead in the face. "Chris, I'm pregnant."

"What?"

"I'm pregnant!"

He takes a step back and leans against the wall. "I was wondering when you were going to tell me."

"You knew and didn't say anything?"

"I know you and your body, Destinee. Your mannerisms, changes to your face. You've been tired, and you are starting to show. I was waiting for you to tell me."

I exhale noisily, a great sigh of relief now that he finally knows.

"How far along are you?"

"I saw Dr. Johnson for the first time a couple of weeks ago. So, I guess that would make me almost fourteen weeks."

"Really? Stop playing. Why did you wait so long to tell me?"

"I was scared to tell you."

"Why? It's my baby, right?" He looks at me with a smirk on his face.

"Yes, it's your baby. You knowing I'm pregnant would put more pressure on me to get back together with you."

He stands across from me in silence, staring at me while I'm still seated on the toilet. "So, we're having a baby."

"Yes, we are having a baby. Promise not to tell anyone until we go back to see Dr. Johnson."

Chris pulls me up from the toilet and hugs me tightly. He whispers, "I love you" in my ear. I can feel the love from the warmth of his embrace.

We walk back outside and everyone is looking at us, especially Regina. I make my way back to my seat in the little bit of shade there is outside. Ebony is seated next to me with her three-month-old son, Mason. It's been a couple of years since I've held a little baby. They smell so good with their soft hands and tiny feet. I ask if I can hold him, and it hits me that I will be holding my baby in my arms soon.

A tear escapes from my eye before I can wipe it away. Ebony looks over at me and says, "You have that magic touch with babies. He usually gets so fussy when people take him from me." I glance over at Chris standing at the grill next to Charles. He looks up, smiling at me. I smile back.

Regina catches it all and winks at me. "Destinee, you're next! I had a dream about fish." Everyone looks at me like I'm the center of attention. "You know what they say when you dream about fish? That means someone in the family is pregnant." They will all soon find out that she's right, but I think she already knows and is just waiting for us to tell her.

The DJ plays "Better With You In It" by MAJOR. Chris walks over to me and pulls me up out of my chair. I give Mason back to Ebony, and we start to sway to the rhythm of the music. Chris sings along with the lyrics. When the song ends, Chris pulls me close to him and whispers in my ear, "Please forgive me. I'm so sorry I hurt you, and I will prove to you that you can trust me again. You and this baby are my priority."

"You two love birds," Ebony yells out. Despite the tension that's been between us, it feels good to be in Chris's arms and for him to be spontaneous like that.

After all the eating, dancing, and card playing, we start cleaning up. Everyone piles in the kitchen like vultures to make a plate before heading home.

I try my best to help Regina and Sabrina clean up, but I'm too tired. The thought of driving home from Newport News to Virginia Beach makes me more tired. Chris is out front talking to his cousins and his uncle, so I make my way to his bedroom, climb under the covers, and get comfortable. As soon as my head hits the pillow, I close my eyes and drift off to sleep.

Not long after I doze off, I hear Chris talking as he walks toward the bedroom. He opens the door and sees me lying there. He walks in and closes the door behind him, making his way to the bed. "I miss this," he breathes as he climbs in and pulls me close to him. I take pleasure in lying in his arms—something I used to do every night. I let the beat of his heart soothe me to sleep.

The next morning when I open my eyes, Chris is not in the bed or in the room. I lie there for a minute, wondering where he disappeared too. After lying there for a few more minutes, I get up and walk out to the den. Chris is sitting in the recliner, watching television. Everyone else has left for church. I didn't realize I had slept that late.

"You were sleeping so good I didn't want to wake you, so I came out here to watch T.V."

"Yeah, that was some good sleep." I still feel safe lying in his arms.

Chris walks with me out to my car. "Can I stop by later?"

"Sure, I'll be home."

"Want me to bring you anything?"

"Yes. Food."

I know once I get home, I'm not leaving the house again. Especially since it's raining.

I think about what happened with Sean the other night, trying to convince the regret that has come over me to leave. I overruled my mind and instead ran with my feelings. He was familiar and there was a connection, but I shouldn't have let my feelings lead me to get too involved. I don't think our intention was to lead each other on, but by me spending time with Sean I may have led him to believe we could be more that what we are.

I grab my phone off the sofa and call Sean before Chris gets to the house. He answers on the first ring. "Wasn't sure I would hear from you today."

"I wanted to apologize about the other night."

"No, no need to apologize. We are both grown, and we both wanted the same thing. I don't regret it, and neither should you."

"That's the thing. I feel like I may have led you to believe we could be more than friends. I don't want us to be in a situationship. I want us to continue to be friends."

"Situationship?"

"I just don't want our friendship to change." I sit down at the kitchen table and fiddle with place mat in front of me.

"Okay ..."

"I told Chris about the baby."

"Glad to hear that." I can tell he's manipulating his voice to sound happy.

"So, you're okay with being friends?"

"I was hoping we could be more than friends, but I respect your decision. I just hope you can still spend time with Najah once she moves here?"

I take a minute to think about how to respond. For me to see Najah, I have to see Sean. That might not sit too well with Chris. But I did promise while I was in Atlanta that we would get to spend time together when she moves here. I can't break my promise to a little girl.

"Yes, I will still spend time with Najah."

I hang up with Sean, and Chris knocks on the door. I see a happy-face plastic bag in his hand. Must be Chinese food.

"You wouldn't have to open the door for me if my key still worked," he says as I open the door.

"We're not gonna go there." I walk into the kitchen, grab a cup from the cabinet, and fill it with ice from the refrigerator door. We sit at the table and I contemplate telling him about what happened with Sean. Technically, we weren't together when it happened, but that's not going to lessen any hurt he might feel.

"You got something on your mind? You look deep in thought."

"Just thinking."

"I've been thinking too, and I think we need to have a serious discussion."

Oh God, he knows about what I did. He sounds so serious, scary serious, but he's right. We do need to talk … about everything. That is the only way we are going to be able to move forward.

"We need to talk about us and all that has been going on." He reaches across the table for the clear plastic top to cover the remaining food in his container. "I know the hurt I caused you will not go away overnight. Just know I wasn't out here looking for someone to replace you. I made a mistake. I am truly sorry for everything, and I apologize for doing that to us."

"I don't understand. I thought you were stronger than that." It's disappointing because I thought we were strong enough to handle anything, and I have always been there for Chris.

"I wasn't out there looking for someone else, but I shouldn't have let it go as far as it did. I knew what she wanted, but I was just trying to be a friend. It went too far, and I regret everything."

"What's everything?"

"Everything?"

"You regret *everything*?"

"I'm not trying to go into detail unless you're gonna give details about what happened with you and college boy."

The silence between us speaks for itself. We both want details but don't want to say too much in fear that it will make things worse.

Chris breaks the silence "Listen, I was wrong and if I didn't do what I did, you wouldn't have ended up doing whatever you did. I think a part of me wanted you to find out what was going on so I didn't have to tell you."

"So, were there others?"

"No, and there shouldn't have even been that one."

"You're right about that."

"I just want to move forward and for us to be honest with each other going forward." He lets out a heavy sigh. "Can I ask you a question?"

I already know what it is. I'm just praying he'll let it go. "Just ask me."

"Who is this guy you've been hanging out with?"

I get up from the table, grab my empty container of food, and put it in the trash. I do not want to have this conversation. I walk into the living room and reach for the remote on the coffee table. Chris grabs it before sitting down next to me on the couch.

"I don't have a problem telling you anything you want to know."

"If you tell me everything, I am pretty sure we won't be moving forward in this relationship."

He leans back in the corner of the couch. "You really feel that way?"

"Yes, I do."

"I don't want this to lead to an argument."

"Me either, but I'll tell you this. I met Sean in college. He and Troy were close friends. I saw him when I went out that night to the club with Kim, and again when I went to Atlanta. Before that, I hadn't seen him since HU's homecoming six years ago."

"Wait, you went to Atlanta with him?"

"No, we just so happened to be on the same flight to Atlanta."

"So, you mean to tell me that this guy *coincidentally* ended up on the same flight with you to Atlanta?" I wish he would listen instead of being so quick to respond. Chris picks the remote up from the couch and turns on the television. "I don't want to hear anymore, Destinee."

I was trying to give him what he wanted, but I guess it's too much to handle. He didn't even let me get to the juicy part.

I sit back on the couch and don't say another word. I want to watch my shows I recorded, not talk about Sean.

"Destinee, can we put all of this in the past and move forward? I just want you in my life, and I hope you still want me, too. We can take things slow and see how it goes."

I'm okay with taking things slow. We can't rebuild our relationship overnight. There is so much more I want to say, but I'm full and the bed is calling my name. I give Chris two options: come upstairs and get in the bed, or leave. He locks the front door, puts his keys on the table, and walks upstairs to the bedroom.

I wake up in the morning to the sound of the shower running. I sit up in bed and see Chris's clothes laid out at the foot of the bed. How did his clothes get here? He didn't have anything else in this house.

Chris walks out of the bathroom with a T-shirt and boxers on. "Good morning, sunshine."

"Where did you get clothes from?"

"I had a bag in my truck. Went to get it last night. You were knocked out."

I must have been sleeping hard because I didn't hear anything, and I am usually a light sleeper. He walks out to the hallway to grab the iron and ironing board in the closet. I get out of bed and fumble through my closet, trying to find something to wear.

I'm about to go in the bathroom to take my shower when Chris stops me. "I need to get something off my chest before I leave."

I can't keep having this conversation with Chris. As much as I don't want to hear what he has to say, I stop what I'm doing and sit at the end of the bed.

"I'm putting in my resignation today. I was offered another job."

I gawk at Chris. "Congratulations? I didn't know you were looking for something else. Thought you loved that job."

"I need to remove myself since Izabelle still works there. My focus is on getting us better than we were before. I can't do that and still work at the same company as her. I need you to trust me, and I just wanted to be honest about that."

My eyebrows rise a notch. I get up from the bed and walk back into the bathroom. He follows me and stands at the door.

"Can I come back home now?"

CHAPTER
TWENTY-ONE

My mother is starting to suspect that something is going on with me. I've been M.I.A. for a few Sunday dinners and we usually talk during the week, but I've been so tired that I only want to be in the comfort of my own home.

I would stop by and see her, but I don't want to give away my pregnancy news, so I call her.

"Ma, what are you doing?"

"Online looking for a bathing suit."

I smack my lips. "Why do you need a bathing suit?"

"Me and Mr. Evans are going on a cruise."

I love seeing my mom happy, and I'm glad she's still able to do the things she loves with someone who cares about her.

"What's going on with you?" I hear her nails tapping on the keyboard.

"I decided to pass up on the Atlanta opportunity."

The tapping stops. "Why?"

"Now is not the time for me to relocate. Plus, Chris and I

decided to work on our relationship."

She clears her throat and says, "Do not let a man, especially a man that is not your husband, get in the way of advancing your career."

"Yes, Ma, I know." I get where she is coming from, but she will understand why I made that decision in a few more days.

After speaking with my mom, I call Michelle to check up on her and fill her in on what's been going on with me before my mother does. I'm excited to hear that she decided to go back home with Kevin and the children. She says she talked to Kevin about the baby situation, and they came up with a plan they both agree on. She's going to have the baby, but Kevin has to get a vasectomy. *Ouch.* He wasn't having it at first but then came around. They both agreed this would be the last baby for them.

When I tell her about Chris coming back home and us trying to work on our relationship, she's a little surprised. "I didn't think you would be able to forgive him." I didn't think so either, but I'm trying.

Chris told Regina and Ebony that we're working things out. I traded a few text messages with Ebony, and she told me she can see and hear the difference in Chris. He's happier. He told her he felt so bad about what he did and promised that if we were to get back together, he was going to do everything in his power to keep me. "You two are meant for each other," she said.

Since Chris started his new job, he's been different. He comes straight home after work and cooks dinner. He hired another mechanic to help Charles at the shop, so now he only goes to the shop twice a week, and he installed cameras so he can see what's going on at any given time. Charles has stepped up a lot and has been doing more when it comes to the business. It's about time he got his life together.

I've been trying to connect with Kim, but she either ignores me or tells me she will call me back then never does. When Kim is stressed, she tends to shut people out. I usually give her some space for a little while then try to get her to come out of her bubble.

Sean has reached out to me a couple of times to ask when I'm going over to see Najah. I really want to, but I don't want to lie to Chris about it. We are finally in a better space, and I don't want anything to get in the way of that, but I really do want to see Najah. Plus, I promised her I would visit her when she moved here.

I've been busy with work, but I'm not letting anything stress me out. I told Chris that carrying another life is scarier this time around. I don't want to do anything wrong. I want to have a safe pregnancy and delivery so I can bring my baby home with me.

Every time I think about going to the doctor, I get anxiety. But I try to have faith and stay positive. I don't remember being this tired when I was pregnant with CJ, especially so far into my pregnancy.

Whenever Chris and I have a conversation about the baby, he brings up how serious he is about us getting married before the baby is born. He practically begged me to put my ring back on. Just a couple of months ago, he would change the subject whenever I brought up planning a wedding or getting married, but now he brings it up almost every day.

I'm hesitant about getting married, especially now. He can't blame me for feeling this way. In a perfect world, we would already be married before this baby comes, but I'm not going to be rushed into it. Plus, I don't want to walk down the aisle pregnant. I want my dress custom made, and I want to stand in front of my soon-to-be husband surrounded by flowers and family at the botanical gardens.

Chris mentioned doing something small with just immediate family and close friends. Then after the baby is born, we could have a big wedding and reception. It sounds like a waste of money and time to me. I'm only getting married once, and right now, I just want to focus on this baby.

I take the day off for my follow-up appointment with Dr. Johnson. Chris takes a half-day and meets me at the doctor's office. He has done a good job keeping me calm, as usual, and reassuring me that the baby will be okay.

I have a flashback when we walk into the exam room and the nurse tells me to lie on the table so we can hear the heartbeat. Chris looks at me and notices that I'm tensing up. He gets up from his chair and holds my hand. The nurse puts the gel on my stomach. Chris squeezes my hand and looks at me. "Everything is okay." I lie there with my eyes closed, listening for the heartbeat. Finally, I hear it and we both breathe a sigh of relief. But I tense up again when I open my eyes and see the nurse's face.

"What's wrong?" Chris asks.

"I think I hear more than one heartbeat."

I look at Chris and then we both look at her.

"What do you mean, 'more than one heartbeat'?" I ask.

She tells us she can hear one clearer than the other, but it definitely sounds like two. The nurse walks toward the door and tells us Dr. Johnson will be in shortly.

A few minutes later, Dr. Johnson opens the door and walks in. "I am so happy to see both of you, together."

I can't say anything, so I smile. I just want her to tell me what she hears in my stomach.

"My nurse tells me she could hear more than one heartbeat in that belly. Let's take a listen." She squeezes the gel on my stomach and then rolls the fetal Doppler around until she hears the heartbeats. "Well, I hear two heartbeats. You know what that means, right? Twins!"

"Twins?" I can't believe what I'm hearing. Four years ago, I lost my son, my first born. Now I'm having twins. She measures my stomach and notices that my measurements are much higher than my last visit. She wants me to have an ultrasound to check the babies. *Another ultrasound*? I can't believe I'm carrying twins. I put my hands over my face and cry.

"Look at God," Dr. Johnson says, smiling at us.

I knew this pregnancy felt different. All jokes aside, this baby bump got three times bigger overnight. I was just getting used to the fact that I was carrying *one* baby, and now I find out there are *two* in there.

During the ultrasound, she asks if we want to know the sex of the babies. I'm amazed she can tell us this soon. Chris and I look at each other and say yes. I don't want to be surprised this time around.

"They're girls," Dr. Johnson says.

Chris looks at the screen and says, "Girls as in plural, or a girl and a boy?"

"Just two girls."

It doesn't matter to me. I'm just praying for a full-term pregnancy with healthy babies.

After leaving the doctor's office, Chris and I grab something to eat. We're both excited and shocked about having twins. We finish eating and walk next door to Marshalls, and I find these adorable pink, baby girl booties with lace trim on them. I hold one set up on each side of my baby bump, and Chris takes a picture. We send a mass text to some of our family members and close friends: "We will be arriving on or about January 14th!"

Michelle is the first person to call me. "I can't believe we are pregnant at the same time, again."

My mom calls me next, screaming, "Oh my God, twins. Why didn't you tell me?" She was starting to worry about me because she hasn't seen me in a while, and I haven't been myself lately. Now she understands why. Then she lets it slip that Landon's wife is pregnant too, but they don't want everyone to know until after her first trimester because she has had a couple of miscarriages. This is crazy! All three of her children are about to have babies just months apart from each other.

I don't hear from Kim, which is surprising.

Troy usually picks Jordan up on Wednesdays from daycare. I contemplate stopping by her house later so we can catch each other up without any interruptions. I talked to Sean a couple of days ago, and he mentioned that Troy has been worried about Kim. He's not sure if she's dealing with depression or overwhelmed with work. I thought the same thing—it seems like she wants to close herself off from everyone.

On my way home, I get a call from Troy. He never calls me unless he needs something or something is wrong.

"Hello?"

"Hey, Destinee. Have you talked to Kim lately?"

"No, she's been really short and distant with me lately." I stop at a stop light and decide to turn around and head over to her house now instead of waiting until later.

"I noticed the same thing and was hoping you knew what's going on with her."

He sounds worried. I know the divorce has been hard on her, and Troy's been asking her to go to counseling to work things out, but she refuses.

"I called her job, and she didn't answer. She's not answering her cell phone either. Can you check on her?"

I hope nothing is wrong. She's worrying everyone. I call Chris to let him know what's going on and make my way to her house.

Her car is in the driveway, but when I ring the doorbell, she doesn't answer. I knock on the door. Still no answer. I call her cell phone again and it goes straight to voice mail. So, I start banging on the door, yelling out her name. Finally, she comes to the door. She looks horrible. I mean, I know I haven't seen her in a couple of weeks, but dang. She doesn't have makeup on, her hair is not done ... that is not like Kim at all. She is always on point, even if she's staying in the house all day.

She lets me in and walks back to her bedroom. "Hello to you too," I say sarcastically. I walk in the house, close the door behind me, and follow her. Her room is dark, the curtains are closed, the television is off, and her room is junky. She's got clothes coming out the drawers and hangers on the floor with clothes on them.

"Kim, what's going on. Why won't you talk to me?"

"I just want to be left alone. I don't want to be bothered."

"You want me to leave you alone?"

"Yes, I do."

"That's not going to happen because I am worried about you,

and I'm not the only one worried. Are you depressed? Talk to me."

"Yeah, I'm depressed! I feel like everything that could go wrong in my life has. My husband cheated, I'm getting a divorce, my career is over, and my health is declining."

I look at her, confused. I know about the divorce, but she hasn't said anything to me about her job or her health. I keep trying to get her to talk to me, but it's like pulling teeth. Finally, she yells out, "I'm being laid off. My last day is Friday. That's not all. I just found out I have cancer."

"Cancer? What type of cancer?"

"Cervical."

I can handle her losing her job, but not the cancer part. Kim has always been the health freak; she eats healthy and exercises regularly. She is all about her health and everyone else's.

How can I be happy about these babies when my best friend is dealing with all of this?

She breaks down and starts crying. I am known as the cry baby, but I try to hold back my tears to be supportive. I plop down on the bed next to Kim and hug her tightly. *I can't lose my best friend. I have to be strong for her.*

"I've been holding this in for weeks."

"We gotta stop keeping stuff to ourselves. We're supposed to be there for each other." I walk to the bathroom and get some tissue.

"When I saw you at the doctor's office, I was having my annual pap smear. They called me about a week later to come back into the office because it was abnormal."

"Why didn't you call me?"

"I thought it was nothing and that the second results would be different, but they weren't. They noticed cancerous cells on my cervix." She leans on my shoulder and lets out a loud cry. It sounds like she needed to let it out. "Jordan is too young to lose his mother, and I want more children. I don't want to die."

I fight back my tears as I tell her she's not going to die.

"I have an appointment with a gynecological oncologist tomorrow, but I don't want to go alone."

"Have you told anyone else? Does Troy know?"

"No, you are the only one who knows." She apologizes for burdening me with this news, especially since she just saw my text about the twins. "You're already stressed and worried about the babies. I don't want to make it worse."

"Stop it! I am here for you, and I'm glad you finally told me so I can help you fight this."

"I don't want to tell Troy because he already wants to try and work things out. Telling him this will make things harder. I can't handle all of that right now."

"Troy is worried about you. He called me today." She's gonna need all the support she can get right now. I convince Kim to get out of bed and take a shower.

While she's in the shower, I fumble around in the kitchen and try to find her something to eat. I call my mom to come over to Kim's house to talk to her about what she's about to go through. She's a nurse and dealt with my dad's cancer diagnosis and treatment. She'll know what to do and say. Plus, my mom has always been like a second mother to Kim.

I call Troy, too, and ask if he can get someone to pick Jordan up from daycare. "This must be serious," he says. "I'm on my way and I'll have my mom pick up Jordan." Kim might be mad at me for doing this, but we all love her and just want to be there to support her through this.

Kim makes her way into the kitchen. I let her know I called my mom and Troy to come over to talk. "I'm okay with your mom but not Troy."

She walks into the living room and lies across the chaise. She seems a little disappointed but will just have to get over it.

A few minutes later, Troy knocks at the door. I open it and he lets himself in.

"What's going on?"

Kim frowns at him. "We are going to wait for Destinee's mom to get here. I can only say this once."

Troy looks at me and I turn my head. If my face doesn't give away that it's something serious, my tears would.

My mom walks through the door and straight to Kim. "What is going on with you?"

Kim breaks down crying and can't get a word out. She tries to catch her breath so she can talk.

"I have cervical cancer."

Troy's jaw practically drops to the floor. "When did you find this out?"

"I've known for about a week. Right after finding out that I am being laid off."

"Why didn't you tell me?" He leaps out of his seat and embraces Kim.

"I have an appointment tomorrow."

"I'm going with you."

She turns and looks at my mother. "I would rather Mrs. Eunice or Destinee go with me. Mrs. Eunice, can I talk you in my bedroom?"

Troy sits with his head down. "I can't lose my wife, Destinee. I just can't."

I hear him sniffling, so I walk over and sit next to him. "We believe in a higher power, and God has the ultimate say, not these doctors. We are going to trust and believe that God will heal Kim."

He lifts up his head. "I am so sorry for everything I did to Kim. She didn't deserve any of it. This is all my fault."

"You are to blame for some of what's going on, but not for all of it."

"When Kim found out I was cheating, the first thing she did was go get tested for STDs. The test came back positive. Can't remember what it was, but I know they were able to treat it with medication."

"She never told me."

"She was embarrassed and ashamed. So was I."

This is a shock to me. We're supposed to be best friends, yet I feel like we've been keeping so many secrets from each other. I know Kim still loves Troy, but she doesn't want to be married to him anymore. I hope he can be there for her and not push to get back together. Troy loves Kim, and I know he is not going to let her go through this alone. Neither am I.

It scares me that I can't fix this for her. I know it's going to take more than me being there physically for her. I will be an ear to listen when she needs to talk and a shoulder for her to cry on when she can't find the words to speak. I want to be angry and show my frustration, but she doesn't need to see that. I can't imagine what she's feeling now. The things that are running through her mind and her worries.

My mom walks out the bedroom into the living room and looks at Troy. "You know I've never been one to sugarcoat anything. So,

I'm going to give it to you straight. Kim needs you right now more than ever, and she needs you to be strong. So does Jordan. She's definitely still hurt over what's happened in your marriage, and no doubt she may continue to lash out at you. Don't let that get in the way of your obligation to her. You are still her husband. Don't you forget that."

"Yes, ma'am."

I walk my mother out to her car. She tells me that Kim is adamant about Troy not going to the appointment. "Someone needs to stay with Kim tonight and take her to her appointment tomorrow."

I can't hold back my tears any longer. My mom pulls me in for a hug and then grabs me by my shoulders and lifts my head up by my chin.

"Listen to me! We serve a mighty God. There is no need for you to worry. I'm believing God will heal Kim, that he will strengthen her in more ways than one. Things happen for a reason, even though we question them. I'm praying that Kim and Troy's marriage will be restored, that she will find it in her heart to forgive him. He still loves her and is truly sorry for all the pain he has caused her. I need you to be strong and healthy for your babies. Try not to stress, and just be there when you can to support Kim. I'll meet y'all tomorrow at the doctor's appointment."

I go back inside to talk to Troy. Kim is still in her bedroom. He doesn't want to leave, but I reassure him that as soon as the appointment is over, I will call him. This is his scheduled night with Jordan, so he'll drop him off at daycare in the morning like he normally would.

I kind of feel bad for Troy. He has been trying for the past year to get back with Kim, but I don't think she's going to change her mind about moving forward with the divorce. I ask Troy if he knew about her being laid off. "I had no idea. She won't talk to me unless it has something to do with Jordan." If he would stop pressuring her about them going to counseling or working things out, maybe she would talk to him more and tell him what's going on.

I call Chris to fill him in. He agrees that I should stay with Kim tonight, so he packs me a bag and brings us some dinner. He stays for a little while and tries to get Kim to laugh. After he leaves, we straighten up her bedroom. We stay up half the night reminiscing about high school and college, and wondering about the future.

It's been years since we stayed up late at each other's house, talking and joking, especially with no alcohol involved. We both lie across her bed. She reaches over, rubs my belly, and starts to cry.

"Why are you crying?" I ask, reaching over to still her hand.

"I just feel like every time one of us has a happy moment in our life, the other experiences something tragic. Look, this is one of the happiest moments of your life and the saddest moment of my life."

"Please don't cry," I say, my voice thick. "You're going to make me cry. We have to trust and believe that God is in control."

"It's hard to have faith when I know I did everything I was supposed to do with my life. I got married and had Jordan. I was faithful to my husband, took care of my health and my body. I've always been health-conscious and active, and now I have cancer. I went to college, got good grades, started my career. Now I'm being laid off from a job I've had since graduating college. What did I do to deserve all of this? Why me?"

"I know it's hard, but you can't think that way." I try to find the right words to say to her. I can't compare my losing CJ to her illness, but I remember the things people would say to me to try and make me feel better when all I wanted was for them to be quiet and let me be. So, that's what I do: let her be and get some rest.

Kim's appointment is first thing in the morning. I'm so glad my mother is meeting us there. She is a huge support for Kim and helps her better understand the process. The doctor tells her they want to run more tests to determine the best treatment for her.

As promised, I call Troy right after we leave the doctor's office to let him know what they said. Kim was upset with me for calling Troy, but I have to keep my promise. Plus, he is still her husband.

My mother takes us to breakfast after the appointment. I know she has a hidden agenda because after ordering our food, I see her getting into counselor mode. This is when she gives advice, whether you want to hear it or not.

"Kim, how many times has Troy asked you to go to counseling?" she begins.

"So many times that I lost count," Kim replies.

"How many times has he apologized?"

"So many times, I stopped counting."

"Do you believe Troy when he tells you he is sorry for all that he's done?"

Kim takes a minute to think. "Honestly, I don't know. Just like I don't know and will never understand why he did what he did. Sometimes it's better for me to block him out because I'm still hurt by his infidelity. I still love him but can't forgive him and stay married to him because I'm too afraid that he will hurt me again."

I watch them go back and forth like I'm watching a debate team. With each one's response, I try to anticipate what the other one will say. My mom has seen her husband, friends, family members, and patients with this disease, and she knows Kim will need all the support she can get.

Kim gets quiet for a minute, looks at my mother, and asks, "How do you move on when you've been hurt by someone you love?"

My mother smiles at her with a knowing look in her eyes then says, "Prayer changes everything."

CHAPTER
TWENTY-TWO

Watching Kim battle cancer and knowing there's nothing I can do to make it go away has been the hardest thing for me. She tries to act tough and not show her pain, but I see right through her. I see how the chemo takes its toll on her body. She's weaker and moody. Her long, thick hair is almost all gone. Now she rocks colorful scarves every day that match her outfits—fashionable as always.

I watch her as she take off her scarf. It looks like she tried to cut some of her hair off, but she says every day a little bit more falls out, leaving her with bald spots on her head. Frowning at herself in the mirror, she says, "What am I going to do now?"

"Maybe you should consider cutting it all off."

She seems skeptical, and I don't blame her. I have never seen her with short hair; that's more my style. After a few looks in the mirror from different angles, she makes a firm decision. "I need to cut it all off."

The next afternoon, we go to Chris's barber, Jay. Kim sits in his chair and tells him to shave it all off. We watch as her hair falls to the floor.

When Jay finishes, he swirls the chair around and hands Kim the mirror, but she refuses to look. She gets up from the chair, gives Jay back the mirror, and reaches into her purse so she can pay him.

Before she can get her wallet out, I jump in Jay's chair. "Okay, I'm next."

I tell him to give me the same cut he gave Kim. They both look at me in shock. Kim sits down in the chair diagonally across from me, tears escaping her eyes. "Are you doing this for me?"

"Let me tell you something. There is nothing in this world that I wouldn't do for you. You are my best friend, my sister, and I love you to the moon and back."

Jay is hesitant. "I'll edge you up, but I don't want Chris coming after me because I cut all your hair off." He makes it sound like I have long hair. My sides and back are already shaved.

"Just take some off the top and clean me up." Chris will be okay and if not, he will get over it. Jay picks up the clippers and goes in on my head.

Each time Jay runs the clippers over my head, Kim cringes. When he's finished, I grab the mirror out of his hand, walk over, and sit next to Kim. I put my head next to hers and lift the mirror up so we can see our bald selves for the first time, together.

"Damn, I still look good," she says.

"Yes, you do, and so do I. Hair doesn't define who you are. If it doesn't grow back, we'll go get us some bundles." We both crack up laughing.

I pull out my wallet to pay Jay. "It's on the house, ladies. Kim, I admire your bravery. And Destinee, I admire your loyalty to Kim."

After dropping Kim off at her house, I head home. I find a scarf in my purse and wrap it around my head so that if Chris is home, he won't see my hair cut right away. When I walk in the house, he's in the kitchen standing in front of the open refrigerator.

I give him a kiss and lean up against the counter. "How was your day with Kim?" he asks.

"I have something to tell you."

He closes the refrigerator and leans on it. "Okay, what is it?"

"You have to promise you won't get mad." I stand up and lift my hands up to my head.

"I can't promise, but I will try my best."

"Okay, close your eyes."

"Just come on."

"Close your eyes first." Once his eyes are closed, I take off my scarf. "You can open your eyes now."

He opens his eyes and looks confused. I give him a couple of minutes to see if he's going to say anything.

"You don't like it, do you?"

"Totally unexpected."

"I did it for Kim. We both went to see Jay today."

"Jay did that?"

I try to hold back my tears. I'm already emotional because of the pregnancy, and with everything else going on my emotions are at an all-time high. "You don't like it, I can tell."

"I mean. You left this morning and you had hair. Now you don't. Gonna take some getting used to."

I don't think it looks bad. When I tell him I did it for Kim because all of her hair was coming out, he calms down. He laughs and says, "Y'all gotta find your own barber, though."

Watching Kim go through chemo is not easy. Every day it's something new. Of course, she has her good days and her bad days but she continues to fight and tries to keep faith that everything will work out. Troy has not left her side. He put his foot down and told her he was moving back into the house and would take over the guest room. She didn't put up a fight. I think it hit her after that first doctor's appointment that she needed Troy. She is blessed to have the support system that she has.

Since she's not working, she insists on helping Chris and I plan our wedding. I gave in to Chris. Figured maybe we should try to get married before the babies are born. Nothing big, just family and close friends. I told him if we do it now, I'm not doing it again after the babies are born. So, I want my miniature dream wedding.

I worry it will be too much for Kim to handle, but party planning is her life. She loves to plan and put things together. She was a project manager for a tech company before she was laid off. She promises me she's up to the task and says it will help keep her mind off everything else going on in her life.

We made a promise to each other in high school that we would be in each other's wedding and be there for the birth of each other's children. I pray every day that she can fulfill that promise. I was there when she married Troy and when she gave birth to Jordan.

I never fantasized about what my wedding would be like. I just knew I wanted it to be a beautiful outdoor wedding with the perfect man. I'm going to get that, but I'm feeling down about not having my father walk me down the aisle. I ask my mother if she will do the honors, along with Landon. She agrees, and Landon is honored that I asked him.

I'm not fussy about the decorating details; for God's sake, I can't even decorate my house. Chris and I agree on the colors—navy blue and gold—and that's about as detailed as I will get.

Even though we want an intimate ceremony and reception, we both have big families, and the guest list continues to grow. My mother is excited that her baby girl is finally getting married, and she's been bugging me about shopping for a dress, but I want to have my dress custom made. I will be seven months pregnant when we get married, and I have to make sure my dress fits the way I want it.

My mother worries that I might not be able to fit into my wedding dress, and she's a little upset with me because I won't let her see the dress or go with me to my dress fittings. I don't want anyone to see my dress until the day of the wedding.

Kim arranges a meeting with the event coordinator at the Norfolk Botanical Gardens. I'm still tripping off of the guest list. I tell Chris we need to scale it back, and he tells me not to worry because he has it under control.

I'm nervous about walking down the aisle, especially with a big belly. The plan was always to get married first and then have babies. I guess technically we will be married before the babies come. I just pray that I'm making the right decision to say, "I do" after what we've been through. I've seen a change in Chris for the better. He's communicating with me more, which I appreciate.

I never thought planning a wedding would be so much hard work, especially when you only have three months to plan. Flowers, food, table settings, music ... This is so overrated.

It will be a small wedding party, just a groomsman and a bridesmaid. I want Michelle to be in the wedding, but we don't need two pregnant women walking down the aisle. I wasn't sure if Kim would be up to it, but she tells me she will be by my side even if she's in a wheelchair.

Chris is adamant about us buying a bigger house, together this time. He says he wants his children to grow up in a spacious house with a big yard and not have to move around. Plus, if we have more children, we won't have to move anymore. I would much rather stay where we are until we get a handle on being new parents. I realize that we are getting married and our family is expanding, but with a bigger house comes more responsibility. Plus, having twins won't be cheap.

The closer we get to our wedding date, the more nervous I get. I know and feel in my heart that I am marrying my soul mate. No one is perfect, but Chris and I are perfect for each other. We love each other and no matter what, we have always been there for each other.

Kim wants me to have a bachelorette party with strippers, but I'm not down with all of that. I can't drop it like it's hot, pick it back up, or twerk. I've got this big belly and lower back pain. I suggest a nice evening with just the ladies, good music, and food. Good food is a must. My mother decides to have me, Kim, Michelle, and Erica stay at her house the night before the wedding. Kim and my mom plan the whole evening, all the way up to when we check into the hotel before the wedding.

Mom makes a taco bar for dinner and strawberry cheesecake for dessert. After dinner, it's girl talk. *This will be interesting.* I'm pretty sure they will share the good, bad, and ugly about marriage.

But I'm looking forward to hearing all about it.

My mom tells us to go sit in the living room. I'm full from eating so many tacos, and I'm ready to go to bed.

My mom sits in the recliner across from the television. Michelle lies on the floor, legs stretched out, her shirt midway up with her pregnant belly showing. Erica and Kim are sitting on the sofa. I stretch out on the love seat with my feet resting on the arm rest.

"Destinee, I need you to pay attention to what we are about to tell you," my mother says.

Everyone looks at me, smiling with anticipation.

"Oh boy, let me brace myself for this."

"We just want to share some marriage advice and words of encouragement since you are the last one to get married."

I know just about everything that has happened with their husbands. Maybe they will share some advice they should've used in their own marriages. I sit up on the love seat and give them my undivided attention. I tend to get emotional when my mother gives me advice. Maybe I need to grab some tissues.

My mother begins to speak softly, yet her voice is strong and she speaks with such insight. "I am going to give you the same advice my mother gave me when I married your father and some things I've learned over the years." She gets up from her recliner and grabs a tissue from the coffee table. "Never go to bed angry at your husband because tomorrow is not promised. That will make you more frustrated with him. Never bring up mistakes of the past. That will only make things worse. Last but not least, let him lead. You are his helpmate, and he is the provider and protector. Stand beside your man and let him do his job."

"Okay, my turn," Michelle says. "Always make time for yourself.

You are no good to your husband or children if you are worn out. Sex does matter after marriage. Keep it spicy and don't slack off. Buy some nice toys and lingerie every now and then to keep things interesting. Believe me, he will appreciate it. You and Chris developed a friendship before you decided to make this commitment, so always remember that and value that friendship. Most importantly, don't let anyone or anything compromise what you two have built."

Michelle turns and looks at Kim, gesturing that it's her turn to go next.

"Marriage is hard work," Kim says. "I've learned that firsthand, and you have witnessed it all. As the both of you grow, you will have to fall in love with each other over again. Don't let that push you away because that's when eyes start to wander. As you may already know, there will be times when you will be furious with Chris. Remember the reason why you said, 'I do.' That will help you get through. And last but not least, trust your gut. A woman's intuition never lies."

Erica looks at me and laughs, then says, "I haven't been married long, but what I have learned so far is to encourage your man and support his goals, but don't give up on your own in the process. Learn how to compromise. Try not to yell at him because most likely it will go in one ear and out the other."

I laugh because I know Landon hates when people yell at him or get too loud. At the end of these speeches, we are all in tears. I can feel the love and support from all of them. It feels good to know I have these strong women to lean on.

Later that night, as I try to fall asleep, I think about Chris and all that we have been through, and I wonder how he's feeling. Is he nervous? I know he is missing his uncle and wishes Greg was still here to witness our union.

Today's the big day. I wake up to the sound of a car alarm sounding off. My eyes open. I take a deep breath and put my arms behind my head. I hear the text notification from my phone, which is charging on the dresser across from the bed. I want to get up and check my phone, but my body is paralyzed because I'm so deep in thought. In a couple of hours, I will be Mrs. Richardson. In a few months, we will be parents to two girls. So many blessings in such a short amount of time.

I roll over to the other side of the bed so I can get up and check my phone. It's a text message from Chris: "Good morning, sunshine. Guess what today is? I look forward to seeing you walk down that aisle at 6:00 p.m. sharp. Don't keep me waiting any longer. I love you!"

I sit down at the chair in front of the desk. Snot runs from my nose, and my eyes are bloodshot red. Kim walks in and sits down across from me on the bed.

She's wearing another exotic scarf to hide that she no longer has long hair. Her skin is so dry from the chemo, so she's always covering up her arms and legs. The dark circles under her eyes reveal that she's tired, but she will never admit that to anyone. Kim always takes on more than she can handle, and trying to get her to slow down or let someone help her is impossible.

"You alright?" she asks.

I hand her my phone so she can read the text message.

"Well, look at you two love birds. I am so happy for you, Destinee."

It's a happy moment. I just wish she wasn't so sick.

"Thank you! I don't know if it's my nerves or what, but I can't contain myself. Today is the day I marry my soul mate."

"Yes, it is. Now wipe away those tears and go brush your teeth because your breath is fire right now."

We both laugh and hug each other. I smell bacon cooking in the kitchen, which means my mother is preparing breakfast. I wash my face, brush my teeth, and head downstairs. Michelle and Erica are sitting at the table talking to my mom while she cooks. She's making all of my favorites again: bacon, eggs, corned beef hash, cheese grits, and biscuits. She makes the best biscuits, and they are always from scratch. I've tried for years to master her recipe with no luck. Every time I try, Chris tells me to leave the biscuits to my mother.

I feel like I need to make sure the wedding stuff is in order, but Chris told me he didn't want me to worry about that today. He said he would make sure things go smoothly, so I try not to worry about the table settings, caterer, and everything else.

The makeup artist is on her way to the house, and Michelle begins doing everyone's hair. Kim and I don't have much that needs to be done to our hair, just makeup. Michelle is surprised I'm not doing anything different with my hair, especially since I told her I'm ditching the creamy crack and going natural.

Everyone has been trying to get their eyes and hands on my wedding dress, but I'm not giving anything away. It will be delivered to me personally once I get to the hotel. The only things they have seen are my nails and shoes.

Kim's dress is navy blue with gold accessories and shoes, my mom's dress is gold. Although they are not in the wedding, Michelle and Erica's dress are also navy blue.

On the way to the hotel, I get a call from Sean. I think about letting it go to voice mail, but I decide to answer it.

"Hello, Destinee! I'm surprised you answered. Was expecting to get your voice mail."

"Nope, you got me, not my voice mail."

"Do you have a minute talk? I know it's your big day." There's a bitter undertone in his voice. And a little sarcasm. Our last conversation didn't end too well. He was questioning me about my decision to marry Chris. He told me I was too quick to forgive Chris.

"Sure, Sean. I can talk." If Chris finds out about this conversation, he's going to be pissed.

"I was calling to congratulate you. I know we haven't talked a lot lately, but I just wanted to call you real quick. You know, since we are still friends and all."

"Sean, we will always be friends but nothing more. I apologized to you before if I misled you in any way. "

"I appreciate that." He sighs and is silent.

"Well, I gotta go and finish getting ready."

"Okay, I understand. I was just calling to congratulate you."

I hear the sincerity in his voice. I wasn't expecting his call, but I'm thankful for it.

Kim looks at me and asks, "What was that was all about?" I tell her it was Sean calling to congratulate me.

"Really, Destinee? Don't let another man come between you and your husband."

"It's not like that, Kim. We are just friends."

"You should've let that call go to voice mail."

I get that she is concerned, but there is nothing to worry about.

I know me having a friendship with Sean is something Chris will flip out over. I care about Sean and Najah, but I know how Sean feels about me and that puts our friendship in a dangerous situation.

We arrive at the hotel. My mother hands me my room key, and I tell everyone they won't see me until it's time to leave for the ceremony. The photographer will be here at 4:30 to get some pictures. Once I am dressed and my makeup is fully done, I will call them to the room.

My mother tenses up and walks away without saying a word. I know she wants to sit with me while I get my makeup done and get my dress on, but I want her to see me after everything is done.

My dress arrives right on time, and it's beautiful. I try not to cry when the dressmaker removes it from the blue garment bag. It's a beautiful off-white, one shoulder, A-line chiffon dress. Nothing but belly and ass popping out this dress.

I try it on and it fits perfectly—no adjustments needed. *Thank God.* Shane arrives next and starts on my makeup.

Everything comes together, and the photographer captures it all. Once my makeup is done and my dress is on, I call my mom and tell her to come down to my room and bring everyone else. She walks in the room and when her eyes catch me standing by the window, she stops and stares at me. Eyes wide, she takes a deep breath in and exhales.

"Mom, are you okay?"

"No, look at you. You are so beautiful! I wish your father and grandparents could be here to see you."

Michelle and Kim walk in behind my mother, and Michelle says, "They are here in spirit." They each have a bag in their hand, except

Michelle.

My mother takes a black box out of the bag. "I've been holding onto this for some time now. Your grandmother made me promise that I would hold onto this until your wedding day. Well, here we are."

She opens the box to reveal a note and pearl earrings. We all try hard not to cry so we don't mess up our makeup. She hands me the box, and I take the note out and read it.

"Destinee, today must be your wedding day. I am sure you are marrying a man that exudes all the qualities you deserve. I wish I was there to support you on this special day. Since I'm not, here are the pearl earrings your grandfather bought me for our thirtieth wedding anniversary. Today they are yours. This is your something old that represents continuity. May your union be forever blessed. I love you, baby girl!"

I can't believe my mother kept these for me all these years. I had no idea my grandmother saved these for me and never thought she would write such a touching note for my special day. There's not a dry eye in the room. I am so glad my mother has kept with this tradition.

My great-grandmother and her sisters started this tradition with their daughters. On the bride's wedding day, she was to be gifted with something old, something new, something borrowed, and something blue before walking down the aisle. Each item represents something different. When my mother married my father, my grandmother gave her the earrings she wore when she married my grandfather. My mother promised her mother that she would do the same with her daughters, so my mother gave those same earrings to Michelle when she married Kevin.

My mother continues. "Okay, blot the tears, ladies, so we don't mess up our makeup. I have one more thing for you. I know it's not as grand as what your grandmother gave you, but I have your something borrowed."

She hands me something wrapped in tissue paper. It's a pearl illusion necklace my father gave to her as a Christmas gift one year. "This represents happiness. I wish you and Chris all the happiness in the world. Always remember that no one is perfect, therefore no marriage is perfect. But as long as you both keep God first, work together, and encourage each other, everything will work itself out. I love you."

Michelle says, "Okay, my turn," and pulls a blue garter belt out of her bra. "This right here represents loyalty and fidelity. Remember, from this day forward you and Chris must remain devoted to one another and depend on each other. I love you, baby sis, and I wish you and Chris the best. You both deserve each other, and I am happy you found someone who loves you like he does. By the way, I left out purity. As we can see, that's out the door. Look at that belly."

We all laugh.

Kim walks over to me and hands me a box. "This is your something new, which represents optimism for the future. Live each day like it's your last. Love like it's the end of the world. Never give up on each other. Now, before you open it, I have a message for you from Chris."

She opens her phone and reads, "Destinee, today is the happiest day of my life. Today I marry my best friend, the love of my life, the mother of my children. I am so blessed to have you in my life. I spoke with your mother, and she let me in on the family tradition.

So, in the box is your something new from me. I'll see you soon. Love you."

Kim tells me to open the box. I slowly open the lid and see a diamond tennis bracelet. Shane is going to have to come back in here and fix our makeup.

There's a knock at the door. It's Landon and Erica. He's looking good in his navy-blue tuxedo and gold tie. Erica looks almost as big as me. Three pregnant women: Michelle, Erica, and myself. All due weeks apart from each other. This is not what I pictured for my wedding, but I feel so blessed.

"Look at you, DeeDee. You look beautiful, big belly and all."

"Thank you, Don!"

"The limo will be here soon. I just wanted to stop by really quick before we meet downstairs for pictures. I am honored to walk you down the aisle and give you away with Mom. Dad would be so happy and proud of you, and I know he is here with us in spirit."

"Thank you. Okay, no more tears. I can't cry anymore tonight. My makeup is already messed up."

After Shane fixes our makeup, we make our way downstairs to take more pictures. When the limo arrives, we all get in and make our way to the ceremony. On the way there, Chris calls Kim. I can hear them talking about the food and making sure everything is good.

When we arrive, Michelle, Erica, and Kim get out first to check on everything. Kim comes back with the wedding coordinator to let us know the coast is clear. Then she leaves to meet up with Charles, the groomsman.

The wedding coordinator directs me, Landon, and my mom

outside. As we walk, I hear the processional music begin and the pastor asks everyone to stand. *Here we go.*

Landon looks over at me. The corners of his mouth crinkle as he smiles at me. "Are you ready? If not, we can make a run for it."

We both laugh, but it's not funny. I'm nervous as hell.

"Stop it, Landon! I'm ready for this."

"Okay. Let's go."

My mom is on my left side and Landon is on the right side. As we get closer to the altar, I see Chris wiping tears from his face. We lock eyes and I smile, trying not to cry.

We get to the altar and the pastor says a prayer before asking, "Who gives this woman to be married to this man?"

Landon and my mom look at the pastor and say, in unison, "We do."

Landon shakes Chris's hand and hugs him, then gives my hand to Chris. The pastor says some words and then lets everyone know that we have prepared our own vows.

Chris reaches in his pocket and pulls out a piece of paper. "Proverbs 18:22 says it best: he who finds a wife finds a good thing. I found a good thing that day I saw you at the gas station. You didn't want anything to do with me, but I knew that wouldn't be the last time I saw you. You didn't seem interested, but that didn't stop me from pursuing you. You did too, after our first dinner, you just didn't want to admit it. I was drawn to the way you carried yourself, your determination, and that beautiful smile. You have always supported me through everything that has come my way. I am blessed beyond measure to have you in my life, and I am so happy to be marrying my best friend, my soul mate, the mother of my children. Today, I choose you to love forever. I will protect, respect, and honor you. I promise all these things always and forever."

I take a deep breath and try to stop my tears so I can say my vows. "Everything happens for a reason. That's why I know it's no coincidence the way you came into my life. If I had done even one thing differently, I might not have met you. From the beginning, I made it clear that I was focused on school and my career, but you didn't pay that any attention. You kept calling and texting. The more time we spent together, the more I fell for you. I thank God you didn't stop pursuing me. You're good for me, and I'm good for you. We are meant to be. I can't promise you that everything will be perfect, but I can promise to love you unconditionally. I promise to always be in your corner, to respect and support you, and to pray with you and for you. I will be there to bring out the best in you. I promise all these things for a lifetime."

Charles hands the pastor the wedding rings to be blessed for the ring exchange. After the exchanging of the rings, the pastor says, "I now pronounce you husband and wife. You may kiss the bride." Chris places both hands on my face and pulls me in for a kiss.

While everyone gathers in the garden with cocktails, Chris's family and my family make our way to take pictures before heading in to the reception.

Once we're done taking pictures, Chris and I take a minute to catch each other up on our day.

"So, how was your night with the guys?" Maybe I shouldn't have asked him that.

"It was just Charles and a couple of my cousins. They wanted strippers, but I didn't need all of that."

"You know Kim wanted to get some strippers too, but I told her no."

"I wanted to call you but didn't want to interrupt your night."

And what an emotional night it was. But he doesn't need to hear about all the marriage advice I was given, and I don't need to hear what the guys talked about. I'm just glad he had a good time and things didn't get out of hand.

We make our way to the reception. The DJ welcomes us as Mr. and Mrs. Richardson. Chris reaches down to grab my hand, and we make our way to the dance floor for our first dance as husband and wife. So much pressure. All eyes are on us.

We stop in the middle of the dance floor, and the DJ changes the song to our first dance song: "Why I Love You" by MAJOR. Chris kisses me on my lips and looks me in the eyes. "Mrs. Richardson, may I have this dance?"

I nod and wrap my left arm around his neck. He places his hands around my waist. My emotions begin to get the best of me and the tears flow like a waterfall. I wish I could get closer to him, but these babies are in the way. As the song continues to play, I place my head on his shoulder and Chris wipes the tears from my face.

After our dance, we make our way to our seats. The DJ picks up the microphone and thanks everyone for being here and asks the pastor to bless the food.

After we eat, the lights get dim. Chris walks over to the DJ and grabs the microphone. My face flushes because I'm sure he's going to embarrass me. He grabs a chair from one of the tables and tells me to take a seat, which I do.

"Y'all, this woman right here is the love of my life. I am so blessed that she is now my wife. I never had the pleasure of meeting her grandparents, but Destinee spoke so highly of them. I met her father a couple of months before he passed away. I told him I was going to marry his daughter. He told me, 'Bullshit.'"

We all laugh because that is something my dad would say.

"I am thankful he was able to meet the man that would marry his daughter. I wasn't sure if I should do what I'm about to do, but after speaking with Destinee's mother, brother, and sister, I knew I had to do this. Destinee, when we started planning our wedding, you were disappointed that your father wasn't here to walk you down the aisle and give you away. And that your grandparents aren't here to see you get married. But they are all here with us today in spirit. I wanted to do something special for you."

I look around and there is a projection screen with pictures of my father and my grandparents. I cover my face to try and hide my tears. I look over at my mom, and she's blotting her eyes with tissue so the tears don't mess up her makeup. I need tissue. *Somebody please bring me some tissue.* I can't believe he thought to do something like this for me.

Landon walks over to Chris and grabs the microphone. "Destinee, I know this moment is supposed to be between the father and the bride. I am not trying to take Daddy's place, but I am going to step in and have this dance with you. I love you, and I am so happy for you. Now let's get out on that dance floor and show them what we got."

By the end of the night, I'm no good. My back has been hurting me all day, and my feet hurt from dancing and walking around talking to friends and family. I just want to get to bed and go to sleep. I had the time of my life and feel blessed that we were able to share our big day with our close friends and family.

Chris and I leave the reception and go back to the hotel. It's only a few miles from the venue, but I'm asleep before we arrive. When we get to our room, Chris helps me out of my dress. I jump in the shower and stand there, letting the hot water hit my body. I scrub the makeup off of my face before getting out of the shower then I throw on a sexy lace piece of lingerie I picked up for this occasion.

I lie across the bed and Chris lies down next to me.

"Mrs. Richardson."

My face lights up with a smile. I turn my head toward him and say, "Yes, that's me."

I am Mrs. Richardson, finally. It feels good to hear him call me his wife.

"I love what you are wearing, but I need to take it off." Chris slides the straps off my shoulders. His lips make their way to my shoulder and up my neck. He stops at my ear and whispers, "Turn over."

CHAPTER
TWENTY-THREE

This third trimester is no joke. Everything is uncomfortable. My back aches and I'm even more exhausted because I can't sleep on my stomach. Four more weeks to go, and our bags are all packed and ready. These babies are moving and kicking up a storm—I'm loving every minute of it. It reassures me that everything is okay in there.

My energy feels nonexistent, and Dr. Johnson has me coming in every week now. At my last visit, she told me and Chris that she wants to set a date for me to be induced. I would rather let things flow naturally, but I understand her concerns.

I still have been working from home a lot more lately, and I've been helping out with Jordan since Kim has gotten sicker. Everything that's been going on with Kim has made me realize that tomorrow is not promised. I need to hold the ones I love closer and not take anyone or anything for granted.

I blame myself for letting her be so involved with the wedding, but she seemed to enjoy it and was feeling okay. If she wasn't doing well, I wouldn't have let her help. It's like she pushed through so she could make it to the wedding, and after that she just crashed.

She's been admitted to the hospital twice since the wedding. Every time I visit her, she looks defeated, like she's too tired to keep fighting. It's not surprising that she isn't much for talking today. She's been having difficulty breathing, so I just sit and watch television with her. I promise Troy I will pick Jordan up from daycare so he can stay longer at the hospital with Kim. As I'm preparing to leave, I walk over to her bed and give her a hug. She reaches over and puts her hand on my stomach.

"You feel that?" I ask her.

"Yes, those babies are ready to come."

"I know, and you are going to be here to see them."

She doesn't respond right away, but I can see the look of doubt on her face. Eventually she says quietly, "I'm tired, and don't know how much more I can take."

Troy gets up and leaves the room. He hates hearing her talk like that. We all do. He said he can't stand to see her weak; she can't keep anything in her stomach. My mom keeps in constant contact with Troy. She saw my dad at his worst and knows what it's like to care for a spouse with a terminal illness. One thing's for sure—he hasn't left her side since her diagnosis and makes sure she has everything she needs and wants.

It's been a while since Kim mentioned anything about her divorce, and looking at the two of them now, you can't tell they were going through a divorce. Troy has made his way back into the house, and they've even had some date nights when Kim feels up to it.

When I walk out of Kim's hospital room, Troy is standing in the small waiting area in the corner, talking to Sean. I walk toward them and remind Troy that I will pick Jordan up from daycare and drop him off tomorrow. I wish there was an exit close by so I didn't have to see Sean.

"You're not going to say hello?"

"Hello, Sean." I give him a hug and turn to Troy. "Call me when you leave the hospital."

"Destinee, wait." Sean walks up to me and asks if we can talk for a minute.

I stand with my back toward him and mumble, "What do we need to talk about?" I slowly turn around, and he walks over to me. "Sean, I have to go pick Jordan up from daycare."

"I know, just give me a minute."

I glance down at my watch. He better make it quick. Time is ticking.

"What is it?"

"Why are you still avoiding me?"

You've got to be kidding me. I turn and start walking toward the elevator. Sean reaches for my arm and grabs it. I turn around, roll my eyes, and sigh. "We've talked on the phone. Don't act like that."

"We have, but it would be nice to see you from time to time. Najah would like to see you, too."

I feel bad that I haven't seen Najah, but Sean makes it seem like Chris will be okay with me going to his house or him stopping by my house. I was naïve to think Sean could be content with just being friends. "Sean, you know I can't."

"Because of Chris?"

"Because I am married, and my husband would rather I not talk to you or see you."

"But we're friends."

"We are, but I still think you want more than a friendship and that's not possible."

"I would, but I respect the fact that you are married now."

"If you respect my marriage, then you should understand why I can't see you."

I miss Sean's friendship, but I keep my distance because I know he still has feelings for me. He should be more careful what he tells Troy because Kim finds out and then it gets back to me. Sean thought I would forget about Chris because of the time we spent together and our one heated night. I had a good time with Sean, especially that last night with him, but I am happily married now and don't want anyone or anything to mess that up.

I pick up Jordan up from daycare. When the teacher calls his name, he looks over at me and smiles then skips to me and gives me a big hug. "Auntie," he yells out. I know he's probably hungry, but I'm not in a mood to cook. I stop at McDonald's to get Jordan a happy meal. Hopefully that will hold him over until Chris gets home and we figure out dinner.

"Don't forget my toy. Last time they forgot it."

I laugh and look back at him. He's sitting with his arms crossed and a frown on his face. "I will make sure they give you your toy this time."

When I pull away from the drive-thru window, my phone rings. Troy's name and number appear on my car display. My heart skips a beat as I press the button on my steering wheel to answer the call.

"Hey. I just picked up Jordan, and we are on our way to the house."

Jordan yells, "Hi, Dad!" from the back seat. When I glance back at him, I can tell he's uninterested in conversation. He's trying to open the toy from McDonald's.

"Can you disconnect your phone from Bluetooth?"

I grab my phone from the cup holder and disconnect it from the Bluetooth.

"Okay, what's going on?"

"They just moved Kim to ICU because she's still struggling to breath and her blood pressure dropped."

He sounds like he's about to break down.

"I'm on my way back up there."

"I can't lose her, Destinee."

I want to pull over and cry, but Jordan is in the back seat.

"Don't talk like that. I'm going to drop Jordan off with Chris, and I'll be right there."

I glance up at the rearview mirror at Jordan. He's playing with the toy and munching on his french fries. I wipe away the tears as they fall down my face. Jordan can't lose his mother. I can't lose my best friend.

I remind myself that God has a plan. We may not understand it, but he has one.

I remember the first day I met Kim. She had long twists in her hair, braces, and thick red glasses. She was the bold new girl. At lunch, she walked into the cafeteria and sat directly across from me. I wanted to say something to her but just sat there like I normally do and ate my lunch. She looked at me and asked, "Are you always this quiet?" I didn't know what to say, so I just looked at her and shrugged my shoulders.

"That's okay," she said. "I'll talk, and you can listen." And it's been that way since we were eleven years old. When she talked too much, I would tell her to take a deep breath and go on mute for a little while. Now I wish she would talk my head off.

The chemotherapy caused inflammation in her lungs, which is making it difficult for her to breathe. I hate looking at her, lying in the hospital bed. Her pale face with the breathing mask tightly fitted around her nose. Pumping air into her lungs. She looks defeated, like she's had enough. That's not the Kim I know and love.

The back-and-forth to the hospital and taking care of Jordan has been taking a toll on me. My feet are swelling and my blood pressure has been high. My mind won't shut off. I'm constantly thinking about Kim. Praying she gets better and can go home.

I manage to get up and get ready for church. Afterwards, Chris and I stop for breakfast, but I don't have much of an appetite. I'm not feeling like myself. When we get home from breakfast, Chris makes me get in bed and rest.

"You're running around here, trying to take care of everyone. You need to rest."

He's right. I do.

If I feel up to it later, I'll stop by the hospital to visit Kim before going to my mom's for dinner.

While I rest, Chris hangs up photos around the house and promises he will put together the girls' dresser. He's going to hang their names on the wall over their cribs: Aja and Anaya.

I rest for about an hour or two and then roll out of bed to use the bathroom. I hear Chris on the phone, fussing. I walk into the nursery, and he tells whoever he's talking to that he's finishing up the girls' dresser, and then he hangs up the phone.

"Everything okay?"

"I don't know. It's always something with Charles. He asked to borrow some money. I told him I would stop by the shop when I finish."

I plop down in the rocking chair in between the twins' cribs. He has finished putting the dresser together and adds the last knob to the drawer. Then he grabs the letters for the girls' names. "Where do you want me to hang these?"

As I show him, he says, "I can't believe they will be here in a few weeks."

"I know. Are you nervous or excited?"

"Both. What about you?"

I stand up as he puts the letters on the wall to make sure they are not lopsided. "I think I'm more scared than anything."

"Don't be. Everything is going to be just fine."

"I hope so."

"Thank you."

"For what?"

"For marrying me and having my babies. You know I want more babies too, right?"

He laughs and walks over to me, kisses me on my lips, and then kisses my stomach twice. It's not funny.

Once he finishes hanging the letters on the wall, he leaves the house to go meet up with Charles.

I take advantage of that time to check on Kim at the hospital. I want to go back to sleep, but I promised Troy I would make my way up there today. To my surprise, she's awake, and it looks like the color is coming back to her face. She removes the mask from her face to give me an update from her doctor.

"He wants me to do a clinical trial."

I'm confused. She just finished chemo and was supposed to start radiation. *Why does she need to do a clinical trial?*

"The clinical trial is a new treatment that would find and attack the tumor cells."

"Is that what you want to do?"

"I want to live. That's what I want to do. Whatever I have to do to keep living, I'll do it. The doctor told me I can do palliative care along with the trial to help with pain."

I try not to break down. Palliative care is for when there is no cure. There's got to be a cure. I place the mask back over her face and hold her hand. I'm at a loss for words. Tears escape the sides of her eyes and fall onto the pillow. I get up from the chair and wipe them from her face. I'm unable to find words to express what I'm feeling.

I know she's worried about Jordan. He's only four years old. What would losing his mother at this age do to him? Kim knows how it feels to lose a parent at a young age. Would Troy be able to take care of Jordan on his own? If I'm thinking about it, I know she is too.

I pray the treatment works and she will beat this thing. All she wants is what every typical woman wants. To be healthy, happy. To have a career, a good marriage, and some children.

I sit with Kim for a little while longer in silence and then make my way home. On my way, I call Chris to see if he made it back home and is ready to go to my mom's for dinner. The call goes straight to voice mail. I try calling him again, but again, it goes to voice mail.

He knows we are going to my mom's house for dinner, so I'm not sure why he's not answering or returning my calls. Not to mention, I could go into labor at any minute.

I waddle upstairs to get my phone charger, and as soon as I get to the top of the stairs, my phone rings. I know I won't make it back downstairs before it stops ringing, so I continue walking to the bedroom. If it's Chris, he'll call the house phone since I didn't answer my cell. I grab my charger and relieve my bladder before making my way back downstairs.

I have two missed calls and a voice mail. One call is from Regina, and the other call and voice mail is from my mother.

I listen to my mother's voice mail, thinking maybe she wants me to stop by the store on my way to her house. "Destinee, call me back as soon as you get this."

I call her back, but it goes to voice mail. What is up with everyone's phone going to voice mail?

About ten minutes later, my doorbell rings. It's my mother.

"Mom. What are you doing here? I just got your message."

Her eyes are wide and watery like she's been crying. She walks in the house and closes the door behind her. "Why didn't you call me back?"

"I did, and it went to voice mail. I've been trying to reach Chris too, and his phone goes straight to voice mail. Didn't ring or anything. I just got back from the hospital. Went to see Kim." I turn around and take a couple of steps toward the kitchen.

"Well, we need to go back to the hospital."

I freeze up and my arms fall down to my sides. "Oh, God. What happened with Kim?"

"No, it's not Kim."

"Mom, please tell me what's going on. You're scaring me."

"I need you to sit down for a minute."

I walk into the kitchen and sit down at the table, nervous because I'm not sure what she needs to tell me.

"Destinee, something happened to Chris."

My heart skips a beat, and I spring up out of the chair. "What do you mean something happened to Chris?"

"Regina called me and said she got a call from Charles that they were taking Chris to the hospital. He was shot. She said she tried to call you but didn't get an answer, so she called me."

I grab my phone, jacket, and pocketbook, and walk out the door. I walk toward my car and unlock my doors, but my mom stops me. "You do not need to be driving. Get in my car." She's right. I am not in the right headspace to be driving. I try to call Regina, but she doesn't pick up. *Who shot Chris? What was he doing?*

When we get to the hospital, Regina and Ebony are sitting in the waiting room.

I stand in front of Regina and ask, "What's going on? What happened to Chris?" My heart is racing, and I'm slightly out of breath from walking so fast.

"Somebody needs to tell me what's going on. He was only meeting Charles at the shop and coming back home."

"He's in surgery."

"Surgery? For what?"

I take a seat next to Regina, and she tells me what she knows so far. Chris met Charles at the shop. When he got there, Charles was out front arguing with two guys. Chris got out of his truck and approached them to find out what was going on. When Chris stepped in to separate Charles from the men and get them to calm down, one of the guys pulled out a gun. He told Charles to give them what he owed them and they would leave. Chris stepped up and told them he wasn't giving them anything until someone told him what was going on and to put the gun down.

Charles reached for his pocket, and the guy shot off two bullets. One hit Chris in the stomach, and the other one grazed Charles's arm. The guys took off in a black sedan.

This can't be happening. I shake my head in disbelief. "I'm his wife. Why am I the last to find out?"

"I tried calling you." One call. One missed call and no voice mail.

"Why didn't the police call me, or Charles?"

"Not sure. Charles called me because they took him down to the police station for questioning."

They need to lock him up. Charles stays in trouble and always calls on Chris to save the day. I knew he was still into something bad. That's why Chris installed all the cameras in the shop. *That's right, the cameras.*

"Did Charles tell the police about the cameras in the shop?"

"What cameras?"

"Oh, never mind. How is Chris? Where is he?"

I'll let the police deal with that. I just need to know how my husband is doing.

"When I got here, they told me they needed to control the bleeding and he needed to go to surgery. We've been sitting here, waiting to hear something."

I can't lose my husband. I pray he pulls through all of this. We just moved into our new home. "The big house" is what Chris calls it. These babies will be here any day now, and we just got married. Kim is upstairs fighting for her life, and I can't even tell her what's going on.

"Richardson family."

A male and female doctor walk into the waiting area. I try to stand but lose my grip on the armrest and fall back into the chair. Mom and Regina lend me their arms for support and I manage to stand up.

"Mrs. Richardson."

"Yes, that's me."

My mom stands close to me with her hands on my back, her feet planted firmly on the floor as if she is bracing herself for my fall.

"Chris is out of surgery, but he lost a lot of blood."

"What kind of surgery? Can I see him?"

There is hesitation in their delivery of this news, which is making me feel uneasy about what they are about to say.

"Chris is in ICU. We had to rush him to surgery so we could stop the bleeding."

"What was the cause of the bleeding?" my mother asks.

"Well, the bullet went through his small intestines and pancreas. The bullet exited his back just a few inches from his spine. But it did a lot of damage to his duodenum."

"What is that?"

I'm trying to focus on what the doctor is saying, and it all feels so dreamlike. Like someone is going to pinch me and wake me from this nightmare.

"His small intestines. There's a lot of swelling. We need it to decrease so the tissues can heal. We are doing everything we can. We need to watch him closely. These next forty-eight hours are critical, and we need to make sure no infection sets in."

"Can I see him?"

"He is sedated. Only two people at a time."

I look back at my mom and Regina. "I'm going to see my husband." I follow the doctors through the double doors.

I pass the glass window and see Chris lying there with tubes and machines hooked to him. Before I can make it to his door, I break down and lean up against the wall. That's my world lying there, hooked to those machines. *Why is this happening?*

I don't think I have the strength to put one foot in front of the other and walk into his room. The tears won't stop falling from my eyes. I know I need to be strong right now for Chris, but I don't know how. I reach in my bag for some tissue and wipe my face before walking into the room. I pull the chair close to his bed, place my hand on his stomach, and start praying.

"Dear God, I pray that you will lay your healing hands upon Chris. God, please be his healer and comforter. Your word says that prayers of faith shall heal. I pray that my husband receives your healing by faith. Apply your resurrecting hands to his wounds. Restore my husband, and show your mercy as you heal him. Please give me and my family the strength to endure this tragic situation. In Jesus's name I pray, amen.

"Chris, you are so strong. I know you will pull through this."

I lay my head down next to his and whisper in his ear, "I know you can hear me. Everyone is here and we are all praying for you. Remember when we first met? You knew right away that you wanted to spend the rest of your life with me. It doesn't stop here. Baby, I need you here with me, and so do Aja and Anaya."

Regina walks into the room, and I can tell she's trying to keep it together. She grips the doorway when she sees Chris. The nurse walks in shortly after and tells us we have a few more minutes then we have to leave.

"I can't leave my husband here. I need to be here with him when he wakes up. I'm not leaving this hospital until Chris is awake."

Regina walks over to the bed. "You need your rest, Destinee. Go home, get something to eat, and come back in the morning."

I grab Chris's hand and kiss it. I'm not leaving this hospital. I look over at Regina and tell her, "I can't go home without Chris. I just can't."

She walks over to me and places her hand on my shoulder. "I know, but you need to take care of yourself and those babies."

I can take care of myself right here. I'm not going anywhere. "Look at him hooked up to all these machines, fighting for his life. Because your son doesn't know how to live his life right."

Before Regina can get a word out, the nurse and my mom walk in the room.

"I'm going to need you all to leave."

I give Chris a kiss, tell him I love him, and walk out to the nurse's station to make sure she has my contact information.

As I'm walking toward the exit, Regina stops me. "I know Charles hasn't made the best choices in life, but he is devastated about what happened to Chris."

"As he should be," I say and continue walking.

I can't keep it together. I start sobbing in the hallway and lay my head on my mother's shoulder.

"Destinee, you staying here at the hospital is going to cause you more stress. All these nurses are here to take care of Chris. Let them do their job."

I feel like when life seems to be on track, something bad happens. I don't know how much more I can take.

"I don't want to go home to that big house by myself." I sit down in the waiting area. Erica sits next to me and grabs my hand. "Destinee, there's nothing you can do sitting here all night. They are not going to let you back there to see him until visiting hours tomorrow. The best thing you can do is get some rest and some food. Chris would want you to take care of yourself and those girls."

She's right. I need rest and strength right now but I will be back first thing in the morning. Mom drives me home and decides to stay the night with me. I walk through the door and notice the pictures I asked Chris to hang up throughout the house. Pictures of us from the wedding, maternity pictures, and some random family photos. Pain grips my chest as I look at the pictures and how happy we were. Especially in the maternity photo. His smile is so bright as he stands in front of me with his hands crowning my belly like a basketball. My body locks up in rage when I think about Chris fighting for his life and not home with me. I wish he would've stayed home instead of going to meet Charles.

I plop down on the sofa and lay my head back.

"The devil's been busy, but we're gonna trust God will heal Chris. He's gonna pull through this."

I look up at my mom standing in the arched doorway. I place my hands over my stomach. "Mom, I can't do this without Chris."

"You won't."

"I can't take anymore losses. I really can't."

"I know what you mean."

I know she's trying to keep my mind off of everything that's going on, but it's not working. I close my eyes and see Chris lying in that hospital bed with all the machines hooked up to him. Every time my phone buzzes or chirps, my heart drops to the pit of my stomach in fear that it's the hospital calling. It seems like the news spread fast because everyone is calling me to see what's going on and how I'm holding up. I can't talk to another person or respond to another text message.

I'm tired, but my mind won't settle down enough to let me get any sleep. When I finally manage to doze off, I dream about CJ. I can't see his face, but I know it's him. I wake up in a panic, screaming and crying. My mother runs into my bedroom to check on me. Said she heard me screaming from the guest bedroom.

"I saw CJ."

"What?"

"In my dream, I saw CJ. We were walking in the park. He was walking next to me and I was pushing a stroller. He was talking to Aja and Anaya and told them he will always be their big brother and will watch over them. The last thing he said was, 'Daddy told me to tell you he loves you and everything is going to be okay.'"

She sits down on the bed next to me. "It was just a dream. Don't think too much into it."

"It's a warning." I am crying hysterically and my mom tries to console me.

"He's just letting you know he's going to watch over his baby sisters."

"But ..."

Before I can complete my sentence, she stops me. "It was just a dream. Try to go back to sleep."

All I want is to lie in bed with Chris and feel his warm body next to me. After that dream, I'm not going to be able to fall back to sleep. I go downstairs to watch television in the living room. Before I make it halfway down the stairs, water gushes down my leg.

"Oh shit!" I yell.

"I heard that. What's wrong?" Evidently my mother can't go back to sleep either.

"I think my water just broke."

"Are you sure you didn't pee on yourself?"

"Yes, I'm sure."

"Are you in any pain?"

"Just my back, but it's been bothering me all day."

"Why you didn't tell me? You could be having back labor pain."

"I gotta call Dr. Johnson."

"I'll call, you go get cleaned up."

My mom calls the after-hours phone number for the doctor, and I go take a shower and change my clothes. When I finish, my mom yells up the stairs, "The doctor wants you to go to the hospital."

I try to stay calm and focused on our way to the hospital. "Chris should be here with me." All of this shouldn't be happening without him. When we arrive at the hospital, we go straight to Labor and Delivery. I get checked in. My nurse starts my IV and hooks me to the baby monitor, which is uncomfortable as hell.

The last time I was in one of these rooms, I didn't have all these monitors on me. I had a bereavement nurse helping with the delivery. This time around, I should be happy and excited. Instead, I lie in the bed unfazed by everything that is going on.

The nurse confirms that my water broke and that baby A, Aja, has more amniotic fluid than baby B, Anaya. They check to see how far I'm dilated. "Five centimeters." Turns out the lower back pain I've been having is contractions.

While I wait for Dr. Johnson to get to the hospital, I call to check on Chris. I want to go up and see him before things get crazy, but they won't let me. When Dr. Johnson arrives, my mom fills her in on what's going on with Chris.

"I know you don't want to hear this, but you need to have a C-section. We've been watching Baby B on the monitor and need to get her out. I don't want to take any chances."

"I don't want to have a C-section, but whatever you have to do, do it. I just need my girls to be okay."

The nurse gives my mom scrubs to put on over her clothing so she can be with me in the operating room. They roll me to the operating room and give me an epidural. They tell me to be very still so they can put the catheter in place. Then they have me lie down on the table with my arms stretched out, oxygen on my nose and a sheet draped in front of me so I can't see what's going on. How can I enjoy the birth experience this way?

A few minutes later, my mom walks in and sits down in the chair next to me.

"Everything is going to be okay." She keeps trying to reassure me that everything is okay, but I know it's not. Nothing but bad stuff has been happening.

I think about how Chris should be the one sitting in that chair, waiting for his babies to be born. He's missing out on all of this. Tears escape my eyes as I lie there with my arms stretched wide.

Dr. Johnson walks in and explains what she's going to do. She says she will be talking to me along the way, letting me know how things are going down there. I feel tugging and the uncomfortable sensation of life literally being ripped out of me.

"Here comes baby A!"

That's Aja. The nurse yells out the time, "3:47," and walks her around the drape so I can see her before the nurse takes her to get cleaned off and weighed. "Six pounds, two ounces, Mom."

At 3:51, Anaya is born weighing five pounds, fourteen ounces. They bring her around so I can see her, too, and then take them both to the nursery. My mom goes with them while the doctor closes me up. Hearing them both cry is such a relief.

I start shaking like a chill has come over me, and it's becoming difficult to breath. I close my eyes, thinking it's panic from just delivering the girls. The last thing I remember is hearing Dr. Johnson say, "I'm trying to get this bleeding under control."

Everything goes black, then I see two people sitting at a table. I walk closer to the table and can tell it's my father and Chris. "Am I dead or dreaming?" Chris stands up and walks toward me. I try to grab his hand but can't. I hear his voice clearly. He says, "I love you and need you to wake up. You gotta wake up for Aja and Anaya."

My dad is still seated at the table, staring at me. Faintly, I can hear his voice but his lips never move. "I can't hear you, Daddy. Speak up."

"It's not your time, baby girl. You are strong, I know you are. You've got to wake up."

Slowly, I open my eyes, and my mother is standing over me. "Thank God, come on, baby. Keep those eyes open."

I look up at my mother and say, "He's gone, isn't he?"

She turns her head away from me and then back. "Yes, he's gone. I'm so sorry."

Like an avalanche, the tears flow down my face and I can taste the salt on my lips. "I saw Chris and Daddy in my dream."

My mother squeezes my hand and says, "At 3:56 p.m., a few minutes after Anaya came out, you started hemorrhaging. Chris died shortly after. He couldn't fight any longer."

The tears won't stop as I lie there, struggling to inhale and exhale. My mother stands at my bedside. She rubs my arm and tells me to breathe. She's no longer holding back her tears.

"Destinee, I'm so sorry," she says.

I just lie there, in silence, staring at the wall. Praying that this is all some kind of sick dream that I will eventually wake up from.

I look at my mother and ask, "How am I going to raise these little girls to know how wonderful and loving their father was? How he was there for every doctor's appointment just to hear their heartbeats and make sure they were growing perfectly in my belly? How am I going to raise these babies without my husband?"

"Destinee, you will tell those girls how wonderful their father was and how much they were loved by him."

There are no words to express the magnitude of pain I feel. This time, when I leave the hospital it will be with two babies and no husband.

CHAPTER
TWENTY-FOUR

The doorbell rings, followed by two knocks. "Who is it?" I call out as I walk out of the bedroom and toward the stairs.

"It's Sean!"

I stop midway down the stairs and throw my hands in the air. *What is he doing here?* I haven't talked to Sean or seen him since the funeral.

I stop at the mirror behind the door before opening it. My hair is a mess. I have bags under my eyes from not getting any sleep and spit-up from the babies on my T-shirt. I open the door. Sean stands there with a box of diapers and two gift bags.

I hold the door open with a smirk on my face. "What are you doing here?"

"I came to check on you."

"How did you know where I live?"

"Don't get mad, but Troy told me."

Troy? "Oh my God! Is everything okay with Kim?"

My heart pounds at the thought that something else might be wrong with Kim. My nerves can't take any more bad news. Kim was released from the hospital the day after Chris's funeral, and she has been under doctor's orders not to leave the house unless she's going to a doctor's appointment. Troy is holding her to that.

"Kim is okay. She's home resting but worried about you. That's why I am here."

"Everyone is worried about me. It's been rough."

I invite Sean in and close the door behind him. I appreciate him coming to check on me, but my days are consumed with changing diapers, making bottles, feeding the girls, and washing clothes. I'm lucky if I can get a shower in when my mom stops by to check on us. I don't have time to sit and chat.

Sean places the bags on the couch and the box of diapers on the floor, and then he takes a seat. As soon as I sit down next to him, I hear crying coming from upstairs.

I hold my head and let the tears fall. "I'm so tired, Sean. I just want to sleep."

"Let me help you."

"Don't take this the wrong way, but Chris should be here helping. It's not fair that I have to do this alone."

"I'm sorry, Destinee. And you're right, it's not fair. But let me help you."

I spring up from the couch and stomp up the stairs like some teenager who's upset because they didn't get their way with something. When I turn the corner to walk into the nursery, Sean is right behind me.

"What do you need me to do?" he asks.

I look him up and down in disbelief. I doubt if he's going to do anything but get in the way.

"I don't know. I've just been winging it," I say, still crying as I walk over to the crib. Both Aja and Anaya are now crying. Sean turns around and walks out of the bedroom. I stand there, watching the door to see if he's going to come back. *Fuck, he's really not staying.*

I turn back toward the crib and reach down to pick up Aja. Sean walks back in the room with his sleeves pulled up. "You thought I left, didn't you?"

"Yes, I did." I laugh and nod.

He walks over to the crib. "I had to wash my hands before touching these precious babies." He looks down into the crib and smiles brightly. "Okay, which one is Aja and which one is Anaya?"

"I'm holding Aja in my arms. Anaya is still in the crib. I try to dress Aja in pink and Anaya in purple because I'm so tired that sometimes I can't tell them apart."

Sean picks Anaya up from the crib, and she immediately stops crying.

I stand there, staring, surprised.

Sean laughs and says, "I have the magic touch when it comes to babies."

I sway Aja in my arms, trying to get her to stop crying.

"It's time for them to eat."

"I'll take them, and you get their bottles."

Sean sits in the glider chair next to the crib, and I place Aja in the crook of his left arm.

There's complete silence as I walk down to the kitchen to make their bottles. I still have bottles sitting on the counter that need to be made. I sterilized them but haven't had time to make them up.

When I walk back upstairs, I hear Sean talking. "I'm going to have to bring my little girl over here to meet y'all. Her name is Najah. She's in school today, but I'll bring her by one day when she is off."

He stops talking when I enter the room and stands up. "You take a seat here and take Anaya, and I will sit here and feed Aja." He sits down on the ottoman in front of me. Then he reaches over to the dresser for a burp cloth and places it under the bottle as he slowly moves it to Aja's mouth.

I sit back in the chair and feed Anaya. I feel frustration building up in me as I watch Sean feed Aja. He's the first man other than Landon and Kevin to hold my girls. I know he's only trying to help, but it shouldn't be him here feeding Aja. It should be Chris.

I think back to the night before Chris was shot. We were lying in bed talking. He was so anxious to meet his girls and proud that we were finally all moved in to what he called our "forever home." He was content with just having the girls but wanted a house with extra space in case we decided to have more children. I told him not to hold his breath because twins were a lot of work. He told me I was going to be a great mother and that he would be here to help with everything. Now he's not here to help with anything.

He was determined to have us all moved in and the nursery completed before the girls were born. "You and the girls are my world," he would say. He said he was going to do any- and everything to make sure we were taken care of and would want for nothing. He kept his word about that. Between the life insurance policy and the mortgage protection insurance policy, the girls and I don't have to worry or want for anything. I can take my time and stay home with the girls until I am ready to go back to work.

Sean lifts Aja up and lays her on his chest to burp her. Then he walks over to the changing pad on the dresser. I finish burping Anaya and lay her down in the crib.

"Let me take care of the girls for a little while, and you go get some rest." I look at the girls and see how calm and quiet they are. Sean looks over at me. "I promise they are in good hands."

I am in desperate need of some sleep, and the girls seem to want him around more than they want me.

"Okay," I say in agreement. "Just for a little while. My mom will be here when she gets off work."

I glance at the girls one last time before walking to my bedroom. I feel defeated when I see the pile of laundry on the bed. I was getting ready to fold it when Sean knocked on the door. I push the clothes to one side and lie on the other side.

When I wake up, the clothes are gone from my bed and Sean is gone, too. I peek in the nursery, and the girls are sound asleep in the crib, swaddled and cuddled next to each other. I walk downstairs, and my mom is in the kitchen, cooking.

"Well, hello, sleepy head."

"Hey, Ma. Is Sean still here?" I look over in the living room but don't see anyone sitting in there.

"No, he left about twenty minutes ago."

"I must have been in a deep sleep because I didn't hear him leave or you come in."

"He told me to tell you that he folded the clothes and finished making the bottles."

My face lights up as I walk toward the living room and plop

down on the couch.

"What was he doing here anyway?" my mom yells from the kitchen.

"He said Kim sent him to help me out with the girls."

"So, you didn't call him over?"

"No, Ma, I didn't call him. Haven't seen him since the funeral."

I sigh and lie across the couch. I stare at the picture of Chris and I taken a few weeks after we met. I close my eyes, and I can see his bright smile. Our first date replays in my mind—our peaceful walk on the boardwalk.

I jump up from the couch. "Ma, can you watch the girls for me for a little while?"

"Sure, where you going? Dinner is almost ready."

"I just need to get some air. I'll be right back."

The sun will be setting soon. I will make it to the beach before it does. I grab my wallet from the baby bag at the front door, and my coat and keys from off the hook. There's a chill in the night as the sun sets. I grab my favorite cup of coffee before walking toward the boardwalk: a large dark roast with caramel swirl and cream.

The wind picks up on the beach as the sun begins to set. I find an empty bench and sit down.

I wish the weather was warmer so I could walk out and feel the warm sand on my feet. I sit back against the bench, pull my hood over my head, and take a couple small sips of my coffee.

On our first date, Chris told me that watching the sun rise or set made him feel at peace, like he was closer to God, and that somehow he just knew things were going to get better. That's why I'm here. I need to find peace with this loss. I need to know things are going to get better because right now my life feels like shit.

These past couple of weeks have been hell for me. Losing the love of my life, almost dying giving birth to two beautiful little girls, and having to plan a funeral from my hospital bed. Then having to come home from the hospital alone with Aja and Anaya to a house Chris and I built together for our family. Learning how to take care of the girls and tend to their needs. Hands down, it has been the most difficult couple of weeks of my life. I'm learning that sometimes life moves in a direction that was never intended or expected.

I know I need to enjoy each day as it is given to me. But that has been hard since Chris is gone. I have days when I break down and cry. Sometimes I don't even know how I will make it through the day, but I know these girls depend on me.

I try to remember that all things work according to God's plan for my life, not according to the plans I have for myself. Raising these girls without their father, my husband, was definitely not part of my plan. I am so afraid that I am going to fail or let them down. Ultimately, I have to let my faith be greater than my fears.

Sometimes it's hard to fathom that loss is inevitable. When we are born into this world, we are guaranteed a death date. We have no control over that. When it's your time, it's your time. I guess it was Chris's time. I will forever cherish our good times and bad times. Chris taught me that all things come to an end so there can be new and beautiful beginnings. These girls are my new and beautiful beginning.

About the Author

Jennifer Johnson is an author who has a passion for inspiring others and utilizes personal stories to complete works of fiction. She understands that life is forever changing, shifting into unknown territory. Jennifer believes that everyone's journey is not the same, but each journey offers personal and spiritual growth which is needed to achieve one's fullest potential.

Jennifer is a graduate of Hampton University and Regent University School of Law. She resides in Suffolk, Virginia with her husband and four children. A true cancer who is nurturing, highly intuitive, and loves spending time with her family.

Acknowledgments

First and foremost, praise and thanks to God for helping me find my passion and purpose. The journey hasn't been easy but I am thankful for it.

To my husband, Ben (Babe). Thank you for always supporting my dreams and goals. Having an idea and turning it into a book takes time. I sacrificed a lot of days and nights writing and editing. Yet you remained patient and encouraging. I love you more than what words can express.

To my children, Tyrell, Kayla, Keyara, and DJ. Thank you for understanding the time I needed to be in the zone and focus on my book. Our motto is "teamwork makes the dream work." You all helped make my dream work.

To my mom and dad, Denise and Edward. Thank you for always encouraging and supporting me. You guys always have my back.

To the rest of my family and friends, thank you for believing in me. I am so blessed to have you all in my life.

Thanks for reading! Please add a short review on Amazon and let me know what you thought!

Follow me on Instagram:
http://www.instagram.com/iamjenniferjohnson